ON A WING AND A PRAYER

"I was just thinking how absolutely lovely you are," he said candidly. He wanted to add that the sight of her slender, graceful neck and shoulders made him think of other things. But he sensed that if he were to tell her what he was truly thinking, she would probably slap his face. He laughed at the thought.

Lauren, eyes flashing, asked "What's the joke? I hope you're not laughing at my expense, Mr. Townsend."

"No, not at all, and please call me Michael. Look, let's call a truce—I think we got off to a very bad start on that flight. I'd really like to get to know you better— and for you to get to know me too. Deal?" he asked sincerely, looking into her eyes. The effect was magnetic and Lauren found herself unable to remain aloof or angry.

What the hell, it's just a party, she told herself. *And I might as well try to enjoy myself in the spirit of getting through the evening,* she thought inwardly. "Okay, Michael," she responded smiling, wondering why each time she looked into his unreadable gray eyes, she couldn't help but also notice the rapid beating of her heart. Lauren turned away from him then, thinking that perhaps another glass of champagne might make her less nervous.

In profile, her beauty was astounding. Michael's pulse began to beat rapidly and he knew he wanted her, wanted her as much and maybe more than he'd wanted any woman in a long time. But he wanted her on his terms and he knew she wasn't ready for that. Not yet anyway.

BOOK YOUR PLACE ON OUR WEBSITE AND MAKE THE ARABESQUE ROMANCE CONNECTION!

We've created a customized website just for our very special Arabesque readers, where you can get the inside scoop on everything that's going on with Arabesque romance novels.

When you come online, you'll have the exciting opportunity to:

- View covers of upcoming books

- Learn about our future publishing schedule (listed by publication month and author)

- Find out when your favorite authors will be visiting a city near you

- Search for and order backlist books

- Check out author bios and background information

- Send e-mail to your favorite authors

- Join us in weekly chats with authors, readers and other guests

- Get writing guidelines

- AND MUCH MORE!

Visit our website at
http://www.arabesquebooks.com

ON A WING AND A PRAYER

Linda Walters

ARABESQUE
★BET BOOKS

BET Publications, LLC
http://www.bet.com
http://www.arabesquebooks.com

ARABESQUE BOOKS are published by

BET Publications, LLC
c/o BET BOOKS
One BET Plaza
1900 W Place NE
Washington, D.C. 20018-1211

All Kensington Titles, Imprints, and Distributed Lines are available at special quantity discounts for bulk purchases for sales promotions, premiums, fund-raising, and educational or institutional use. Special book excerpts or customized printings can also be created to fit specific needs. For details, write or phone the office of the Kensington special sales manager: Kensington Publishing Corp., 850 Third Avenue, New York, NY 10022, attn: Special Sales Department, Phone: 1-800-221-2647.

First Printing: July 2002
10 9 8 7 6 5 4 3 2 1

Printed in the United States of America

I'd like to dedicate this book to my mother, the late Ethel Beatrice Thom, whose love of life, quest for decency, and fearless demeanor inspired me in more ways than I can say.

And to my three sisters—Gloria, Connie, and Delores—who always made me feel that anything is possible, I offer my deepest gratitude.

ACKNOWLEDGMENTS

My sincerest gratitude goes out to all those who gave their unconditional love, support, and encouragement during the incubation of this, my first novel.

Thank you to BET Books; Chandra Taylor, my editor; and each staff member who so graciously took the time and effort to make this happen.

I'd like to extend a special note of appreciation to Donna Hill—my friend, my mentor, my idol—who encouraged me wholeheartedly from the start. Thank you and please know that each and every day I thank God and the universe for our introduction.

And most importantly, I'd like to thank my family—Nikki, Lance, Teylor, and especially Calvin—who tolerated and constantly applauded my concentrated efforts, absolute enthusiasm, and indefatigable dedication that helped produce ON A WING AND A PRAYER.

And the priestess spoke again and said: Speak to us of Reason and Passion

And he answered saying: Your soul is oftentimes a battlefield, upon which your reason and your judgement wage war against your passion and your appetite.

Your reason and your passion are the rudder and the sails of your seafaring soul.

If either your sails or your rudder be broken, you can but toss and drift or else be held at standstill in midseas.

—Kahlil Gibran
"The Prophet"

One

Dawn hovered timidly over Cobble Hill while most of its inhabitants slept soundly, still unaware and for the most part, uninspired by the encroaching new day. Lauren Traynor turned over, raising one arm to shield her eyes from the increasingly insistent light threatening to push its way through to her consciousness. She hit the reset button automatically as the sounds of contemporary jazz filled her bedroom. The fluorescent numbers on the clock face read 5:30 A.M. Taking a deep breath, Lauren swung slim legs to the floor as she headed into the bathroom to shower. Though still groggy, the cascading force of the water enabled her to begin thinking of the day ahead.

A direct flight leaving John F. Kennedy Airport en route to Los Angeles's LAX with a one-hour connection between flights, then on to Denver's Stapleton Airport. The last leg of her trip was nonstop to Atlanta where she would lay over for a full eighteen hours. Scheduled to return to New York late the next evening, Lauren knew she had a very full thirty-six hours ahead of her.

She dressed methodically, yet hurriedly, thinking of the usual early morning traffic headed east of the city toward JFK. Glancing in the full-length mirror lining one wall of the walk-in closet, her reflection gave no cause for unease. The richly dark navy blue uniform with its contrasting burgundy piping at the lapel and cuffs conservatively complimented her figure. Long shapely legs, gently flared hips and a generous, but modestly hidden bustline did nothing to detract from the cool professionalism the austere uniform meant to convey. A crisp white oxford shirt, open at the neck with just enough clearance to reveal standard seventeen-inch pearls, completing the look. Its military styling and clean uncomplicated lines, along with simple navy blue pumps, spelled authority.

Worldwide Airlines, one of the largest domestic passenger carriers covering the Northeast corridor, had acquired a standing reputation in the airline industry for employing only the most professional and dedicated inflight personnel. They also took great pride in having recently added to its existing fleet, several of the newly developed L2000 aircraft, which boasted state-of-the-art radar technology, seating that afforded maximum comfort to all its passengers, as well as the highly touted "upper level" lounge area which its first-class and business clients seemed to truly appreciate. Noise-canceling headsets had also recently been added to complete Worldwide's full compliment of attention to detail in courting its prime passenger market.

Lauren picked up her handbag and overnighter, placing them inside the foyer which led to the elevators. Almost as an afterthought, she walked through the living room to the other side of the two-bedroom apartment and knocked softly at her roommate's door only halfway expecting to receive an answer.

"Gloria," she called. Turning the knob, she pushed the door open to reveal an empty room tastefully done in shades of purple and pale gray. *She's probably still in L.A.*, Lauren thought, realizing that they'd literally cross each other's paths while in flight sometime during the course of the next twenty-four to thirty-six hours. The fact that Gloria's brother, Morgan had called several times in the past two days was not unusual. Lauren's mind touched on the fact that although he always seemed genuinely nice and extremely loving toward his baby sister, his incessant calls and frequent unscheduled visits were a bit much. Although Gloria and Morgan did not share the same biological father, he was extremely protective of his stepsister, sometimes even going so far as to obtain information that was none of his business. Once, he'd even paid for information indicating her whereabouts and when Gloria realized the extent of his digging, she'd confronted him. Morgan and Gloria often argued about his intrusive meddling, to no avail. He followed orders from their father, Gino Sorrentino, and that was the problem.

Lauren crossed the room to close the vertical blinds in Gloria's room, noting several plants lining the windowsill which were sorely in need of water. *I really don't know what's going on with her or maybe I do—she's probably going through changes,* Lauren thought as she walked into the adjoining bathroom and filled a large plastic container with water. She then pulled a pen from her breast pocket and quickly scrawled a note. *Hope to see you on Thursday night. Let's talk. I'll be in Atlanta. Page me!! Love, Lauren. P.S. Water your plants!*

She glanced at her watch. It read 6:35 A.M. Orientation was scheduled to begin at 7:15 for the 8:40 A.M. flight. *Okay, I have about forty minutes to make it to the airport,* Lauren thought, entering the elevator. She pushed "G." As she descended toward the underground garage, her mind once again came to rest on Gloria. Lauren was sure Morgan was somehow involved with less than honorable associates, but she also knew he was extremely good at whatever he did. Though the two young women had not discussed it at length, Lauren knew her roommate had grown up in an extremely well-to-do environment. She also knew that Gloria seemed determined to make it on her own merits now that she was an adult. Her father, Gino Sorrentino, was the problem it seemed. Although he kept an extremely low profile, Lauren realized that he controlled much of what both Morgan and Gloria did. She was fairly certain that if not for the fact that Morgan had given his assurances of staying right on top of Gloria's everyday activities, Gino would never have okayed her living on her own, flying around the country even in a work-related capacity, and having a life of her own.

Lauren, too, had felt the need to separate herself from her past and make a truly independent statement in her adulthood. Memories of her parents' recent divorce were steadfastly embedded in her mind. After almost three decades of marriage, neither of them had been able to explain to her exactly what had happened. She only knew that her mother had been devastated—heartbroken and was only now seemingly on the road to some semblance of recovery.

No, not me, she thought to herself often. The protective wall she'd built around herself was solid and intact. Impenetrable. Although it was sometimes difficult to remain totally detached from the social scene, Lauren was determined to avoid the pitfalls her parents' marriage had so effectively warned her against. Their example was a scathing testimony and all she needed to confirm to her what was obvious—love and marriage was not a tangible reality. Thirty years of marriage had ended without explanation and that seemed to be more the rule than the exception.

She had her work, which she loved and although she sometimes dated, it was always casual. Very casual. No two dates in the same week with the same man. Those were her rules and anybody that wanted to play the game had better abide by them was her attitude.

Lauren stood 5'7" in her stocking feet and weighed 127 pounds. Up until the age of about fifteen, she had been skinny and gangly, seemingly all arms and legs. Her skin, darker and more olive complexioned than her mother's—who credited her Cherokee grandmother with the coloring as well as the cheekbones—had always been prone to acne.

Thank goodness for her dad's medical benefits, which had included the orthodontist. Having to wear braces for three years was torture of another kind with the kids at school yelling "Metallica" anytime she was within earshot. She'd handled it though, choosing to ignore and shut out anyone who was so ridiculously intrigued with something they should just ignore. Then, the following year, everything had changed. Her hair, a glossy mixture of silky brown with auburn highlights had suddenly seemed even thicker and the orange hues took on an almost golden glow with the sun's natural bleaching effects. She had spent almost the entire summer at the beach, having gotten a job at The Scoop, a local boardwalk ice cream parlor. Her skin, thanks to twice monthly visits to the dermatologist, had begun to clear up and her golden brown complexion took on a healthy sheen. Her weight not only shifted into all the right places, she even put on a few pounds, rounding out her figure. The hollowness of her cheekbones, which had sometimes been so pronounced as to give her an almost gaunt look filled in creating an earthy, almost exotic look. The high curve of her cheekbones also accentuated her warm brown eyes. And suddenly, Lauren had metamorphosized from a thin, gangly teenager with braces and an unruly thick pigtail into an intriguingly beautiful teenage girl.

When several of the male seniors at her high school started dropping into The Scoop on a regular basis to chat, order milk shakes and subsequently ask her out, she realized that they too had somehow noticed the changes in her. It made her nervous though, and she resolved then and there that boys and dating were in the category of "mysterious" and "off limits."

She knew she loved to travel. She'd spent her entire childhood moving from country to country, city to city with her parents. She made up her mind that year that the easiest way to continue to do it would be by joining the airline industry.

Inserting her key into the door of the baby blue Saab 900, Lauren inwardly prayed that the Belt Parkway would be traffic free. Her prayers were answered and exactly one hour and ten minutes later, after fifteen minutes of orientation, she stood in the front section of the L2000, microphone in hand, instructing the 117 passengers on board Worldwide Airlines flight number 234 en route to Los Angeles to fasten their seat belts and observe the no-smoking signs. She then proceeded to the rear of the first-class section and watched as the two junior flight attendants gave further instruction in emergency procedures as part of the pre-flight safety instructions and precautions mandated by FAA regulations.

As senior flight attendant, Lauren served as liaison between all crew members including the captain, first officer and flight engineer. Her responsibilities also included all first- and business-class passenger needs as well as overall responsibility for the remaining cabin crew members. Now, in only her second year of flying, she had proven herself to be both capable and extremely dependable early on in her flight training. Promotion to the rank she now held had come after only one year of flying for Worldwide Airlines, a position that usually took a minimum of three years or 3,750 hours of in-flight time to reach.

After graduating from Rutgers University, she had applied to and been offered the position with Worldwide immediately. Flight attendant school had been a breeze. Lauren managed to complete her training at the top of her class and she immediately set up a list of rules and priorities for herself. So far, she had accomplished and kept in order her list of priorities—one of which had been to obtain a senior position within the first two years of flying. The rules, however, were another matter. Although she found it fairly easy to conform to most of them—no smoking, no red meat and limited alcohol consumption—there was one that she found to be a constant challenge. That was the "no dating passengers rule." And although this was a self-imposed restriction, Lauren knew that it was and would continue to be the hardest to maintain.

She was approached often, but she took the stance that if she wavered once, it would be that much easier the next time and the time after that. Thinking back to just a couple of weeks earlier, Lauren remembered a flight on which several members of the Orlando Magic's basketball team had booked passage, along with their coach on the red-eye special from Los Angeles en route to New York. Some of the players were really attractive and, one in particular, with the most extraordinarily unusual brown eyes, had written his telephone number on a brand-new set of armbands. He shoved them into her hands as he was exiting the plane in New York saying "Be sure you use these," his eyes twinkling mischievously. Lauren had laughed because he'd been flirting with her the entire trip, ringing the call button to ask for things she knew he didn't need. He'd finally gotten up the nerve to make his move, she thought laughing as she waved good-bye.

Although she'd thought about him once or twice, she'd stopped herself before dialing those digits. Then,

there had been just last week when a young doctor, obviously quite interested in getting to know her, had
given her his dinner napkin with both the hospital and
home numbers scrawled across it. "You can reach me
at the hospital most times," he'd offered. "I'm still doing my residency so I don't really get to spend that much
time at home," he'd added with a smile showing even
white teeth that contrasted nicely against his creamy-
brown complexion. NYU Medical Center was scrawled
across the top and underneath were the two numbers.
It had taken Herculean willpower for Lauren to contemplate adding this one to the mounting collection
she knew she'd never use. He'd seemed genuinely nice
and not at all pushy or conceited, but the thought that
nagged her were memories that were deeply ingrained
in her mind. "I don't want to be another statistic," she'd
reasoned.

Looking up from her station now, Lauren noticed the
captain's signal light flashing. She started toward the
cockpit thinking back on how she'd been somewhat
hesitant about the New York to Los Angeles assignment
when she'd first been given her lines for the month.
Sometimes, especially on transcontinental flights, it
could get a little difficult if the crew wasn't one hundred
percent cooperative. But this crew had turned out to
be one of the best she'd ever had the pleasure of flying
with. There were also times when the element of envy
had to be dealt with simply because she was usually
younger than many of the flight attendants and other
crew members she supervised. As yet though, she'd had
no real problems and was sincerely hoping to keep it
that way.

"Yes, Captain," she said crisply upon entering the
cockpit with a mock salute.

"Coffee, Traynor," he said, obviously amused. "I'm
running out of fuel and the flight hasn't even begun

yet. I'm beginning to think my body has been conditioned to function only on high octane Worldwide Airlines coffee—one sugar, no milk, please," he ended jovially.

"Okay, Captain," Lauren said, smiling and turned toward the copilot. "Anything for you, Anderson?" she asked.

"No, just you, baby," he replied automatically, his eyes remaining fixed on the many gauges, dials and devices that filled the aeronautic panel before him.

Leaving the cockpit, a smile still playing about her mouth, Lauren strode purposefully toward the galley, checking the aisle for anything that might have been left on the floor which would constitute a hazard. She began to prepare a tray with coffee and Danish, knowing that Anderson would be the first one to grab something to eat although he'd been too preoccupied with pre-flight routine checks to acknowledge it.

Her thoughts were interrupted by a deeply masculine, though well-modulated voice asking, "Are you planning to eat all that yourself or are you willing to share with a very hungry passenger?"

Lauren, accustomed to dealing with all types of passengers and in particular, with those who were privileged enough to travel first class, turned slowly, smiled tolerantly and said with professional grace, "If you'll kindly return to your seat, sir, the crew will distribute breakfast shortly after we're airborne."

She then turned back to the coffee burners and was surprised when she realized that the passenger had not moved.

"Sir," she said, turning as she looked up to see who this obtrusive person was. The stormy gray eyes she encountered were not quite what she'd expected. He was tall, at least 6'3" and well-built, though slim. The designer shirt and jeans fit him well. The khaki color of the shirt accentuated the warm olive tones of his skin. His hair was what stood out the most though. Dark, dark brown and curly, it almost gave the appearance of being black. His nose, straight, but not too thin, with gently flaring nostrils gave him an almost rugged, animal look.

Lauren felt her pulse quicken and her breathing become more rapid as she sought to regain her professional composure. Her faltering had not been lost on the passenger, however, and he took her momentary hesitation in, weighing it as he continued to thoroughly gauge her also.

"Sir, if you will kindly take your seat, I will even personally assure you that breakfast will be served momentarily," she replied coolly. Her voice did not give a clue to the rapid pounding in her chest. Inwardly she chided herself for her reaction. *Calm down. He's just another man—just another passenger,* she told herself. But his piercing gray eyes continued to hold her as she struggled to retain a detached, yet professional stance.

Michael Townsend, or Maestro M as he was known in some circles, was sizing this little flight attendant up. He believed women came in two categories, those whom he wanted to spend time with socially, and those whom he could put to some other good use. Right now, he was trying to decide which category this one fit into. He was vaguely aware, in an unpretentious way, of the impact his dark good looks had on most women and knew he could have his pick of the litter. He picked often and never felt the need to make the slightest commitment. His work was his mistress.

Michael had been sixteen when his best friend, Roger's mother had seduced him. Though she and Roger's father had been divorced for several years, Michael had still felt guilty about sleeping with his best friend's mom and ended the affair after six months.

But in that time, Michael had reached a level of sensitivity and skill in lovemaking most men achieve much farther down the road in life. He ended the affair with all the tact and diplomacy his sixteen years of experience could muster. He just stopped answering her calls and stopped showing up. Since that time, he'd pretty much had any woman he wanted. But he always chose carefully. He believed he could read a woman in six seconds flat. Generally, he was right on target, but right now he was trying to read this flight attendant without much success.

He hadn't really been all that hungry, but he'd noticed her as she walked by his seat and glided toward the cockpit a few minutes earlier. He couldn't help but notice her authoritative air and something else that she herself wasn't even aware of. She walked like a woman on the verge of knowing herself. He'd also noticed her body. Although the severity of the uniform sought to effectively detract from the natural curves, its tailored lines only served to accentuate the full bosom, narrow waistline and rounded hips. Her legs, long and slim, were well shaped, but what had really caused Michael to get up and approach her had been her hair. Shoulder-length and silky, its thickness was shimmering lights of bronze with golden auburn highlights. Now, standing this close to her, he realized it was natural and almost matched the golden brown of her eyes, which were unbelievably large and cat-like in their slant. Those eyes were staring right into his and he had the uneasy feeling that she might not be so easy to conquer after all.

She was studying him, too, he realized. Lips parted, showing even white teeth. *She is really something.* Standing there wearing her professional calm, she was coolly waiting for him to take his seat.

"Look, I didn't mean to interrupt your schedule, but I really am hungry," he said earnestly, surprising even himself. "This trip was rather unexpected because I had no advance notice that my partner was going to con me into going to L.A. this morning," he added, nodding toward his seat next to which another passenger sat, head bent in concentration over the *Wall Street Journal.*

"So, Miss Traynor," Michael said glancing at the nameplate she wore, "can you help a brother out?" he added, smiling, which only served to deepen the grooves on each side of his mustached mouth.

"Actually, we're almost ready to begin our in-flight service of breakfast," she replied, smiling in spite of herself. Her face warmed as she realized that her passenger was truly enjoying his little power play.

"Fine. I guess I can hang on a little longer," he added resignedly as he turned, heading back toward his seat in first class.

His legs were long and trim, the jeans molding themselves to his thighs as if made for them. His derriere was strong, too, and Lauren couldn't help but notice that his rear looked as if you could flip a quarter off its resiliency.

Nice buns, she thought inwardly, a smile playing around her mouth. Lauren's heart continued to beat rapidly as she turned to finish preparing the tray for the cockpit crew. *Just what I need,* she thought, *a flirtatious pain in the neck. But what a smile.* And the magnetism she'd felt just standing next to him. And that voice. *Where have I heard it before?*

Wanda, one of the junior flight attendants broke her train of thought as she came into the galley moments later. "So, who was the hunk I saw chatting you up?" she asked as she began to prepare the breakfast trays for distribution.

"Just another hungry passenger," Lauren replied, then added "and a pain in the neck too. Come on, let's get this breakfast rolling before we have half the passenger list breathing down our necks," she said, a hint of irritation in her voice.

The remainder of the flight had been uneventful. As passengers prepared to deplane upon arrival at LAX International Airport, the crew manned all exits of the aircraft, one of the many FAA regulations. Lauren waved good-bye to a six-year-old boy still bubbling with excitement at having completed his first airplane trip. She turned, still smiling to the next passenger.

Michael Townsend murmured, "Great flight," and in one stride closed the distance between them. He reached up, unable to stop himself from attempting to touch a stray curl of Lauren's hair and his hand brushed against her face lightly.

"Great crew too," he said, looking directly into Lauren's eyes.

"Thank you," she responded coolly, but his touch was so heated she was sure her face showed traces of being branded.

"Look, if you're ever in New York and you're not busy, look me up. I can be reached at this number." He handed her an embossed business card.

Lauren dropped it into her uniform pocket and said politely, "Thank you, but I don't think so." She immediately noticed the darkening of his eyes, but then his face masked over and he murmured, "Well, if you change your mind, just call." He turned and walked through the jetway into the Worldwide Airlines terminal.

Almost against her will, Lauren reached into her pocket and pulled out the business card. *Michael Townsend—Program Director—WJZZ Jazz Radio.*

"So that's why his voice sounded so familiar," she murmured.

WJZZ was one of New York's most popular stations. It emphasized jazz, R&B and other urban contemporary music. Lauren had listened to the "Michael Townsend Element" countless numbers of times, including just that morning as she dressed for work.

I did not know he looked like that, she mused, smiling to herself. She was half tempted to tear the card up and throw it away before even leaving the aircraft. Instead, she left it inside her uniform jacket pocket, knowing she'd soon add it to her mounting collection of never-to-be-called prospects.

He probably has a woman in every city from New York to L.A. I'll de damned if I'll be part of the fan club, she thought as she gathered her gear.

Some minutes later as she exited the aircraft, Lauren could still feel the heat of his touch against her temple.

Two

"Good evening, ladies and gentlemen. Welcome to WJZZ and the Michael Townsend Element, where we not only listen to good music, we discover it. Tonight for your listening pleasure, I'd like to spin something you'll really like. It's new, it's hot, and it's most certainly gonna be a big hit. They're probably one of the hottest duos on the scene today—Boney James and Rick Braun. Here's the latest release entitled 'Grazin in the Grass—Can you Dig It.' They're already number one on the Billboard charts and their tour is currently selling tickets like mad."

"Just to keep your groove going, next in line is a new group out of the West Coast—straight from Newport Beach in sunny California. Remember the name Ultra Light—'cause the sound is heavy. I want you to know, too, that they have one of the baddest keyboard players I have ever had the distinct pleasure of listening to—his name by the way is Mitch Tyrell. Don't forget it because this young man is going to be around for a long time to come! Okay, here it is from the CD of the same name, the hot new single entitled 'Follow the Signs.' "

Michael turned the audio to "off" on his mike as the sounds of contemporary jazz filled the control room. He then began to set up the remaining CDs for the evening's programming.

He was worn out both physically and mentally. Los Angeles was always exhausting. He hated the pretentious people, the constant sunshine, and the miles of endless freeway. Then, too, there were the obligatory press parties both he and his partner, Duke Hayes, were required to attend. The primary reason for this most recent trip had been to attend the promotional coming-out parties of two new groups, The Skeffington Five and Ultra Light, whose Virgin release was set to flood the airwaves after the Boney James/Rick Braun single played. Both jazz groups had a distinctive sound, but Michael already suspected that the Ultra Light CD was going to be a success. He usually knew a hit when he heard it and his audience respected and counted on his continuous play of easy listening, smooth as silk, always dependable contemporary urban jazz.

Duke walked into the control room, coffee mug in hand and sat down. "Hey," he said lifting a cowboy-boot-clad foot onto the nearby desk. Michael nodded in greeting and continued to monitor the audio on his playback gauges.

"What happened to you after the party? I thought you and that cute little chick from the public relations firm were hitting it off in a major way. Then wham, I looked up and you were nowhere in sight. She was on the other side of the room looking as if she'd lost her best friend," Duke continued between gulps of coffee.

Michael laughed as he continued to concentrate on the control panel before him. "Hey, man," he said finally, "don't tell me you were actually worried about how I was making out—you looked awfully wrapped up in Simone or whatever her name was," he added, smiling.

"Well, I have to admit that dancers have always intrigued me," Duke said smiling as he smoothed his beard, reminiscing. "They have such incredible balance and dexterity. And what an imagination," he added laughing.

"Spare me the intimate details," Michael said. "I knew it was time for me to get going when she started talking about what a great singer she was! I just knew that if I laid one finger on her, she would probably expect a five-year, two-album recording contract to materialize. Honestly man, I think I'm getting too old for that scene," Michael added as he continued to monitor the programming controls. "You know, I never thought I'd be so turned off to chasing women," he ended, shaking his head in amazement.

"Mike, let me tell you something, you're not getting too old. You sound like you're just tired of all the game playing, man," Duke said putting his cup down. "I went through the same thing once. And do you know what put an end to it?" The rhetorical question hung in the air much like condensed particles in a vacuum—but only for a few short seconds. "Marriage," he said answering his own question with certainty.

"Yeah, and need I remind you that only two years later you're divorced. Thanks, but I don't want to go that route," Michael said shaking his head slowly. "Well, hell nobody wants to go that route, it just happens," Duke responded defensively.

"Well, I don't have the time nor the patience for it in my life. I'll just keep on doing it like I have been," Michael responded. "No promises, no entanglements, no commitments," he added.

"Yeah, that's what you say now, Mike, but do you know what I think? I think you're already over the edge—ready for the plucking," Duke said smoothing his beard again, smiling all the while.

Michael laughed and turned toward him. "Duke, my friend, you're full of it. Marriage is one cliffhanger I think I'll pass on," he said with finality as he flipped the control panel's power switch to off. "Come on, that's it for tonight. I've taken care of the weekend programming, but we are still waiting for the ad spots on Tenneco Industries to come in from the agency," Michael said, signaling the engineer in the audio booth with a thumbs-up sign to conclude and finalize the tape.

"I'll speak to the agency representative on Monday morning," Duke said, rising from his chair. "Keep your chin up, Mikey," he added. "Hey, by the way, are you going to Morgan Pryor's party Saturday night? I hear it's supposed to be a real blast." He walked toward the exit.

"No, I don't think so." Michael picked up his briefcase and sunglasses. "I am a.w.o. after our bit in Los Angeles—all wiped out, if you know what I mean."

"Oh, come on, man," Duke said, throwing his hands up in feigned exasperation. His six-foot-three-inch, 205-pound frame filled the doorway as Michael stood ready for the onslaught which he knew was about to come. Wearing jeans and a dark blue turtleneck, Duke was an impressive sight by any standard. His hair, a combination of gray and black was almost shoulder-length and somewhat curly. A full beard matched the salt and pepper as if by design. He was in good shape due to an almost fanatical obsession with pumping iron.

"I hear the party is at his baby sister's crib," Duke added obviously warming to his subject. "I also hear she is something else. Gorgeous, with a body to die for. It'll probably be worth your while just to get a good look at her. Not to mention the establishment of that all-too-important social camaraderie. After all, Morgan Pryor could very well be our next partner," he added soberly.

"You know, you're incredible," Michael said, shaking his head. "You never cease to amaze me." He laughed, at the look of shock and pain on his partner's face. They both knew that Duke loved women.

"No way," Duke acknowledged. "This is about business—it might be wrapped up in a pretty package like a dinner party or social engagement, but make no mistake, partner, this connection could stand to be very important to us. The sad part is that I've got a previous engagement for that evening. You remember the team from IPI International? Well, they're flying in and we're going to finalize their advertising commitment for the new campaign. You know the deal—dinner, drinks, entertainment—otherwise I'd try to make it to Morgan's bash myself."

"Man, I was looking forward to just being at home, listening to some good music, relaxing and catching up on the pile of *New York Times* that's just inside my doorway, you know," Michael said.

"Yeah, sounds like the kind of weekend I wouldn't wish on my worst enemy," Duke kidded back. "Seriously, partner, Morgan Pryor could very well be the key to the deal we're trying to swing with WTTS and KKSU. I know you realize he's the man behind Cityscape Broadcast Network."

"Of course I'm aware of this dude, Morgan Pryor and his extremely successful radio stations in some of the fastest growing markets—L.A., NY, Chicago and Miami. Actually, I met him in Puerto Rico about three years ago at the annual Radio Technological and Engineering Convention. I think almost any and everybody who was involved in the industry was there that year."

"Right you are, partner, and the endorsement of Morgan Pryor could mean the support of just the investors we'll need when it comes time to pull together the financing for our planned expansion," Duke added.

"Yeah, yeah, okay, I see your point," Michael answered resignedly. "I'll be there. Listen, did we get an invitation or anything?"

"Oh, right," Duke said and reached over to the intercom on Michael's desk. "Caroline, bring that invitation to the CBN party in to Michael will you, sweetheart? I think it's on the credenza in my office," Duke added, turning toward Michael. "Listen, have a good weekend, partner, and don't do anything I probably haven't at least thought of," he added, laughing as he headed toward the outer offices.

"Sure, you too," Michael said. Instinctively, he knew that Duke was right in his estimation of the importance of many of the industry's social nuances. He also knew that if they played their cards right, the next moves would ensure their ability to reach the next level. They had planned it that way and it was, thus far, unfolding according to plan.

Michael picked up the telephone and dialed the building garage. "Hey Rick, this is Mike Townsend. I'll be down in about five. Bring the car around front please," he said quickly and hung up.

The midnight blue Jaguar XJ6 was parked in front of the building when Michael exited the elevators some minutes later. He stepped in, started the motor and inserted a CD marked "For Demonstration Use Only" by Intrigue, a new Swedish jazz group. The clear, sweet sounds of a flute solo filled the car's interior. Michael could physically feel his body begin to instantly unload some of the day's tensions.

Music affected him that way. It always had. Heading uptown on the East River Drive, his thoughts were reminiscent of his childhood. His father, a lieutenant with the New York City Police Department had hardly ever been at home and his mother, a reserved, sensitive woman, had quietly begun to drink. An only child, Michael was often aware of the changes in her personality depending on just how much alcohol she'd consumed that day. He was often alone, but never lonely. His constant companion: music.

He'd sit by the radio, listening to the rhythmic sounds coming out and find comfort in the tones, the notes, and the melodies. At the age of nine, when his dad had surprised him and brought home a small guitar, he'd been hooked. The lessons had been expensive, but Michael had loved playing so much and had been so naturally good at it that his father felt compelled to continue the lessons.

Michael, along with his best friend, Roger Garner, formed a band with two older boys the year they both turned fifteen. Roger played horn, Eric was on percussion, and Gary played keyboards. It had been great fun for a while, but then some of the guys had begun to miss the weekly rehearsals. When they did show up, they were more interested in smoking pot and drinking beer than they were in jamming. Michael became disgusted. He vowed from the age of fourteen to keep as far away from drinking and drugs as he could. He'd seen what it was doing to his mother. There were times when he even sometimes went so far as to pour out the liquor he often found lying around the house, replacing it with water. She always seemed to manage to find more, drinking herself unconscious on many afternoons.

The year he turned eighteen was a pivotal point in Michael's life. It was the year that he graduated high school, it was the year he came to the realization that he wanted a career in the music industry, and it was the year in which his mother died. Her liver had not been able to take the many years of alcohol abuse. Neither he nor his dad had been aware though, that Monica Townsend had lived her life being a relatively well-off woman. Content to live on her husband's salary, it seemed her father, a talented and innovative leather craftsmen who had migrated from Barbados to the United States, had had the foresight to invest heavily in utility stocks.

He'd accumulated quite a cache of staples like Consolidated Edison, Brooklyn Union Gas and even some Bell Telephone.

Monica Townsend had somehow known that the end was near and, two years before her death, had transferred all certificates into her only son's name. As fate would have it, Michael also won a full scholarship to Northwestern University in music appreciation. Midway into his sophomore year, Michael made the decision to change his major to engineering and to minor in music. As it turned out, what he actually studied were the females. Tall, short, light, dark, sorority sisters, homegirls, all shapes and sizes. Michael had them all. His dark good looks seemed to attract them like honey. He always let them know, though, right from the start, that all he was interested in was having a good time—and he in turn made sure they had fun too.

The only indulgence of his inheritance he'd allowed himself was the purchase of a brand-new spitfire red Alfa Romeo two-seater and it became his trademark. The tall, dark, good-looking engineering student who could also play the hell out of an electric guitar became legendary for zipping about the small college town, always with an interesting girl at his side, but never the same one twice.

He'd met Douglas Theodore Hayes, better known as "Duke" in his junior year at Northwestern. Duke had been a senior then. The son of a drugstore chain owner, Duke had been tall and good-looking in an Ivy League sort of way. The two had met more as competitors than as anything else. They were both dating one of the school's most popular students, Deirdre Marshall, who also held the distinction of being sophomore class vice president, captain of the cheerleading squad and assistant editor of *The Legionnaire*, the school newspaper. As it turned out, neither had taken the co-ed seriously and she'd ended up dumping them both for a third-year law student, but it had served to bring them to each other's attention. They became inseparable, and after graduation continued to keep in touch. When Duke had been offered the purchase of station WJZZ through the National Broadcasting Service Investors, his first thought had been of Michael Townsend as a senior partner as well as program director. He'd contacted him back in New York and the deal had been set.

The station had done exceptionally well after they'd switched the direction of its programming from pop/rock to adult contemporary jazz. Michael seemed to possess an innate gift for spotting upcoming new music and new talent specifically geared toward their rapidly growing listening audience. He knew his audience and what they wanted to hear it seemed, before they did.

Duke was the force behind the financial end of the operation. A business major with a high quotient of credits in marketing, he was a financial whiz at corporate investments and capital outlay. They were currently in the process of attempting to acquire two new stations—KSSU in Los Angeles and WTTS in Atlanta. Although revenue was not a problem, they both realized that a thorough, in-depth analysis of the market was absolutely necessary before any green light could be given to the deal.

One of the major potential investors in the stations to be acquired could be Morgan Pryor, an independent financier who had a reputation for tying the knots on some of the most lucrative deals ever consummated in the radio broadcast industry. He was also the major decision maker for the network of radio stations he owned throughout the United States. Cityscape Broadcast Network had consistently posted above-average audience numbers for the past three years and had a list of advertisers which were enviable industry wide.

Word on the street that Pryor was somehow mob related certainly set the stakes at a different level. Michael knew from having done his homework that he and Duke needed to seal this merger if they were to get to the next level. What he was unsure of was exactly how motivated Morgan Pryor was. He also knew it would most certainly be in his and his partner's best interests to find out.

He intended to do just that.

Three

The persistent ring of the doorbell awakened Lauren from a dream-filled sleep. Turning on the video monitor to the lobby as she stretched lazily, she wondered who could be coming to visit at this hour. Her bedside clock radio read 7:15 A.M. The screen was filled by the image of a deliveryman, cap in hand, impatiently pacing.

"Yes, can I help you?" Lauren said into the receiver mounted on the wall nearest the bedroom doorway.

"Yeah, lady, we have a delivery for apartment 4F. Steuben glassware," he muttered, clearly impatient.

"Glassware," Lauren repeated more to herself than anyone else. "Are you sure you have the right apartment?" she asked thinking he had probably just rung the wrong bell.

"The name on the order is Sorrentino—apartment 4F," he repeated with exaggerated calm.

"Oh," she exclaimed suddenly remembering that it was the tenth. Morgan and Gloria's dinner party was scheduled for this evening.

"Okay, look, you'll have to go around to the freight elevators," she replied. Pressing the electronic buzzer that activated the doorman's telephone, Lauren hurriedly pulled on a pair of jeans and a sweatshirt with "Columbia" emblazoned across the front.

"Max, there are some deliveries being made. Please show them to the freight elevators," she said.

"Sure thing, Miss Traynor," he answered quickly.

Knocking twice on Gloria's door, Lauren was not at all surprised to see her roommate's prone form with a pillow covering most of her head.

"Come on, sleeping beauty," she said softly while tugging at the pillow gently. "You have to sign for a delivery in a minute—get up and throw something on," she added as she continued trying to rouse her unresponsive roommate.

"You sign for me," Gloria replied sleepily while turning over.

"Sorry, pal, but I can't. They're in the Sorrentino name."

"Oh, for heaven's sake," Gloria finally grumbled as reality made its painful way through her slumber-induced resolve.

"Where is it?" she asked, sitting up and tossing her pillow away from the rumpled bed with impatience.

"They're on the way up—you'd better throw something on. I'll make some coffee—you look as if you could use it," Lauren said over her shoulder as she made her way toward the kitchen.

That was to be the first of many deliveries made that day. Mikasa china arrived next, then cases of imported champagne, Russian vodka, Scotch, bourbon, rum, and rye whiskey. Two cases of dinner wines, red and white were also delivered as both Lauren and Gloria stared in amazement at the sheer abundance of everything.

"I thought you said this was going to be a small, informal dinner party," Lauren said quizzically.

"I know, I know. But you know how Morgan and my dad are," Gloria answered, throwing her arms up in exasperation. "This doesn't even come close to my definition of small or intimate," she added, shaking her head.

The caterer, chef, and serving staff from Maxwell's Plum arrived at about 4:30 and began setting up the serving tables. They laid out the china and crystal as two chefs began to prepare the evening's fare. Spinach salad supreme with fresh mushrooms, cold broccoli and pasta with pesto salad along with a huge seafood salad containing large chunks of lobster, shrimp and lump crab meat were prepared. Avocado souffle, ratatouille, chicken parmesan and fresh hot pasta were the evening's entrées. Appetizers consisting of miniature vegetable quiche, smoked salmon on rye wafers and assorted crudites with a curried yogurt dip were to be circulated among the guests during an informal cocktail hour.

Fresh pineapple slices, papaya, mangoes, kiwi fruit and assorted cheeses adorned one buffet table. Each serving station held a centerpiece consisting of an oversized crystal vase filled with one dozen peach roses, baby's breath and eucalyptus. The colors complimented the warm earth tones of the foyer magnificently.

By 6:30, the disc jockey, a.k.a. "Groove Mix Master" had completed his makeshift booth that housed his necessary equipment. Dual turntables, two 250-watt amplifiers and what appeared to be miles and miles of wiring were painstakingly attached to four six-foot speakers distributed strategically around the large living room.

By 7:00, both Lauren and Gloria were dressed. Lauren had chosen a one-shouldered white tea-length dress she had purchased from a small consignment shop in the east 80s. Designed by Emanuel Ungaro, it undulated in flattering ripples whenever she moved. The wrapped lines of the bodice outlined the swell of her breasts while slight gathers accentuated her tiny waist and gently flaring hips. Black patent leather sandals with two thin straps that crisscrossed at the instep complimented the elegance of her outfit. Her hair, shimmering brilliantly from the lemon rinse she'd used after shampooing, cascaded down and around her shoulders. Just before leaving her bedroom, Lauren decided to add a winding gold bracelet to her bare-shouldered arm. She then selected a mother-of-pearl comb, pinning her hair back behind one ear. The effect was stunning, but to her she appeared her ordinary self, a trifle dressed up she thought, for what had been billed as a "casual dinner party."

Gloria had selected a strapless black beaded bustier. The matching black taffeta skirt hugged her slender form as if by design. Purchased from Saks Fifth Avenue, it had an inverted pleat that opened to reveal more beading, creating the optical illusion of a slit directly up the center. Her hair, a rich charcoal black, was pulled severely back from her face and twisted upwards into a classic knot. Small black onyx-and-diamond earrings adorned each ear. They'd been a Christmas gift from her father, purchased at Tiffany's. Gloria couldn't wait to see his reaction. Gino hated her in black.

The first guests arrived shortly after 8:45. From then on, it was difficult to keep track. At Morgan's insistence, his chauffeur, Reggie had been stationed just inside the small foyer which led directly from the elevators into the apartment. His instructions were to greet the arriving guests, check their invitations and show them to the entrance. In the next hour, the normally spacious, uncluttered, ultra-modern apartment overflowed with people of every imaginable persuasion. Singles, couples and groups arrived. An interesting blend of businessmen, creative people, professionals and radio personalities completed the mix—the cream of the New York crop. Morgan had compiled the guest list with a specific goal of expansion in mind. All the guests arriving reflected that objective. Morgan had done his homework.

Gloria and Morgan were in conversation with Danton Arias, a fashion photographer whose latest work had graced the covers of *Elle* and *Vogue* magazines. The son of a member of the Venezuelan Consulate, Danton had been educated in London's finest schools. At his mother's insistence—she was American, born in Texas—and over his father's objections, he'd attended Northwestern University. He'd then moved to Paris where he'd studied at the Sorbonne for two years. During that time, he'd worked with some of the major fashion houses on the Cote d'Azure. The training and experience he received showed up brilliantly in his work. Since returning to the United States, he'd literally taken New York and the fashion industry by storm. Danton looked up now and could hardly believe his eyes.

"Michael," he called out, practically shouting to be heard over the music and the drone of conversation in the room.

Michael Townsend, having just exited the elevator, stood just inside the entrance and produced his invitation for the attendant's inspection, then waited for his eyes to adjust to the subdued lighting. Dressed in a tobacco-colored linen suit, he made a strikingly handsome appearance. His shirt, open at the neck, was collarless and of a tan slightly darker in hue than the suit itself. The muted colors set off his dark hair and gray eyes dramatically. Hearing his name and with surprise plainly etched on his face, Michael smiled broadly and crossed the room in long, purposeful strides.

"Danton, what the hell are you doing here?" he asked, his hand outstretched. The two former classmates shook hands, then clasped each other in a mock bear hug.

"Hey, didn't you know I was back from Paris?" Danton replied with feigned indignation. "I know I called

your place and left a message at least once," he stated
with certainty.

"Sure you did. I even saw the spread you did in *Harper's Bazaar.* That was some layout, especially those jungle scenes. And forgive my not getting back to you
sooner, but sometimes I'm overwhelmed by the station's
demands," Michael added laughing.

"Yeah, it was an incredible shoot—hot as hell in the
Florida Everglades though."

"Hey man," Danton said suddenly breaking into a
huge grin, "I, along with the rest of New York City's
avant garde population have been listening to your station and I want to tell you that's some fantastic stuff
you play. You were always heavy into the music though,
even back at Northwestern." He reached over and patted his alumni buddy on the shoulder, adding fondly,
"Damn, it's good to see you."

"You too, Danton, you too. And it's great to hear that
you're into the station's programming. You know we
realized that we'd captured a good portion of the New
York audience, but it definitely does my heart good to
know that we're reaching the A crowd," Michael noted
enthusiastically.

A waiter approached, carrying champagne-filled
flutes and they each removed one from the tray offered.

Suddenly, remembering Morgan and Gloria who had
since become engaged in conversation with a very short,
very pretty blonde dressed in red silk pajamas, Danton
turned and began introductions.

"Michael Townsend, I'd like you to meet our host,
Morgan Pryor," he said as the two men shook hands.
"Michael was at Northwestern with me. You've heard
of WJZZ. Well this is the man behind the station," he
added proudly.

Michael had actually noticed Morgan and Gloria
when he'd entered the room. Although they'd never

been formally introduced, he knew enough about the industry to be able to recognize anyone who was of any importance.

"This is some bash," he offered, noting the cut of Morgan's suit, the fine fabric and the faultless fit. Morgan Pryor was obviously a man who spared no expense in fostering the absolute best in his appearance.

"Why thank you. It does seem to be turning out quite well," Morgan agreed, turning to survey the now-packed apartment. "I'd like you to meet a very special young lady, my sister, Gloria," he said draping one arm protectively across her shoulders.

"I'm very pleased to meet you," Gloria said as she looked Michael straight in the eyes and extended a very businesslike handshake with a surprisingly firm grip.

Michael liked that. It meant this sister of Morgan's was no pushover, although her "big brother" seemed to not as yet have gotten that message. Duke had been right though, she was a knockout. But for some unfathomable reason, he had absolutely no desire to hit on her. *Duke's right, I must be losing my touch*, he mused inwardly.

"Didn't we meet in Puerto Rico at a broadcasting convention about four years ago?" Morgan asked, interrupting his thoughts.

"You know, I think you're right, we certainly did," Michael said, realizing that Morgan's mind was obviously as sharp as his clothes. He hadn't expected that the venture capitalist would remember that minor, inconsequential meeting.

"My partner, Duke Hayes and I had just closed the deal on our first station. We're now in the process of negotiating for a couple of new acquisitions."

"Well, I happen to know that you guys did a beautiful job of turning WJZZ-FM around—and in record time, too," Morgan said handing Michael his card. "Call me if you want to discuss financing strategies and perhaps, some creative maneuvers. We own stations in all the major markets," he explained.

"Sure. I'm very aware of your network holdings and have also admired some of the maneuvers I've come to realize were orchestrated by your organization," Michael said carefully. "I wouldn't consider myself effectively plugged in if I wasn't aware of CBN and how well it's doing."

Michael noticed that Gloria, who had been quietly sipping her champagne, listened with mild interest while scanning the room.

Lauren, having gone into her bedroom with a mild headache some minutes earlier, was seriously considering making a quiet exit for a much-needed breath of fresh air. She would be glad when this party was over. After checking her makeup she made her way, once again, into the now overly crowded living room area. Gloria spotted her almost immediately and motioned for her to join them.

All right, all right, Lauren thought with a small degree of annoyance as she slowly made her way toward the group consisting of Gloria, Morgan and a tall gentleman whose back was to her. *I hope this is not one of Morgan's sidekicks,* she thought.

"Lauren, honey," Gloria said, ignoring her roommate's look of *I'm gonna kill you.* "I'd like you to meet Michael Townsend. Michael, say hello to my roommate, Lauren Traynor," she added, completing her introductions.

Turning toward her, Michael smiled, his surprise masked by a cool veneer. "I think Miss Traynor and I have already met," he said as he held out his hand.

"Yes, a few weeks ago en route to L.A.," Lauren said

with amusement and surprise etched on her face as she politely took his outstretched palm. The contact was electric.

"Well then, I'll leave you two to get reacquainted," Gloria said as she drifted off to continue mingling.

"Michael, I'll be looking forward to hearing from you soon," Morgan said once again extending his hand in a final handshake.

"Count on it," Michael responded decisively, knowing that Duke would be impressed by how easily he'd made the contact that this evening was all about.

He then turned his full attention to Lauren, taking into account her outfit, her fragrance, her demeanor, and most of all, her presence.

"You look great," he said in the deep, rich voice she remembered only too well. As a waiter approached with a tray of champagne, his eyes drank of her taking in every curve, every cleft and every line of her body.

"Why thank you, Mr. Townsend," Lauren replied as she sipped her champagne rather nervously. It did not escape Michael's notice.

"If memory serves, you were going to contact me, Miss Traynor." An impudent smile played around his mustached mouth as he awaited her reply.

"I don't know what gave you that idea." Anger began to bubble up within her. She was also angry at herself for not being able to turn away from looking into his incredibly penetrating eyes—they spoke volumes to her even if what seemed to come out of his mouth made her want to laugh in his face. If he thought that his looks, charm or his success was some kind of "free pass" to accumulate women—that she was going to tumble at his feet like some brainless bimbo, he had another thing coming. She was fuming, but she'd be darned if she'd let him see her anger.

"I am sorry," she said slowly, enunciating each word

carefully so that he'd get the message quickly and definitively. "I don't make it a habit of calling or dating passengers. In fact, I don't date passengers at all," she added emphatically.

"I see," Michael said, not wanting to believe her. "And I'm sure you have your reasons for that particular rule so I guess it was fate that I ran into you again. I'm not a passenger now, am I?" he countered with obvious amusement.

"No, but this isn't a date either," she volleyed.

They both laughed, realizing each would be a formidable opponent. She had to admit that he was at least quick on his feet, but then that too was part of the game. She smiled then, realizing it was going to be an interesting evening after all. She noticed that his eyes which had appeared gray a moment before, now appeared to be almost black.

"Why are you looking at me like that?" she asked when she noticed that he appeared to be almost staring at her throat.

"I was just thinking how absolutely lovely you are," he said candidly. He wanted to add that the sight of her slender, graceful neck and shoulders made him think of other things. But he sensed that if he were to tell her what he was truly thinking, she would probably slap his face. He laughed at the thought.

Lauren, eyes flashing, said, "What's the joke—I hope you're not laughing at my expense, Mr. Townsend," she added cautiously.

"No, not at all, and please call me Michael. Look, let's call a truce—I think we got off to a very bad start on that flight. I'd really like to get to know you better—and for you to get to know me too. Deal?" he asked sincerely, looking into her eyes. The effect was magnetic and Lauren found herself unable to remain aloof or angry.

What the hell, it's just a party, she told herself. *And I might as well try to enjoy myself in the spirit of getting through the evening,* she thought inwardly. "Okay, Michael," she responded smiling, wondering why each time she looked into his unreadable gray eyes, she couldn't help but also notice the rapid beating of her heart.

Lauren turned away from him then, thinking that perhaps another glass of champagne might make her less nervous. In profile, her beauty was astounding. Michael's pulse began to beat rapidly and he knew he wanted her, wanted her as much and maybe more than he'd wanted any woman in a long time. But he wanted her on his terms and he knew she wasn't ready for that. Not yet anyway. Duke's words of the week before flashed through his mind: *You're ready for the plucking, man,* but he pushed them aside.

"Would you like to dance?" he asked, reaching for her hand.

"Sure," she replied softly. "Just let me finish this first." She attributed her nervousness to the fact that until now, she'd been stone-cold sober. Something about this dark-haired man caused her to lose her composure. She finished the second glass of champagne in three gulps.

"Do you normally do everything so quickly?" Michael asked as he guided her toward an area where several couples were dancing.

"Only when I'm in a hurry," Lauren replied coolly, choosing to ignore his insinuation.

As they began to dance, Lauren felt the pulsating music take over her body. A good dancer from the time she could walk, she'd studied ballet from the age of seven until she turned twelve. Five years of training showed itself now in the fluid, almost sensual movements of her body. Michael, who prided himself in being a quick study of human nature, observed and marveled at the sensuality she displayed. Hair thrown back, slender neck exposed and that slender curvaceous body gyrating to the beat, she was really testing his resolve to keep his distance.

Control yourself, he thought. *She's just another chick. Yeah, but what a body,* he thought and those eyes, slanting upward, their bright amber color enhanced by long thick lashes. She reminded him of a sinewy alley cat enclosed in the body of a beautiful, sophisticated, untapped goddess. Wow, just the thought of all that raw, unrefined power sent his senses reeling, he realized suddenly as they began to dance.

Lauren's thoughts were with the music. The two glasses of champagne she'd consumed had begun to relax her and she now focused solely on the music. It inspired an impulse to totally abandon her normal conscious self, and that abandon showed in her complete involvement in the beat. She danced as if there were no tomorrow, no tonight . . . time had ceased to exist as did her surroundings. A small crowd began to gather, encouraging her. Only then did she notice the surprise and obvious enjoyment on Michael's face. The record ended and she felt as if she were climbing up out of some dense fog.

She felt Michael's arm encircle her waist as he whispered, his lips very close to her ear, "Let's get some air, Lauren." She breathed in great gulps of air when they reached the terrace.

"I don't know what got into me in there," she said, her face flushed from exertion. "I'm a little embarrassed."

"Don't be. You were having one hell of a good time from the looks of it," Michael said laughing. "And you made me look good too," he added. "Where did you learn to dance like that?" he asked with genuine curiosity.

"I don't know. Some of it just came naturally, but my parents were sticklers for dance lessons all throughout my formative years," Lauren responded, laughing now too. "I just know that I love music and whenever I hear something with a good beat, it sets me off—especially after two glasses of champagne." She smiled, realizing that she was probably a little bit drunk.

"So, Lauren Traynor with the uninhibited dance moves, where are you from originally?" Michael asked, smiling gently into her eyes.

"Well, I was born in West Germany. My father was a captain in the army then, and we lived mainly in Europe while I was growing up—Germany, then France and finally Spain. We came back to the States when I was about eleven. Dad was stationed at Ft. Dix in New Jersey. By the time I entered high school, the summer vacation crowd at the Jersey shore was as much a part of my life as breathing. Wildwood, Cape May, Seaside Heights, those were my playgrounds as a teenager and I found work each summer at the boardwalk concessions."

"I see—so you're obviously well traveled which helps to explain your sophistication. Where did you go to school?" he asked, now fully interested in all the nuances of the fascinating creature before him.

"I went to Rutgers University and after graduation, applied to Worldwide Airlines—and was accepted. So, here I am, based out of New York's John F. Kennedy Airport."

Michael, who had been listening intently, found himself wanting to hear more. It wasn't that her story was any more fascinating than the many others he'd heard. He was, in fact, fascinated by her. She possessed a freshness, a candor that he knew was real. And that was rare . . . rare indeed. "Thirsty?" He asked as he signaled a waiter carrying trays filled with more champagne.

"Yes, I am. Are you trying to get me drunk so that you can seduce me, Michael?" she asked as she took a sip from the champagne flute he handed her. Momentarily caught off guard by her seriousness, he looked directly into her eyes. "My intentions are honorable and above board. I plan to wait until you do the seducing," he said pointedly.

"Well then, I guess neither of us has anything to worry about," she countered defiantly.

Michael was finding it more and more difficult to control a natural urge to take her in his arms. Outwardly though, he appeared his usual composed self.

"So, you're hell-bent on giving me a hard time, aren't you?" he said, smiling, and her breath caught momentarily in her throat.

"What else would you expect of an army brat, Mr. Townsend?" she countered with feigned indignation. Lauren laughed, tossing her hair back from her face. Despite her initial reservations and reluctance, she was having a good time.

Michael reached out, unable to stop himself from lightly stroking her hair's silkiness. He wanted to bury his face in its mass. Her eyes stared intently into his. She knew he wanted to kiss her, could feel it in his touch and see it in his eyes. Yet, something held him back.

"I think you are going to be a big problem for me," he said finally.

"Really? Why, are you married?" she heard herself ask quietly.

Michael's laughter was like a glass of cold water in her face. "No, and I don't have any plans to be," he answered calmly.

Hot with indignation she answered, "Well, that's fine with me. I feel the same way. You know, my parents were married for twenty-seven years. My mother had to constantly adjust to living in all kinds of places, foreign countries and different cities. Lots of times, it was damn rough on her. I was a child so it was a little easier for me to adjust, I think. And Dad had the military to help re-orient him to the locale," she added with a trace of bitterness in her voice. "Well, they were divorced about three years ago—after twenty-seven years of marriage. All those years down the drain, wasted—I don't want to end up like that. I'm never going to marry anyone," she ended vehemently.

Michael said nothing, yet continued to observe her, unable to tear his eyes away. She was beautiful, stubborn, vulnerable and everything he'd ever wanted. "Well, that's a relief. Now all we have to worry about is how much champagne you can put away in one evening," he said, breaking the mood. They both laughed.

The sky was lit by pre-dawn light as Michael took Lauren's hand and whispered reluctantly, "I'd better be going, it's getting late." Several times throughout the evening, he'd almost given in to an overpowering urge to kiss her softly pouting lips. He sensed a degree of genuine reticence on her part though. Maybe it was this that caused him to hold back—or maybe it was the uncertainty of where it would lead. There were still a few couples talking quietly in the living room, music playing softly in the background.

"I'd like to take you to dinner sometime if that's okay," he said as they walked toward the elevator. "Why don't I call you?" It was a statement, not a question.

"I'm not really into dating, Michael—so really, what's the point?" she said, figuring he'd give up if she really appeared disinterested.

"Look, it doesn't really have to be a date. Actually,

I'd like to hear more about the time you spent in Europe. It's something of a pet peeve of mine that I've never been although I've been almost everywhere else. Okay? You'd be doing a friend a favor," he ended somewhat convincingly.

"Well, okay, fine if you want to," Lauren responded carefully with a slight note of caution in her voice.

Michael noted her hesitancy, but dismissed it immediately. He knew that if he backed off now, she'd be off and running. Running away from him and any other man who represented a threat to the safe little world she'd concocted.

"Are you listed in the book?" he asked as they approached the foyer where Reggie had been stationed earlier in the evening. It was deserted now, the overhead lights dimmed to a golden glow. In this light, tiny flakes of golden glitter appeared to adorn Lauren's face, hair and shoulders.

"Yes," she answered in a small voice as though pondering if she trusted herself to give even this small an amount of information.

Michael turned toward her then, tilting her chin upward to meet his lips in a kiss that was soft and undemanding. Her lips clung to his as the kiss went on and on, slowly deepening in intensity and heat. Lauren felt her entire body begin to respond as he slowly enticed her, running his tongue lightly across her lips before he tentatively found his way into the warm inner recesses of her mouth.

She surprised herself by boldly returning his play, but his response, immediate and sure, was anything but playful. She felt the pure maleness of him, sensed the thorough engagement of his senses and knew that this was not a man with whom to indulge in unfulfilled passion. She also realized that she was helpless to stop herself as her responses were not so easily within voluntary reach anymore. Her pulse quickened along with her breathing as he began to explore the inner recesses of her mouth languidly yet thoroughly, her body responding with an unknown urgency of its own. Her lips, no longer uncertain, parted as she began her own, somewhat timid, exploration in return. Her arms wound around his neck as she pressed her body into his.

Michael's surprise at her sudden abandon nearly caught him off guard. All reason left him as she daringly molded her soft body to the length of his. He slowly, methodically trailed kisses from her mouth to her neck and gently grasped her head, reveling in the feel of her soft silky hair. His hands moved lower as he caressed her shoulders and back.

Lauren felt as though she were being drawn into some unknown vortex.

He began to gently explore the sloping curves of her breasts, the slow circling motion causing her nipples to become erect under his practiced hands almost immediately. His breathing became harsh, his mouth more insistent and his hands increasingly more daring.

"Let's go back inside," he murmured thickly against her mouth. With her back now against the wall opposite the elevator doors, Michael continued his ministrations, thoroughly acquainting himself with every crevice, every corner of her soft mouth, and slowly moved to the swell of her breasts over the bodice of her dress.

"No," she managed to murmur, tearing her mouth away from his suddenly, his hands on either sides of her body shielding her effectively from any further movement.

"No?" he repeated, his lips hovering just above hers in a questioning stance. Lauren surprised herself then, making the first move and reestablishing the connection. She lifted her lips to his, throwing caution and

modesty to the wind as she provocatively slid her tongue
into his mouth.

His response was immediate. His mouth traveled
slowly down the slope of her neck and shoulder to
the creamy smooth expanse of flesh which he'd exposed by somehow lowering the single strap, as all
rational thought fled her being.

This has to stop, she told herself inwardly even as the
pounding in her chest found its way to the heart of her
womanhood. Yet, she couldn't bring herself to break
the contact. She felt his breath on her breast, the heat
of his tongue warm and wet encircling the cone, teasing
it lovingly with his tongue as the nipple responded to
his ministrations as if by order. Lauren's knees grew
weak and she realized she only remained standing because he had taken her weight onto his frame—his hips
molded to hers boldly. She took a deep breath, drawing
on willpower once relegated to "reserve strength," put
both hands against his chest and pushed gently, tearing
her lips away.

"I think you should leave now," she managed to
quickly utter through lips still swollen from his kisses.

Michael's confusion was evident, yet he asked no
questions, his gray eyes unreadable. He had been surprised by her responsiveness, but he had been thoroughly caught off guard by his own reaction to the
nearness of her. She definitely spelled trouble, but he
had never backed away from a challenge in his life and
he wasn't about to start tonight.

"It is definitely time for you to go home," Lauren
repeated, her breath coming in shallow bursts. She
pushed the elevator button quickly, struggling to regain
her composure.

"Right," Michael said as he stepped into the elevator.
"Are you sure you don't want to continue our discussion

of your tortured childhood?" he asked. "I think I may have some answers for you."

She laughed then and he realized that he had enjoyed this evening more than any he'd experienced in a long time.

"Great party," he said as the elevator doors opened.

Lauren could still feel her heart pounding as she smoothed her hair, restored her dress and took several deep breaths before returning to the interior of the apartment. Her attempt to restore order to her outward appearance was easily accomplished; her heart, her mind and body were another story.

Four

Morgan Pryor leaned back in the buttery-soft fawn-colored leather chair, his gaze focused on the view below him. His thoughts, however, were a million miles away. Forty-six stories below, the Madison Avenue lunch-hour crowds hurriedly made their way, unaware of their casual observer. The plush interior of his office served to detract somewhat from the harshness of Morgan's own private reality of late. Warm bronze tones, beige highlights and accents of stark chocolate brown reigned throughout. A long sleek sofa, covered in deep brown suede lined one wall elegantly. A low, squat glass rectangular coffee table of equal length sat solidly in front of it. His desk, uncluttered and gleaming in the afternoon sunlight was constructed entirely of glass with thick brass legs. The executive styled high-back chair which sat behind it was done in sumptuous tan Brazilian leather.

In one corner, a large wooden totem pole towered, an authentic replica of a Cheyenne ceremonial piece. It had been a gift from Morgan's stepdad, Gino Sorrentino, delivered with the note, "Not worth a plugged nickel" attached. Morgan had kept the card as a kind of keepsake, but he actually loved the pole.

The thick pile carpet brought to mind rich, dark espresso with random, angular splashes of cream. It ex-

tended upward and fully covered the raised platform
on which Morgan's desk sat. The ceiling-borne high
hats were powerful lighting elements, but had been
dimmed to a mere glimmer. One wall featured a circular clock constructed of a single slab of bronze-colored
onyx, its large black hands making both a design and
practical statement.

Amid this plush interior lived a man who was on the
verge of desperation. He had no qualms about his financial condition—that much was solid. His radio network, Cityscape Broadcasting Network extended
throughout the major markets of the United States.
That much accessibility to any media form meant
power. But Morgan was no fool. He knew his power had
limitations—serious limitations. He also knew that he
was about to put those limitations to the test.

Thus far, his relationship with his stepfather, Gino,
had remained under control. It had been during his
senior year at New York University where he was major-
ing in law that his mother had informed him of her
intention to remarry. He'd been shocked. He hadn't
even known she was dating. Grudgingly, and after much
verbal persuasion, he'd agreed to meet his stepfather-
to-be. Morgan guessed right off, and correctly so, that
Gino was a wiseguy, but what he couldn't believe was
how much his mother seemed to adore the man.

The name Sorrentino had bothered him the entire
time he was smiling, shaking hands, and making nice
with Gino. It wasn't until he'd arrived back at school
that it came to him. Any dedicated student of law
would have recognized that name. *Gino Sorrentino*. His
was one of the foremost names in the Kent investigations which had been ongoing for the past three
years. The probe, conducted primarily by the FBI, involved New York City, Chicago and Miami with the
Grand Jury seeking an indictment against at least

three men reputed to be underworld crime kingpins. At the head of this formidable list was Gino Sorrentino. The problem, it seemed, was that each time the Grand Jury sequestered a witness who could corroborate any of their evidence, something happened to that individual. There had been at least four such cases over the span of three years. Two were found in the trunk of an abandoned Jeep parked underneath the West Side Highway with their heads blown off, one had suddenly been admitted to Bellevue's psychiatric ward in a catatonic state suffering from a complete and total breakdown, and a fourth had disappeared altogether. Efforts to locate the individual had, as yet, been unsuccessful. Though the FBI and local police departments of each city had provided an intensive dragnet, no significant case-breaking clues had been found as to how these *coups de grace* had been expedited. The why was evident. Someone did not want their testimony to reach the stand and had gone to a lot of trouble to make sure of just that.

Morgan had never discussed Gino's background with his mother. She wouldn't allow it. And when they were married in a civil ceremony six weeks later, Morgan vowed that he'd protect her from any exposure to his stepfather's world of unwritten rules.

He hadn't found out until much later that he would also be inheriting a stepsister. And although he originally vowed not to like her, not to interact with her and to spend as little time as possible with her, she'd ultimately grown on him. Some seven years his junior, Gloria had become an important part of his world. He wanted to protect her from all that his stepfather's inner circle had to offer as much as he wanted to protect his mother. He wasn't sure if he could pull it off though because Gino was in fact, her father. A product of his first marriage, Gloria was his only biological offspring and that made things even more sticky. Gloria had attached herself to her "big brother" like a barnacle to an old, rusty salvage tanker. Morgan hadn't expected that, but in time he'd grown to tolerate it and of late, even come to appreciate the relationship he shared with her.

What he really hadn't anticipated was Gino's generosity. Not only did he see to it that Morgan finished NYU Law, he'd also exposed him to contract litigation little by little. By doing so, he'd insured himself a vested partner in his newest business enterprise—radio.

Morgan Pryor became one of the youngest investors in a radio network spanning the east coast market. With his background in corporate law helping to insure some of the most ironclad deals ever constructed, his fate was sealed. That had been twelve long years ago.

Now, Gino Sorrentino was a silent partner. Therein lay the problem. Morgan wanted him out. It had become increasingly apparent that Gino was losing control over his people and his own fate. Not only had there been numerous arrests and convictions, but a new federal probe had just been launched into racketeering and Morgan knew it was time to throw in the towel. There was only one way to go and that was legit. But how much time and money would it take to set up all the necessary mechanisms and put the appropriate controls into place? That was the number one question plaguing Morgan Pryor and no easy answers were forthcoming.

The party he'd given at Gloria's apartment had been a huge success—both from a social as well as a business standpoint. He'd been diligent in creating the guest list and it had served to accomplish just what he'd had in mind. He leaned over and pressed the intercom—"Jennifer, get me a Michael Townsend over at station WJZZ and if he's not in, ask for his partner, Duke Hayes," he said, the business card laying directly in his line of vision.

A moment later, the intercom signaled, with Jennifer announcing Mr. Townsend on line one.

"Hey, how's it going," Morgan said quickly, using the speakerphone.

"Fine, just fine," Michael replied, a little surprised that he'd heard from Morgan Pryor so soon.

"Well, I thought it would be a good idea for us to get together—perhaps over lunch sometime in the coming week if your schedule permits," Morgan stated.

"Just let me check with my secretary on that—hang on a minute." Michael put the call on hold. He came back on the line several moments later. "Okay, how about Wednesday at, say one o'clock?"

"That's good for me too," Morgan said. He'd already calculated the exact amount of time it would take the consultants to complete their ongoing research. Tuesday morning had been the determined deadline and would allow ample time for dissection, absorption and even correction if necessary, to the crucial reports they would deliver.

"Do you know Hurley's on Sixth Avenue?"

"Yes, I do—they reportedly have some of the best steaks in New York City." Morgan's obvious attention to detail could only mean one thing—he was serious about the meeting. And that was a good sign, Michael surmised.

"They most certainly do," Morgan agreed. "Okay, and bring your partner along too—we might as well get the necessary feedback from all interested parties. I just think it's about time we sat down and decided what the future of radio in this sector of the country should be for the next decade," Morgan threw in, knowing that this could indeed secure just the future he wanted for both himself and the Cityscape Broadcasting Network.

"I like the way you think. I have to check with Duke about his schedule, but as it stands now, I'm ninety-five percent sure we'll be seeing you on Wednesday," Michael added enthusiastically.

Inwardly, he wondered just what Morgan Pryor was really up to. He knew that Duke's schedule was clear for Wednesday as their secretaries kept them apprised of each other's commitments. He also knew that this was indeed a meeting that Duke had been vying for all along because CBN could be the final answer in their quest for expansion.

"Duke." He waited for his partner to respond over the intercom system.

"Yeah—what's up Mike?"

"Wednesday at one P.M.—you, me and Morgan Pryor from CBN at Hurley's Steakhouse on Sixth."

"Wow, you didn't waste any time in hog-tying that dude," Duke exclaimed excitedly. "Good work, partner."

"Yeah, well that's what happens when you send a man to do a man's job," Michael said, laughing at his own egotism.

"So I see—and what about that sister of his—was she as fine as I heard?"

"Definitely—she was cute, but haven't you learned that it's not good to mix business with pleasure?"

"Yeah, I was really just kidding about her anyway. But I am sincerely impressed by your ability to have made a lasting impression on Morgan. Good work, buddy," he said sincerely, knowing that this connection was one that they'd both worked toward.

Michael realized that it was not Morgan's sister that had left a lasting impression on his mind—it was Lauren Traynor. Now that Duke had brought the dinner party up, he knew he had to come to terms with exactly what, if anything, he wanted to do about it. Lauren had been on his mind, but he'd not given in to the temptation of reaching out to her.

Not yet, anyway.

Five

The captain's voice resonated throughout the cabin, "Ladies and gentlemen, we're now on approach to Denver's Stapleton Airport and should be landing in approximately fifteen minutes. The temperature is a mild seventy-eight degrees with clear skies and no precipitation. Thank you once again for choosing Worldwide Airlines. We hope you'll think of us when you choose to travel again."

Lauren then disengaged the wall-mounted hand microphone. Speaking in a well-modulated tone she began, "Ladies and gentlemen, please observe the fasten seat belts sign and raise your trays into their original upright position. For those of you sitting in window seats, the majestic white-capped land formations visible on the left side of the aircraft are the Rocky Mountains. On behalf of Captain Woods and the other crew members, thank you once again for flying Worldwide Airlines."

Lowering herself into the nearest jump seat, Lauren fastened her seat belt as FAA regulations called for all personnel to be seated during takeoff and landing. She was still feeling the ill effects of the night before, but began to tally her beverage sheet as her head continued to pound. The remainder of the trip included a two-hour layover in Denver with a connecting flight headed

back to New York's JFK. She couldn't wait to get home
and into a hot tub.

Never again, she scolded herself inwardly. *Champagne
and I do not get along well,* she thought as she tallied the
column of figures incorrectly for the third time. Reaching into her breast pocket, she withdrew a tiny pocket
calculator and began to rework the numbers. Thoughts
of clear gray eyes invaded her mind causing her to mentally betray all that she'd managed to hold sacred. She
could still feel the pressure of his lips on hers once
again and could almost feel his arms around her and
she realized that she was in trouble. Too much of her
control was lost in his presence. The realization that
this one man could possibly spell disaster to the emotional fortress she'd constructed unnerved her, but also
made her resolve that much stronger.

*I am resilient, determined and infinitely more in control
than he could ever be,* she defiantly told herself as Flight
234 concluded and the plane landed. *I can handle this,*
she thought as the remainder of the day unfolded. Her
brain still would not allow her to forget all that had
taken place only twenty-four hours earlier.

Some four hours later, Lauren pulled into her parking space tired, hungry and very much in need of two
Advil. Once inside the apartment, she quickly stripped
off her uniform and headed toward the bathroom. Adjusting the bath water, she added two ounces of Zen
milk bath and searched the medicine cabinet for relief
of the headache that had plagued her for the past several hours.

"Thank goodness," she whispered when she found a
half-filled bottle of Advil. She then proceeded to wash
her hair quickly in the basin, adding a deep conditioner
before entering the bubble-filled tub. The water felt like

silk as she lay with her head against the back of the tub. Eyes closed, she was once again reminded of a pair of gray eyes mocking her, challenging her. From far away, came the sound of a muffled ring, but Lauren didn't have the strength nor the will to answer. She relaxed until the water began to cool, hating to leave the warmth and relaxation her bath had offered.

Stepping from the tub, she realized that she'd not eaten since breakfast as she heard her stomach growl emptily. Entering the kitchen, Lauren spotted a hastily scrawled note on the refrigerator door. "Sorry—we're out of everything . . . let's do shopping together on Wednesday. Love, Gloria." Opening the refrigerator door, Lauren saw that her roommate had not exaggerated. A half-filled container of cottage cheese, two bottles of Lowenbrau and a large bottle of Evian were its contents.

"I guess it's Yung Kim's tonight," she said aloud, reaching for the phone. It rang just as her hand touched it and she laughed in spite of herself. Inwardly she hoped it wasn't either of her parents. After the day she'd just experienced, she didn't really want to talk to anyone.

"Lauren Traynor, please," a cool, impersonal female voice recited.

"Yes, this is she," Lauren replied with mild curiosity.

"Hold on, please," her caller advised.

"Hello, Lauren," Michael said, his deep, richly modulated voice causing her heart to thump wildly in her chest. It took a moment for her to respond as she had been caught off guard by his secretary's initial contact.

"Hello yourself," she replied, sounding quite calm and sure of herself despite the pounding of her heart.

"How was your flight?"

"Fine, I just got in about three quarters of an hour ago," she replied.

"I see—I was wondering if you'd like to go out to dinner. Or, have you eaten already?"

"Actually, I was just going to order in," she admitted breathlessly. Why did his voice always affect her this way, she thought. What she really wanted to say was a cool "No, thank you, Mr. Townsend, I'm not interested." But she was . . . she reluctantly admitted to herself. She also knew she was actually anticipating seeing him again, already thinking of what she could wear.

"Listen, I'll pick you up in about an hour," he said without waiting for an answer.

"Okay," she answered slowly, her voice seeming to come from someplace deep inside of her. Placing the receiver in the cradle, Lauren realized two things. Her headache was gone and her heart was racing.

True to his word, exactly one hour and twelve minutes later Michael stood inside the doorway dressed casually in jeans and a gray knit sport shirt.

She'd dressed quickly after blow-drying her hair straight. She took the time to simply bump the ends, which left it long, silky and very sexy. Lauren had selected a simple two-piece black silk dress. The v-neck top had thin spaghetti straps with a matching skirt that reached just above her knees, accentuating her long slender legs. Black suede pumps with sheer lace-topped thigh-high hose from Victoria's Secret completed her outfit. Her makeup consisted of a bronzer, mascara and a honey-colored lip gloss.

She added the diamond studs her parents had given her as a graduation gift and was just spraying Zen on the insides of her wrists, elbows and knees as the buzzer rang.

"Wow, you look great," Michael said walking into the apartment. As Lauren shut the door, he took one step toward her, closed the distance and lifted her chin slightly. Brushing her lips with his own very lightly, he murmured, "That's for being absolutely irresistible."

Lauren stepped back, gingerly trying to compose herself. His lips were warm and firm just like she'd imagined over and over all day.

"Do you think I'm a little overdressed?" she asked, trying to camouflage her emotions.

"No, not at all. I'd planned to stop at my apartment and change. Scouts honor—I'll be on my best behavior," he said, holding up three fingers in the traditional Boy Scout salute. "It just made more sense to stop and pick you up first because my apartment is uptown. I made reservations at Devonshire's in Greenwich, Connecticut," he added.

"Great, I've never been there, but I hear the food is divine," Lauren said reaching for her purse and keys.

As they waited for the elevator, Lauren couldn't help but notice the way his jeans seemed to mold themselves to him. His legs, which seemed endless, were trim, but muscular. He guided Lauren toward a midnight-blue Jaguar XJ6 parked directly in front of the building.

"Oh no," she exclaimed, spotting the familiar orange envelope stuck under his wiper blade. "You got a ticket—didn't you see the sign—no parking—no standing?" She pointed to a red and white parking sign directly in front of the vehicle.

"No problem," Michael responded casually. "I have a very close association with the NYPD," he added, laughing at the puzzled expression on Lauren's face as he guided her into the passenger seat. The entire interior of the car was done in a soft, supple tan leather.

"I see. Another perk associated with the job?" she asked as she stepped in.

"Not quite—my father has been on the force for the past twenty-nine years," he added, shutting the door and walking around to the driver's side.

"This car is an absolute dream," Lauren said snuggling down into the seat, unaware of the effect her uninhibited squirming was having on Michael. He turned away and inserted a CD as the sounds of Bryan Culbertson's newest release, "Something 'Bout Love" filled the interior of the automobile.

As they headed uptown on the FDR Drive, Lauren could feel the tensions of the day leave her. She attributed it to the two painkillers she'd taken, the plush interior of the Jaguar, even perhaps the music—anything but the company she was in. They made polite conversation during the short trip. They exited the highway at 96th Street and headed west. Michael made a sharp turn into the driveway of a brownstone located between Lexington and 3rd Avenues.

Activating a remote-control mechanism, the garage door rose and Michael pulled into its dimly lit interior. They entered the hallway of the main floor. Rich polished mahogany woods dominated both the walls and the flooring. From the burnished banisters to the highly gleaming parquet floors, the town house was a study in classic elegance restored to surpass its original beauty. An authentic nineteenth-century marble fireplace dominated one wall over which hung a large oak-trimmed oval mirror. Leopard-patterned cushions filled a window seat overlooking a courtyard patio on the other side of the room. And facing out onto the Ninety-third Street main entrance, a floor-to-ceiling window entirely dominated one wall. Two huge fichus trees sat on either side of the window with a large standing replica of a panther crouched just below it.

In the center of the room two Brazilian leather sofas faced each other, separated by a triangular beveled-glass coffee table. Lauren stood just inside the doorway and took in the elegance of the room before her.

"Michael, it is absolutely wonderful." The sincerity was plainly audible in her voice.

"Thanks, but I really haven't finished yet. I'm scheduled for an installation of track lighting in about two weeks and then we'll see . . ." His voice trailed off as he began to think how good she looked standing in the middle of his living room floor.

"Wow, how did you ever get those trees to grow to that size," she asked, indicating his two prized possessions which framed the room's massive floor-to-ceiling window.

"Just luck and a lot of sunlight," he answered proudly. "Look, make yourself at home. I'm headed for a quick shower. The bar is over there." He pointed to a circular rattan bar. "Would you make something for me too?" he called over his shoulder as he headed up the staircase to his bedroom and dressing area. "Surprise me," he added.

"Surprise you," Lauren repeated to herself as she began to look over the assorted bottles, glasses and other paraphernalia. The bar, though compact, was well stocked with a small refrigerator beneath it. There was even a built-in mini sink.

"Let's see, he's probably a martini drinker," she murmured as she began to pour Absolut vodka into a shaker. Adding vermouth, and a twist of lemon she shook it vigorously then poured it into a huge martini glass she found in the freezer.

She smiled then, thinking of her father who had always liked martinis. He'd taught her to make them when she was just fourteen. She hated the taste herself, though. She opened a bottle of Evian and waited.

Six

The restaurant was exquisite. Intimate wrought-iron candle holders adorned each table providing subdued lighting. The maitre d', obviously familiar with Michael as a customer, greeted him warmly and seated them at a corner table ahead of several other waiting couples. Soft music added to the atmosphere of casual elegance. He had, as promised, dressed quickly. His hair, still damp from the shower, shone darkly against his mocha-colored skin and the whiteness of his shirt only served to accentuate the contrast. He'd chosen a charcoal-gray suit with a subtle pinstripe. The accompanying tie, also gray, had tiny slanted random charges of a lighter shade of gray giving him the appearance of a Wall Street banker.

Lauren found herself looking at the man sitting across from her and wondered, quite frankly, if she should have come. She knew she was not ready for anything more than a casual date, yet she also knew the man inspired feelings in her that were anything but casual. She vowed inwardly to end the evening early, get some much-needed sleep, and decline any further invitations from Mr. Michael Townsend.

She could feel his eyes on her as she scanned the menu.

"Do you like seafood? The broiled lobster is excellent," Michael said, momentarily breaking her thought pattern. Lauren placed her menu on the table and smiled.

"You must be psychic. I was just thinking of that," she answered.

"Not psychic, just tuned into you." He looked meaningfully into her eyes.

"Two lobsters, broiled to perfection, Tony," he instructed as their menus were taken away. "We'll also have a bottle of Dom Perignon."

"Michael, I really don't know if I should drink anymore champagne around you," Lauren said, a smile playing around her mouth.

"I promise that I will not, I repeat, will not allow you to get out of hand like you did the other night," Michael said with mock seriousness in his voice.

"What? Why you . . ." Lauren sputtered, indignation mixed with amusement written on her face. In the candlelight, she was framed by a beautiful golden-orange glow that accentuated her almond-brown coloring. The black spaghetti straps of her outfit enhanced her breasts and Michael took a deep breath to quiet the sudden hammering in his chest. Inwardly, he acknowledged that the woman sitting across from him had an uncanny and unexpected effect on him. Each and every time she was in his presence, he felt he no longer had control over what would or would not happen. He silently vowed to make this evening different.

Their table overlooked the mouth of the bay in Greenwich, Connecticut. Lights from the many boats moored dockside twinkled incessantly.

"So, how was your flight today?" Michael asked conversationally.

"Fine, it was one of my easier days—New York to Denver and then the return trip back to New York. Unfortunately, I had a headache the entire trip due to my overindulgence in a certain fruit-based beverage. That feeling just seemed to hang on for the entire day."

"That's only because you drank it too quickly," he countered. "Champagne was meant to be sipped slowly, young lady," he added.

"I'll try and remember that," she said, raising her glass in a toast.

"Here's to savoring life and champagne slowly," he said, looking into her eyes.

"I'll drink to that." They both laughed then.

"You know, when I was a kid, I wanted to be a rock musician more than anything in the world. My dad gave me an electric guitar when I was ten years old and I thought I was going to be the next Jimi Hendrix," he said.

"What happened? You strike me as the kind of person who's capable of doing anything he puts his mind to. Why did you stop playing?"

"Well, when I went away to college, my interests just seemed to shift. Somehow, playing a guitar for a living didn't fit anymore. I decided instead to promote the music of those that did. Also, the lifestyle of a rock musician seemed to be pretty far out. I wanted no part of the drugs, alcohol and overall abuse they encounter. By becoming a recording engineer, I switched the direction of my interests a little to the right you might say," he added.

"But the music training and exposure you already had under your belt must have contributed greatly to your ability to select and identify raw, untapped talent," Lauren stated.

"Yes, it did," he answered, suddenly realizing that not only was she beautiful, but that she was intelligent too. He liked that, but he also realized it made for a dangerous combination. He'd have to be careful with her . . . very careful.

The salad course was served, then a gourmet mixture of radicchio, endive, and romaine topped with gorgonzola, chopped walnuts and drizzled with an olive oil and balsamic vinegar dressing.

"So, tell me . . . It must be pretty exciting working with platinum-selling recording artists and top-notch musicians on a day-to-day basis," Lauren mused.

"Not really. Sometimes it can actually be boring just like any other job. But the magic is in the finished product," Michael explained, his face becoming more animated as he spoke.

He reminded Lauren of a small boy who had just discovered the world's greatest secret and was now sharing it for the first time with a best friend.

"Music is like no other entity in the world. Its beauty and its ability to touch and communicate to people regardless of language barriers, races, ethnic background and religion is unparalleled," he added candidly.

Lauren felt her pulse quicken and her heart beat faster as she realized that she was genuinely interested in what he thought and how he felt. Her response to his honesty both surprised and infuriated her simultaneously. She felt herself responding to Michael's impassioned description of his work as if she were somehow a part of him and therein lay the problem. She did not want to be a part of him or any other man—not now and possibly not ever. She couldn't wait for the evening to be over—she was almost sorry she'd agreed to come although she was having an absolutely wonderful time.

Their main course was served then, flaming-red lobsters broiled to perfection and served with drawn butter.

"Here, let me do that for you," Michael said as he deftly cracked the large claws.

"Are you always so helpful?" Lauren asked, watching his hands expertly tackle the task at hand. What was really bothering her was the thought of those same hands and the feelings they had aroused in her only one night before. His hands, long and slender were almost perfect in their dimensions, tapering to neatly trimmed fingernails. He wore no rings.

"I was really prepared to not quite like you, Michael," she said abruptly, forcing herself to tear her gaze away from his hands and how she imagined they would feel on her body again. "I didn't expect you to be so much of a gentleman," she explained, lowering her eyes, fearing he would know her true thoughts or perhaps read in her face the feelings he aroused. She looked up then and Michael was surprised to see the beginning of tears in her clear, softly shining amber eyes.

"What is it about you that makes me want to hold you constantly?" he asked, looking directly into what she felt was her soul.

"Come on, let's get out of here," he said suddenly, ready to signal the waiter for the check.

"But we haven't finished dinner yet and I am starving." Lauren laughed at his impatience, her emotionalism and the picture they'd make if they should leave so abruptly.

"Okay, but this is your last chance to eat, young lady. I have something else planned for us this evening, something I think you might like," he said mysteriously.

"Well, now you've really aroused my curiosity," she stated.

"Well, we're sort of celebrating."

"Celebrating what," she asked knowing as she did that he'd come up with something that would probably have her laughing even harder.

"Well, celebrating our first date which almost didn't take place," he offered as he began to tackle his dinner.

They both laughed, each realizing that they'd reached and survived a major hurdle in the evening.

Some hours later as they were leaving the restaurant,

Michael suggested they exit at the rear, which opened onto the dockside.

"Let's take a walk along the pier, the air will do us good," he said, placing his hand at the small of Lauren's back. She could feel the warmth and the slight pressure it caused. She could also feel herself respond to it despite her feelings earlier in the evening.

"Fine," she answered, moving into the lovely moonlit night. The water was a canvass of velvet stretching out toward some unknown and uncharted destination. The moon shone brightly, casting a funnel of light out onto the bay. Michael took Lauren's hand as they began to walk the length of the pier. It was warm and she was momentarily caught off guard by the level of his attentiveness. Several yachts were anchored on either side of the bay, creating a covelike atmosphere.

"What a lovely setting," Lauren murmured, taking in her surroundings.

"Yes, it is quite lovely, but not as lovely as you," he said as he gently turned her face toward his. "You know you've woven some kind of spell on me, Lauren," he said in a gently accusing tone.

"No spell, Michael," she said softly as he lowered his lips to hers in a kiss that was gentle and searching. The scent of her, the feel of her lips, the warmth of her body pressed into his was exquisite. The sounds of the seagulls circling overhead seemed to echo their unspoken feelings, which now threatened to surface.

Michael could feel the beginning of a strong desire to do more than just hold her in his arms begin to overcome him. Not wanting to lose control or to move too fast, he reluctantly pulled himself away, continuing to hold her and reveling in the moment.

Lauren shivered slightly.

"Are you cold?" he asked.

"Only when I'm not in your arms." Lauren's answer

came without a moment's hesitation and even surprised her somewhat.

"Come on," he said taking his jacket off and draping it over her shoulders.

Lauren could still feel the warmth from his body radiating from it and it brought to mind again what it felt like to be in his arms.

"Where are we going?" she asked with mild curiosity as Michael led her along the marina's walkway.

"Somewhere where we can both be warm," he answered as they approached the opposite end of the pier.

A large white yacht was moored dockside with "Megahertz" emblazoned in bold black letters along her side.

"Hank," Michael called out as they approached the gangway. A man of about fifty or so dressed in a dark sports shirt and white trousers, his salt-and-pepper hair topped by a cap, turned to answer the call.

"Aye, aye, Captain," he bellowed out, welcoming them on board. "She's all ready—whenever you are." He nodded politely toward Lauren.

"Henry, I'd like you to meet a friend of mine, Lauren. Hank here is my first mate."

"Hi," she said, taking his hand politely. She hid her surprise well. The yacht had been totally unexpected, causing her to wonder what other surprises he might have in store for the evening.

"Would you like the grand tour?" Michael offered.

"Sure thing," Lauren responded, her face lighting up with eagerness at the new and unexpected adventure.

The cabin, which was done in varying shades of green with accents of pale yellow, featured walls of magnificent oak paneling throughout. Thick, plush forest green carpet covered all the floors. A sofa in mint green ultrasuede ran the length of one wall with two subtly striped yellow-accent chairs facing it. The galley, which lay at the front end of the ship was comprised of a full-size countertop range, microwave unit, and a butcher-top table that spanned the entire length of that area. Several high-backed wicker stools were placed beneath the countertop, which faced a window seat. Filled with striped yellow cushions, it faced a wall of windows overlooking the bay, creating a spectacular view. A stainless-steel refrigerator with matching freezer was stacked vertically in one corner. Michael led Lauren, hand in hand, and together they took in the breathtaking beauty of the boat room-by-room.

He then led her back into the living room and crossed to a wall panel of dials and controls. The sounds of the Rippington's "Welcome to the St. James Hotel" filled the room as Lauren was once again reminded that Michael's world indeed revolved around music. She also realized that his attention was now suddenly focused on her as he watched her carefully from across the room.

"Is there anything wrong?" Lauren asked softly.

"Not a thing," he answered, crossing the room toward her. "You know, I wondered if you were going to like *Megahertz*, but watching you just now, I don't think I have anything to worry about."

"Well, my dad kept a small schooner moored in Cannes when we lived in the south of France. We used to sail almost every Sunday," she added, smiling at the memory.

"Wow, I'm impressed," Michael admitted candidly. "The French Riviera must be gorgeous."

"Oh, it is, especially in the spring before all the tourists come and the Cannes Film Festival madness takes over," she answered. "Do you spend a lot of time sailing?" she asked.

"Not as much as I'd like," he offered. "Usually I'll spend all day Sunday just outside the harbor, but on long weekends and holidays, Hank and I have been

known to disappear without an itinerary or agenda,"
he added, laughing. "Sometimes, I even hang the rod
and reel over the side to see what I can catch. It gives
me a chance to unwind, sort things out, get away. I always come out here alone," he ended.

Lauren looked at him then and knew instinctively
that he was telling the truth.

"Can I get you something to drink?" He walked toward the galley.

"Okay, no champagne though please." Lauren
laughed.

"How about ginger ale with a twist?" he asked.

She rose from the chair and walked toward him then.
The dress moved with her, her hips rhythmically undulated as she approached and it occurred to Michael that
no matter what she wore, she looked good. She stopped
just at the other side of the counter separating them
and smiled.

"Come here," Michael said softly, the command subtle yet filled with meaning. Lauren hesitated for what
was probably a micro second and then did as she'd been
told. She walked into his arms, and it felt as if she'd
always been there. Belonged there.

As if by design, their lips met and all resolve melted.
His tongue teased, caressed and explored every crevice
of her warm mouth, languidly, as his arms held her
tightly to him. His earlier resolution of keeping things
under control was sorely put to the test. The combination of champagne, lack of sleep and Michael's warm
body pressed against her was also affecting Lauren. The
natural male smell of him mixed with the citrus scent
of his cologne was thoroughly intoxicating and she allowed her hands to wander down his finely chiseled
back until she reached the swell of his buttocks. He felt
so good. . . . Michael's hands slowly explored Lauren's
voluptuous body as he felt the tempo of her breathing

increase immediately. He trailed kisses along her jawline to her neck, his tongue tracing a pattern on the exposed swell of her breasts as he gently eased the tiny straps down her arms. Her breasts were flushed and warm, standing upright as a blush crept its way upward, casting an apricot glow over her entire body. She moaned as he took one nipple into his mouth while covering the other breast with a tauntingly slow circling of his thumb. As she arched her neck backward, the scent of her perfume filled his nostrils.

"Michael," she murmured and he again covered her mouth with his own, stopping the flow of any words she might have uttered. Lauren's knees grew weak and she wondered if she could remain standing for much longer. She also realized that she had somehow made a decision sometime during the evening. Boldly, she pressed her body fully against Michael's and was instantly aware of his excitement as their passion continued to mount.

They moved to the bedroom as one, stopping intermittently to resume their sweltering kisses, brazen caresses and no-holds-barred exploration of each other. Between kisses and mutual caresses, he removed his jacket. Michael brushed her hands away as Lauren tried to reach behind her to the zipper of her dress.

"Let me," he said, his voice husky with desire as he smoothly turned her around, his hands moving to the top of the zipper. He kissed his way down her back as he lowered the zipper.

The trembling as well as the insistent thoughts inside Lauren's head were slowly being erased. A burning desire took its place. As she stepped out of her skirt, she turned toward Michael, clad only in a strapless black bra and thigh-high lace-topped sheer black stockings.

"God, you're beautiful," he breathed into her neck

as he gently kissed her lips, her neck and one shoulder. His hands cupped her breasts and caressed them slowly.

Emboldened by the naked passion she saw on his face, Lauren began to undo and remove his tie, then slowly unbuttoned his shirt. She held him in her gaze as she did so, knowing that there'd be no going back after their next kiss. She walked into his arms then and together they fell onto the king-size bed.

Michael gathered her into his arms, their legs entwined. "I don't want to let you go long enough to take off my clothes," he whispered between kisses.

Lauren reached down then and unbuckled his belt. He lay back, his eyes hungrily devouring the sight of her rounded breasts, the points seeming to beckon him.

"Here, let me help you," he said as he eased out of his pants. His shirt was next.

Lauren raised up on one elbow and watched him, a tiny smile playing around her mouth. Her breathing had returned to a semi-normal pace, but her face was still flushed with excitement.

Michael reached over and pulled her to him. "Your eyes remind me of a cat, always watching," he said, kissing them shut. As their lips met again, they melted together in one blazing entity, passion overtaking all rational thought.

Lauren's body reacted as if empowered by a will of its own. As Michael's hands trailed a blaze of fire down her body, Lauren's breathing again became ragged. He found the core of her and stroked, kneaded and petted her until she became like something wild and untamed.

"Please," she moaned, "please," and yet she knew not what she asked for.

"Not yet, my little kitten," he murmured softly into her ear. He trailed his mouth down her neck, hotly covering her throat with tiny kisses that left her wanting more. The nipples of her breasts were flushed a deep burgundy as Michael alternately suckled and teased each with his tongue. His head moved lower, his hands removing any remaining vestiges of clothing that might have hindered his exploration.

As Michael's kisses found their way down Lauren's heated body, she felt as if a fire was ripping its way throughout her entire being. Tossing her head back and forth, her hands grasped and kneaded his firmly muscled shoulders. She felt his kisses hot and fiery on her stomach and then she tensed as she realized that he was moving lower. When his mouth found her core, spasms of pleasure rippled through her. Lauren felt as if she'd been possessed by some unknown force as her body was engulfed by wave after wave of pure pleasure.

"Michael," she called out breathlessly as he raised himself between her open thighs. She felt the heat of him, the strength of him begin to enter her then and the sensation both surprised and delighted her.

Slowly, very slowly he entered her bit by bit. God she was tight. He smoothed her hair back from her face and kissed her soft lips gently. The realization hit him then. She was a virgin. He began to move slowly and awaited her response. She picked up his tempo as the small measure of discomfort she'd felt subsided and was replaced once again by need.

Lauren began to respond then to the primitive urgings his manhood inspired. A rhythm as old as time was inspired and Michael could feel himself reaching the edge of his control, yet he continued to hold back. Lauren once again felt the gathering of tension in her belly. He thrust more deeply into her core, relishing their fit, their perfectly measured tempo, their synchronized timing. Their lips met again in a burning, throbbing kiss that sealed their fates. Lauren exploded in a burst of passion she had not known possible as Michael found complete release and satisfaction within her tight, hot wetness. They lay together, fingers intertwined, their breathing ragged, still joined as one.

He nuzzled her neck, breathing in her scent and raised his head to look into her eyes, which appeared smoky with residual passion.

"Are you okay, kitten?" he asked, searching her face intently.

She smiled. "Yes, I'm fine," she whispered, returning his gaze steadily.

He gathered her into his arms and kissed her lips softly. Sometime later, they slept.

The sun shone brightly through the porthole as seagulls exercised their God-given right and sung into the wind. Lauren awakened to the delicious smell of coffee brewing. As she opened her eyes, memories of the past night and all that had transpired flooded her mind. A blush crept up her body, creating an enticing glow that radiated into her face.

"I'll never let you return to civilization if you keep waking up looking that, gorgeous," Michael said as he stood in the doorway of the bedroom, admiring his guest.

"Why didn't you wake me? What time is it?" Lauren asked shyly, looking for a clock.

"Time for you to answer one question," Michael answered, setting a tray down on the bedside table. He leaned over and kissed her lips. They were soft and warm and brought to mind the rest of her. Slipping a hand beneath the sheet, he caressed her breast. Lauren reached up and wound her arms around his neck in a firm embrace.

"Why didn't you tell me you were a virgin?" he asked, breaking the kiss, concern written plainly on his face. "I broke a cardinal rule thinking you were probably on the pill or some form of birth control. I cannot believe we were both so careless," he continued, realizing that reckless behavior of that kind was not at all to be taken lightly.

"I didn't know it was something I had to advertise," Lauren responded, a note of slight anger in her voice.

"Telling me was not in the category of advertising, kitten," he said lowering his lips to hers again. When the kiss ended, they were both breathing rapidly. Lauren's eyes had darkened with desire to a smoky topaz and she reached her hand into his robe and found what she wanted.

"Damn, you're just full of surprises aren't you," Michael said under his breath as Lauren guided him back into bed.

"Does it make a difference—my being a virgin last night?" she whispered. Lauren continued to caress him slowly as their bodies molded to one another as if they couldn't get close enough. Michael kissed her hungrily then, desire replacing all thoughts of food.

"No, not anymore," he murmured against her lips. He hesitated momentarily, reached into his robe pocket and pulled out a small silver packet. "Sweetheart, don't ever let that happen again," he said softly, kissing her as he joined her in bed.

"I won't—it's just that I didn't expect the evening to progress as it did," Lauren said honestly. His kisses trailed a blaze of fire from her mouth to her shoulder blades, his hands exploring every crevice, bringing shivers of delight to Lauren's entire body. When she cried out his name for the second time, Michael protected them both, and entered her slowly, a silent prayer somewhere deep in the far recesses of his mind that their earlier lovemaking would have no lasting ramifications.

Seven

Hurley's, a bona fide legend in the circle of restaurants frequented by midtown Manhattan movers and shakers, was nosily and appropriately crowded. Nestled between Avenue of the Americas and Rockefeller Center—home of NBC—within walking distance of CBS Headquarters, and within earshot of both ABC and Time Warner, its location was prime. Its roster of routine lunchtime patrons included some of the most prominent individuals in the communications industry. Morgan had chosen it for just that reason. He'd purposely refrained from bringing anyone from his management team, hoping to put his potential partners at ease. This meeting was also somewhat of a litmus test, as his plans going forward called for many such incremental changes. This would be an excellent testing ground.

Michael and Duke arrived together and were shown to Morgan's table. "Hey, it's good to see you," Morgan said genuinely, extending handshakes all around as they were seated.

"You, too, it looks like you have a little clout. I know the wait list for lunch reservations here is booked for months in advance," Duke offered.

"Yeah, but if you know who to call, it falls in line," Morgan countered.

"I see," Duke said smiling as he and Michael began looking over the menus offered by the attending waiter.

"We were both pleasantly surprised by your immediate response—if we had known there would be this level of interest, we would have contacted you earlier on," Michael offered genuinely.

"Well, initially CBN and its advisory board members were opposed to any discussion of merger and acquisition. However, in the past six months, changes in the marketplace as well as some inherent internal dispositions have allowed us to "rethink" our original position," Morgan said. "Listen, let's dispense with business a little further into the lunch—we'll talk business over dessert and coffee—agreed?"

"Sure, no problem," Duke said as Michael nodded in agreement. They then placed their orders for lunch.

Two hours later, both sides had presented enough of their respective issues, concerns and observations to feel that a "meeting of the minds" had indeed taken place.

Actually, the lunch had gone exceptionally well. Each individual in attendance possessed an enviable level of expertise in his own field; Duke, having handled the financial end of WJZZ since its inception was exceptionally aware of all that would be acquired by merging the two entities. Michael was more than enthusiastic having researched early on the potential market share which would be capitalized by accessing CBN's additional stations.

And Morgan knew that with a little luck and an acquisition of this kind, Cityscape Broadcast Network's prominence in the overall market could, in fact, insure him the leverage he needed to break away from Gino once and for all.

"Look, why don't I have all the paperwork messengered over to your offices by say Monday of next week?" Morgan offered as they finished dessert and coffee. "That way you'll have plenty of time for the 'suits' to go over each and every detail." He laughed comfortably. He liked these two men. They were intelligent, knew the industry inside and out but, more importantly, they were hungry—hungry to get to the next level and he both respected and admired that hunger. He even shared it.

"That sounds fine," Michael said as Duke also nodded in agreement. "Give our people a couple of weeks and we'll get back to you, but if what we've outlined here today holds water on paper, I think we should have a done deal," he added with his hand outstretched. Morgan, Duke and Michael all shook hands as the waiter refilled cups with coffee.

Duke, never one to leave any stone unturned, decided to broach the unspoken question that had been threatening to surface since the meeting began.

"Look, we would be less than candid if we didn't bring up the ongoing Federal probe that was recently launched into Gino Sorrentino's business holdings. What's the most likely effect, if any, that this will have on the proposed merger?" he asked candidly.

"I'm actually glad that you felt comfortable enough with me to touch on that subject," Morgan responded candidly. "As a matter of fact, plans are in the works at this very moment to 'handle' that particular situation and to answer your question—none—there should be no tangible effect whatsoever on our planned acquisition/merger. When you have your people go over the financial and projection analyses we're sending over, you'll see that we have made provisions for every contingency—with or without Gino Sorrentino this deal will be a go," he ended emphatically.

"Very well, I suppose that pretty much covers all the

points we needed to address," Michael said, rising as did Duke.

Morgan rose and shook hands with both men, preparing to leave the table.

"Oh, by the way, I heard it from a pretty reliable source that you and Lauren are dating," Morgan said quite suddenly taking both Duke and Michael by surprise.

"Yes, do you have a problem with that?" Michael asked, attempting to mask the minor degree of annoyance that lurked just below the surface. He was definitely surprised that Morgan was treading into waters so personal—and his timing couldn't have been worse.

"No, no problem at all. I just want you to know that she's like a sister to me and I couldn't be happier knowing she's associating with someone whom I suspect will be my next business partner," Morgan ended.

"As a matter of fact, she's very special to me, but I think we have some 'issues' to work out. You know the drill," he added, realizing that Morgan only had her best interests at heart. And suddenly, realizing that he did too.

Morgan laughed then and the fine line of tension was broken. "Yeah, I most certainly do." He knew that his protective nature, which he'd probably picked up somewhat from his stepdad, Gino, was never far from the surface where his sister Gloria was concerned. And he'd recently transferred some of that concern to her roommate simply because she was often around when he dropped by.

"Actually, I've been trying to reach her for a couple of days and she hasn't returned a single call," Michael admitted, only now acknowledging that it did, in fact, bother him.

"Well, good luck with that—maybe she's flying and

took on a string of overnighters in Los Angeles or something," Morgan offered.

"Yeah, or she could just be avoiding me—I'll find out soon enough," he said candidly as the three emerged onto Sixth Avenue.

"Listen, whatever happens, it was good to meet with you guys and talk radio. Let's really try to put this thing together. I think we'd be a dynamic force to be reckoned with in the industry," Morgan said with certainty.

"I think you're right," Duke agreed.

"Let's move forward then," Morgan offered before he entered a taxi.

"Well, what do you think—do you think the Gino stuff is legitimately settled and unable to affect the deal?" Michael asked Duke as they hailed a cab back to the East Side of Manhattan to WJZZ's offices.

"Hell, if I knew the answer to that I could predict the next numbers on one of those powerball jackpots that offer up $100 million. Partner, we're gonna have to allow our team of consultants and legal eagles to do their jobs and pray that they do it well. If there's anything illegitimate to uncover, they'll find it," he ended. "And by the way, what exactly is going on with you and Lauren? And, more importantly, who is she anyway," Duke asked with a big grin on his bearded face.

"To answer your second question first, she's the roommate of Morgan's sister. Beautiful, smart, stubborn and extremely unpredictable. And to answer your first question, I intend to find out," Michael answered, determination written across his handsome face.

Eight

Lauren was miserable. Although she methodically and mechanically went about the business of carrying out her daily responsibilities, she was quite simply miserable. With each passing day, she was less certain that what she was doing was the right thing, but she could not, would not, allow herself to give in—not now, not ever. The risks were just too high.

Almost a full week had passed since her date with Michael, and she was regrettably coming to the realization that it would probably take at least a few more weeks for her to forget all that had transpired in that one evening.

How could I have been so stupid? Why did I sleep with him? she repeatedly asked herself each day. And although there were no easy answers forthcoming, the mere fact that she'd allowed him to get that close certified the need, in her mind, for Michael's demise. Now all she had to do was convince the rest of her. It was difficult for her to admit, but Lauren physically ached for him.

When she awakened each morning, it was to thoughts of clear gray eyes looking into hers and when she lay down at night, usually exhausted after filling her day with work, errands and anything else to soak up as much time and energy as possible, it was his arms that she could almost feel holding her securely while his lips burned their way into her dreams.

The dreams. They were the worst part of it. She'd awakened on more than one occasion with his name on her lips. Only the night before, she thought she'd called out his name loudly into the darkness. Thank goodness Gloria's bedroom was far enough away that the sounds hadn't reached her.

Lauren was also very much concerned about a conversation that she'd overherad earlier in the week between Gloria and her brother, Morgan. If what she suspected was right, Michael and his partner were negotiating with Morgan to perhaps "merge" their two respective radio enterprises. Lauren knew that Morgan's business partners, along with his stepfather, Gino Sorrentino, were probably not exactly what Michael and Duke had in mind. Oddly enough, she felt no special loyalty to Gloria in this complex web of friendship versus whatever it was she was feeling for Michael Townsend.

He'd called each day, leaving short messages on her answering machine asking that she return his call. Five days—five messages and she had not returned a single one. It had taken more than willpower and she knew she was being ridiculously stubborn by not giving Michael the courtesy of a return call, but she didn't trust herself. Lauren knew that if she heard his voice, or came face-to-face with those piercing gray eyes, she'd lose any measure of resistance she'd managed to build up in the past week. She was determined not to allow that to happen.

On Friday morning, Gloria knocked at her roommate's door at exactly 10:05 A.M. "Lauren, you haven't forgotten your promise to do the grocery shopping with me have you?"

"No, I'm almost ready—just give me ten minutes."

Lauren opened the door with a blow-dryer in one hand. She had dressed in jeans and a sweatshirt with Rutgers University emblazoned across the front. The supermarket was only a short walk from their apartment.

"Hey, I made coffee. I've gotta call Morgan before we leave because he's been trying to reach me all week. The new schedule I'm on makes it almost impossible for me to have any kind of life," Gloria said as she headed back toward the living room.

"Tell me about it," Lauren responded absently, thinking that there was more than one good reason for not having returned calls this past week and hers had absolutely nothing at all to do with any new schedules imposed by Worldwide Airlines.

Court Street's resident Food Emporium as well as the many local gourmet shops lining the main street were only moderately crowded and they were able to complete the much-needed chore of monthly marketing in record time. The tree-lined streets harboring well-kept brownstones created a relaxed and comfortable haven for the business professionals, local artists and avant garde residents who lived within their confines. A stone's throw across the east river stood Manhattan, its skyline impressive even in the afternoon sun as they returned from their shopping.

As they entered the apartment sometime later, arms laden with groceries, fresh flowers and dry cleaning, the phone was ringing. Gloria, thinking that Morgan had returned her call of earlier that morning, raced to pick it up.

"Hello," she said breathlessly into the phone. "Yes, yes, as a matter of fact she is. Yes, thank you very much, it was good to meet you also," she added before handing the phone to her roommate.

Lauren took a deep breath, and braced herself.

"Well, hello stranger," he said and her heart began to race.

"Hello yourself," she responded hoping that he wouldn't be able to detect his effect on her.

"I've missed you," he said and her heart beat faster.

Lauren closed her eyes as a wave of pure desire washed over her. "This is not fair," she said softly.

"No, it's not—it's never fair in love or war," Michael responded candidly, immediately understanding her implicit meaning. "What are you doing right now?"

"Putting away groceries," she responded automatically, her heart on auto-pilot.

"I'd like to pick you up in about two hours. There are some things I'd like to show you." He waited for her reply knowing she was weighing everything he'd said heavily.

"I think you've shown me quite enough already." She laughed.

"I'm not even going to dignify that remark with a response." He laughed, too. "Listen, I'll pick you up at three o'clock sharp. Dress casually," he said and hung up before she could protest any further.

"Damn," Lauren said, hanging up the phone. She shook her head slowly.

"Don't tell me you don't want to go out with him. He's drop-dead gorgeous, is a partner in his own radio station and if what Morgan says is true, may be working out a deal to merge with CBN which will make him a media mogul," Gloria added, her emphatic description washing over Lauren like a cold shower.

"Look, I'm really upset with myself. Upset for being so weak that all he has to do is say my name and I'm immediately reduced to whatever and wherever he wants me to be. And I am especially upset that when I'm in his presence, I'm unable to control what ultimately happens," Lauren admitted.

"Look, Lauren, everyone has the ability to affect someone on the planet that way. Most of us though are never fortunate enough to come into contact with that person whom you affect in the same way. It seems to me that you guys have that mutual thing going on. I say go for it," she added as she continued to place groceries in the cabinets while Lauren filled the refrigerator with produce and dairy products.

"Well, he says he has something he wants to show me. I do want to see him, so I guess I'll get ready." She neglected to mention the dreams, the lack of sleep and the ache that started somewhere near her heart.

"I'd like to introduce you to a most demanding mistress," Michael said as he ushered Lauren into WJZZ's offices. Touring both the studio and the corporate offices, Lauren began to relax and enjoy the experience. Most of the station's personnel were off on weekends so the Saturday afternoon staff consisted of a skeleton crew. Lauren was extremely impressed as well as intrigued by the high-tech equipment that dominated the recording studio, the engineering booth and the overall mechanics behind radio broadcast transmission.

Wearing black capri pants, low-heeled black mules and a stark-white shirt that tied on one side at the waist, Lauren looked both crisp and sexy. She had pulled her hair off her face into a ponytail though some tendrils had escaped, falling softly on the sides of her face and along the back of her neck. As she stood before the engineering control board, she slowly but shyly ran her hands across the many levers, knobs and buttons, being very careful not to activate anything, Michael walked up behind her.

"So, what do you think of your competition?" he asked softly as he slid his arms around her slender waist.

"No contest—I think I give up," she said smiling as she turned into his arms.

"Good answer." He stepped forward and pressed a kiss lightly against her lips. The initial contact was brief, and called for more. He kissed her more deeply as he slowly began to explore the inner recesses of her mouth, warm and sweet. God, she felt good against him. He'd missed her. He knew that now and it hadn't even been a full week since their previous date. *I'm losing the battle, but what a war,* he thought as he continued to hold her, nuzzling her neck.

Lauren's response was immediate—being in his arms was even better than she had remembered or dreamed and they engaged in a heated exchange, mouths slated against each other, each trying to absorb as much of the other's essence as was possible at this juncture.

Michael molded her hips to his as his hands slowly caressed her back and came to rest at her hips.

She could feel his arousal and suddenly realized that she very much wanted to feel him inside her, moving her to the depths and heights she knew he could. But she also resisted with every inch of her fiber the involvement it signaled.

Slowly, ever so slowly, he raised his hands until they found her breasts, circling each in a tantalizing maze that caused her to moan and sharply take in her breath. As Michael gently teased each luscious mound to attention, his breathing became ragged, almost harsh. He continued kissing her, teasing her with his tongue and Lauren felt her resistance slowly slip away as he ran his thumb over a nipple. Waves of pure pleasure assaulted every one of her senses. She could feel him, smell him, taste him, even hear him as he kissed his way down her neck, stopping to momentarily pause at her ear to murmur, "My little kitten" before continuing his exploration of the warmth of her neck.

Feeling her response, knowing he could take the afternoon wherever he wanted it to go, Michael suddenly lifted his mouth from hers and kissed her chastely on lips swollen with passion. He placed one finger on them and looked into her eyes.

"You know you're irresistible, but we don't have time for this." He then smoothed her blouse, straightened her collar in an exaggeratedly formal manner and kissed her on her now puzzled forehead. Taking Lauren by the hand, he led her into his office.

Lauren, shaken by her response to his kisses and the abrupt turn of events, remained cool and composed on the surface. His office was done in shades of black, white and stainless-steel gray; cutting-edge contemporary with clean lines which spelled authority. A black leather executive chair, with chrome arms and base, matched the sofa and guest chairs. A small round conference table in black onyx occupied the corner and was surrounded by four black and white zebra striped guest chairs. The only visible art work was a large black and white print of Miles Davis, horn in tow, looking totally immersed in what had been his life's most serious dedication—blowing his brains out. It had been taken at the Montreaux Jazz Festival in 1988. Framed copies of several dozen CDs filled the expanse of the wall behind Michael's desk.

Lauren looked up from where she sat on the comfortable sofa and realized two things. He wanted her to be there and whatever happened next would determine everything. She'd thought that she had reasoned all of this to a foregone conclusion—put it into perspective so to speak. Now, after kissing him for what had seemed an eternity and experiencing her body's reaction to the nearness of him, Lauren realized that she was no longer in charge of the order of things and she didn't like it. She knew that she was probably in for the biggest fight of her life. With herself.

"So, Michael, what's this I hear about a possible merger between WJZZ and CBN?" she asked quietly as Michael began sorting through some of the paperwork on his desk.

Michael looked up from his paperwork, brows knitted and said summarily, "I suppose your roommate told you," he inquired casually.

"Yes, and I wonder if you and your partner really know what you're getting into. It's been my understanding for some time now that Morgan and CBN have some questionable aspects to the way they conduct business as well as the type of business they're really in," Lauren said evenly, hoping her concern didn't show.

He looked up at her then, rose slowly from his chair, strode across the room to her and bent down on one knee. At eye level, he gazed into almond-shaped eyes which were now filled with mild concern and spoke earnestly. "Lauren, I appreciate your speaking with me candidly about CBN and Morgan Pryor, but you do know that Duke and I have legal representation as well as a team of communication consulting experts. They'll complete the due diligence required to give the go ahead to any possible merger that might take place," he said, taking one of her hands in his.

"Our guys are competent, thorough and highly trained to ferret out any fraud or misrepresentation, so don't worry. We feel confident that this is a deal worth doing," he added to allay her fears.

As she struggled to put her response into the right words, clearing her throat before speaking, he raised her hand to his lips.

"Okay, yes, I know that you and your partner are going to be thorough in your research, but I'm just saying to be really careful. Morgan's people and those guys at CBN are very polished. I think they may even have the ability to doctor the books, repackage research and statistics, virtually make a weed smell like a rose, is what I'm trying to tell you. Don't get me wrong, I love my roommate to death, but I am really convinced that Morgan and Gino Sorrentino could spell trouble," she ended, sincerity clearly discernible in her voice.

"Your concern is really touching. I can't begin to tell you how pleased it makes me to know that you're on my team," Michael said, surprised at her candidness. Touched by her concern, he placed a kiss in the palm of her hand.

"Look, let me finish up here and I promise we'll talk more about this over dinner, okay?"

"Okay," she replied reaching over to pick from a stack of the most recent magazines on the nearby stainless-steel coffee table.

"Wait, I don't remember agreeing to have dinner with you," Lauren said as he walked back to his desk.

"Yes, you did—when I kissed you in the control room. Now be a good girl and let me get some work done," he said with mock sternness in his voice.

Lauren laughed and looked him in the eye with an unreadable expression on her face. "Good girl?" she asked, the political incorrectness hanging in the air like a suspended icicle in below arctic temperatures.

"Hey, it was a simple request backed up by an extremely authoritative demeanor," he said looking across the room at her intently now. He knew she was facing a struggle. Damn it, she'd put him through hell in the past three days not returning his calls and he knew the time to establish rank was now. He continued to watch her from across the room.

"I guess I can handle that," she said finally and began flipping through the magazine.

* * *

Sometime later, they pulled into the garage of Michael's town house. They'd stopped at Gristedes on Third Avenue. Lauren had been surprised at how well Michael knew his way around the supermarket. He obviously shopped for himself often.

"I'll prepare dinner because I know that you probably think I can't," he offered gallantly. He'd come to the realization that Lauren thought he was a spoiled bachelor, either enlisting the aid of females or hired help to help him in day-to-day activities of his home.

"Wow, that's the first time someone has actually talked their way into preparing a meal on my behalf," she laughed in response.

"For your information, I had assumed no such thing, but if you feel you have something to prove, be my guest," Michael said.

He did that and much more. The salmon steaks were grilled to perfection with just the right touch of a tangy lemony dill garnish he'd painstakingly whipped up in his Cuisinart food processor. Delicate angel hair pasta accompanied the dish with a light toss of virgin olive oil, fresh garlic and parmesan cheese. Lauren had prepared her favorite salad mix of radicchio, endive and baby gourmet greens drizzled with a Caesar dressing.

"Hey, no fair that your offering came in a presorted package," Michael responded when he realized she had somehow cheated.

"All's fair in love and war—you said so yourself—and cooking alongside you in this kitchen is definitely war," she chided him. He'd used almost every pot on site creating what was, in the end, a fabulous dinner.

"Come on, I'll help you clean this mess up," Lauren offered, bending over to begin stacking the wall-mounted dishwasher.

Michael, standing in the doorway of his ultra-modern kitchen, hungrily took in the sight before him.

"You know, I don't let just anyone into my inner sanctum," he teased.

Lauren, still in the process of stacking the dishwasher, turned to him. She realized the view displayed and stood up, placing her hands on her hips.

"Listen, you'd better be glad that I'm feeling charitable. I just decided to be nice to you because you fed me such a beautiful dinner," she admitted coolly.

Michael came up behind her as she reached up to the counter for the remaining items.

"Before you do that there's something I have been dying to do all throughout dinner." He lowered his mouth to hers in a scalding kiss. The countertop at her back, Michael at her front, there was no room to retreat. Nor did she want to. Michael's kisses inflamed her with a heat they both felt. It quickly reignited the passion they had previously put in check while at the station, bringing it to a new level.

Lauren realized she was in serious trouble. She was in his house, his kitchen, his domain. His turf, so to speak.

She tore her mouth away abruptly, putting two hands on the wide firm expanse of his chest to push him away. "I'm busy now. If you want my help in cleaning up this disaster you've created, I suggest you back off," she stated firmly.

He laughed, dropped his arms and stepped back. "The lady has spoken," he recited. "You're right. I am guilty of trying to take unfair 'homecourt advantage,' he admitted. "Thank you though, kitten, for coming to my rescue and helping me clean up. I think I got a little carried away this time in an effort to impress you with my culinary abilities." He laughed as he surveyed all the pots, bowls and various other cooking elements he'd employed while preparing his masterpiece of a dinner.

Lauren laughed too as they both attempted to return

his kitchen to its original organized and spotless condition. The evening passed quickly as Michael introduced Lauren to his expansive collection of CDs, DVDs and albums. They listened to Art Blakely, Nina Simone, Charles Erland and Herbie Hancock, Frank Sinatra, Ella Fitzgerald, Billy Holliday and Tony Bennett and of course, Miles Davis. Michael's library of music spanned the last several decades including jazz, pop, rock, R&B and classical recordings.

Lauren had kicked off her shoes and was relaxing comfortably on one of the oversized leather sofas. With her feet tucked underneath her, she leaned her head back against the softly enveloping mass and let out a small contented sigh. Michael, carrying two half-filled glasses of Merlot, smiled. She was like a kitten after all. Purring. He carefully placed the wineglasses on the low coffee table and sat down next to her. Lauren opened her eyes, feeling the sudden shift and found him staring at her.

"Mind if I get comfortable too?" he asked, raising his legs out to the far end of the sofa and placing his head in her lap.

"No, not at all," she murmured, her hands of their own volition placing themselves softly on his chest. She could feel his heart beating and realized that its rapid pace matched her own.

His body, firm and hard in all the right places, made her think of what it felt like pressed against her own. Lauren stared down at his face, his eyes now closed, and studied the chiseled lines. She realized at that moment, for the first time in her life, that she was on the verge of falling in love. The knowledge created a new fear in her—the fear of abandonment. She knew it was silly. After all, wasn't she with him now, at this very moment? But she also knew that life and its never-ending series entitled, Turn of Events with Parts I, II and III had the distinct ability to change what was oh-so-nice into what was ultimately unbearable. At the blink of an eye, things changed.

"I'm not asleep in case you're wondering," Michael said his hand moving up to cover hers warmly. "It's just that it feels so tranquil with you here that I can't help but close my eyes," he added looking up at her now. "You know your eyes are hypnotic," he said suddenly looking at her intently.

"Well consider yourself hypnotized. Now how about passing me that lovely glass of wine you poured," she said, laughing.

"Okay, so you don't believe in the paranormal any-more than I do," he said laughing too as he reached across to the coffee table and picked up both glasses. He raised his to hers in a mock toast. "Here's to hyp-notic trances, catlike eyes and magical, mystical eve-nings," he offered.

"I'm not sure if I want to drink to that—it sounds ominous. How about here's to a wonderful evening and fabulous company," Lauren responded.

"If you keep looking and sounding like that, it's go-ing to be very difficult for me to do the honorable thing and take you home," Michael said, returning to his prior place in her warm, cozy lap.

"Oh, I didn't know the dinner invitation included sleepover rights too."

"It doesn't, but I'm not ready for you to leave yet. Is that all right with you, Miss Traynor?" he asked as he placed his wineglass on his chest. He held it there with his large fingers splayed on either side of the stem.

"Fine," she responded, looking down at him.

They continued listening to music for the next two hours, each wrapped in their own cocoon of content-ment, yet keenly aware of the other's presence. It was 2:10 A.M. when Michael gently pulled Lauren down beside him, kissed her warmly on the lips and said, "I'm taking you home now, kitten."

Lauren was surprised, although she didn't allow it to show. She had thought the evening would somehow end differently. She knew that he really wanted her too, but she also knew that she was grateful that he was being such a gentleman. She was not sure if her willpower would have withstood any pressure.

During the trip from East 93rd Street to Cobble Hill, Brooklyn, the FDR Drive was deserted. The Brooklyn Bridge rose majestically before them and Lauren felt the need to say something she'd wanted to all evening.

"I hope your merger with CBN goes really well. You deserve it," she said.

"Thank you, Lauren," he said somewhat moved that she was in fact interested in something that meant so much to him. "What are you thinking about for your future?" he asked then, suddenly curious as to what it was that would make her ultimately happy.

"Well, I will probably continue to fly for several years, acquiring additional seniority and such so that I can start to have more personal time. Actually, I recently applied for a fairly prestigious spot with the Charter Division of Worldwide Airlines. You know, private charters for specially arranged flights," she added. "The pay scale is about twice what I make now and the flying time is much less." she explained.

"Well, I'm sure you'll get it," Michael offered sincerely. "You were certainly in charge on the flight I initially met you on." He laughed at the memory.

"Oh, stop, it will you. Don't remind me." She laughed too then. "You were determined to be a pain in the neck and it was my duty, no, my obligation to put a stop to it," she continued.

"Actually, you're wrong," he said soberly. "I was just

trying to get to know you better. And now that I have, it's just a matter of time."

"What's just a matter of time?" she asked, intrigued. They approached Lauren's building and she reached for her seat belt. Michael neglected to answer the question, allowing it to hang in the air. He reached over, placing a soft kiss on her lips. The closeness of the space inside the Jaguar, the scent of his cologne, and the memory of the evening just passed were playing havoc with Lauren's senses.

His tongue gently swept her mouth, his hands coming up behind her head to hold her to him more firmly. His other hand found its way to her waist, grasping her softly before moving to brush her rib cage and the soft skin just beneath her breast. His wide fingers reached and cupped that sweet expanse of skin and her reaction was immediate. A sharp intake of breath was accompanied by the hardening of her nipple beneath his gently coaxing hand. When he finally lifted his head from hers, both were breathing irregularly.

He looked into her eyes and said softly, "You'll find out." Michael then unhooked her seat belt and walked around the car to open her door. Extending his hand to help her out, he pulled her to him once more, whispering huskily, "You got off easy tonight, kitten. Next time, I don't know that I'll be able to exercise as much restraint," he said, kissing her lips quickly as he molded the length of his body to hers intimately. She could feel his passion pressing into her flesh and knew that it was pure control he was exercising.

"Good night, Lauren," he said brushing his lips lightly against her temple. He watched as she walked into the building. The doorman waved as Michael returned to the Jaguar.

Lauren's mind was racing as she entered the apartment. Filled with thoughts of Michael, the last twelve hours they'd spent together, and most of all, wondering where she fit into the equation of the possible business merger currently being put together.

The passion they'd shared had once again moved her to her core, but she questioned the way Michael had seemed to effortlessly put it on hold. She wasn't at all sure that most men behaved that way, but hadn't any experience to compare it to.

She realized, quite correctly, that he was definitely interested in her on a personal level, but she also wondered if his real motivations had anything at all to do with the fact that she was currently the roommate of his proposed business partner's sister. As she prepared for bed, she came to the realization that only time would reveal the truth.

She also came to the decision that, in the meantime, she'd keep Mr. Townsend on an extremely short leash.

Nine

Morgan's thoughts shifted alternately between the proposal, which had been delivered that morning by hand carrier, and back again to the mess he now found himself entrenched in. Gino had not been at all receptive to his explanation of the benefits to be derived from clinching a deal with the owners of WJZZ. That was the hard line of it.

Whether it was due to his inability to fully grasp all of the ramifications from a business standpoint, or whether it entailed his detailed understanding of all the nuances the pending deal would offer was unclear. What was abundantly clear was that Gino was dead-set against any suggestion of merger and acquisition.

They'd had dinner, the four of them, at Gino's favorite Italian restaurant, Fiorello's on Saturday evening. When Morgan had begun to fill his stepfather in on the progress he'd made since meeting with WJZZ's two principals, he'd nearly exploded.

"What makes you think this would solve any of our current problems in terms of infiltrating a market we already own?" Gino bellowed, his voice rising in direct measure to his now boiling temper.

"Look, when all is said and done, we're never gonna be able to acquire the market share we really need in the tri-state area without acquiring WJZZ. In addition, this merger would also cause us to obtain two of the most accomplished and respected talents in the business on the east coast—Hayes and Townsend. You can't buy that kind of respectability or the positive publicity that goes along with it," Morgan pointed out.

"Talent, schmalent. And as far as the New York/New Jersey/Connecticut market is concerned, I already told you I have some plans in the works to put everything in line," Gino said, jabbing the air with his fork emphatically. "Just leave everything to me. We're gonna be fine."

"Why is it that every time we try and have a peaceful evening out with the family, it ends up in chaos," Cora Sorrentino asked, clearly upset that her husband and son couldn't seem to be in the same room without a major conflict arising. "And don't tell me it's just business," she stated.

Cora lifted her wineglass to take a sip of the Cabernet Sauvignon Gino had chosen for the table. Elegantly coiffed, regally reared and ensconced in her favorite signature designer Escada, Cora Sorrentino did not look anywhere near forty-eight years of age. Her hair, a rich chestnut-brown pulled back into a classic chignon, appeared almost black, complimenting her olive coloring perfectly and highlighting a flawlessly smooth complexion.

Gloria detested these little family gatherings, but knew they were mandatory. She had worn an olive green matte jersey wrap dress that ended just short of her ankles, with olive green suede pumps accentuating the attractive swing of the A-line inspired skirt. Tiny gold hoop earrings adorned each ear. Her face, normally animated and full of expression, now presented classic boredom to anyone who cared enough to interpret it. It was her contention that this was her father's own personal form of torture and her brother's penance for having entered his world of business. The main thing accomplished at these dinners was that her father and stepbrother were able to talk a significant amount of business. She and her stepmother tolerated each other in feigned compliance and everyone present was miserable.

"Mom, don't get upset again, for God's sake. We have to talk this stuff out and the office is probably bugged. You know the Feds are still trying to make a case of any and everything attached to the Sorrentino name," Morgan quickly pointed out while covering her hand with his own in an attempt to comfort her.

"Well, I think you and Gino should find another medium for your little business meetings too," Gloria added. Agitated from the beginning of the evening by the guise of family closeness, she was also thoroughly fed up with having to sit through the entire evening of business discussions that would inevitably ensue. This had been going on now for some months and it was time that somebody put an end to it.

"After all, Gino, our input has absolutely no value to either of you so why should we be subjected to this?" she questioned defiantly, knowing that the use of her father's first name as well as her overall tone would surely anger him.

"Young lady, you are not being subjected to anything, now eat your food and be quiet," Gino suddenly ordered in a more quiet and subdued voice.

He looked over at his wife, smiled indulgently and said, "Cora, honey, don't let them spoil what should be a lovely dinner. Good food, good drink and good company in Little Italy," he added, raising his wineglass enthusiastically in an attempt to break the overwhelming sense of doom he felt threatening to overtake the dinner table.

"Look, Morgan, maybe you're right about the office

and the Feds," he said, lowering his voice substantially. "You're probably even right about these two guys, whatever their names are, at WJZZ," Gino added. "But I'm telling you for the last time, let me handle the mergers. We don't want any unscheduled or unauthorized additions to our administrative personnel," he said, his meaning obviously cloaked in the unspoken.

"That's where you and I disagree, Gino," Morgan offered soberly. "I think the only way to circumvent the Feds while also bringing some new, wholesome blood into CBN is through a merger and acquisition. A legitimate merger and acquisition," he added, with the emphasis clearly on his usage of the word legitimate.

"You are being your usual bullheaded self and the only thing you're gonna accomplish is to encourage the continued stagnation of the whole damn operation," Morgan continued, his temper now beginning to come undone. He suddenly realized that the deal which he'd thought was signed, sealed and delivered would most certainly be jeopardized by the man seated across from him.

"Look, since when do you get off telling me how to run my operation?" Gino said, his voice now mellowed to a menacing pitch. "I brought you into CBN when you were still trying to figure out which way was up—a smart college kid with absolutely no clue as to what or where it was all about. Or have you forgotten?" His eyebrows arched meaningfully.

Gloria, who had remained silent throughout this latest exchange between the two reigning power moguls, stood up at this point and threw her dinner napkin on the table. "I'm going to the ladies' room," she said with disgust. "When I return, if this conversation hasn't reached a termination point, I'm out of here." She turned and walked briskly toward the rear of the restaurant.

"Gloria, just a minute, I'll join you," Cora said, rising quickly. "She's right and you both know it," Cora said, looking at both her husband and son with a quick but penetrating glare. "This is not acceptable—and we should not have to be subjected to your incessant shop talk," she added as she angrily walked away.

"I hope you're satisfied with yourself," Gino said to his stepson, refusing to acknowledge any part in the dinner fiasco.

"Not only am I not satisfied, I'm not even going to accept responsibility for any of what took place this evening. If you weren't so bullheaded about CBN's future, the discussion would be unnecessary. And, for your information, it's a moot point because the prospectus, all the financial information as well as a full three years worth of projections and full disclosure was delivered to the offices of WJZZ early today," Morgan revealed. He waited several moments for Gino's reaction, dreading it.

Gino slowly shook his head. "You really don't have a clue as to what you've done," he said finally. "Look, when I tried to make it clear to you from the start of the possibility that we had almost zero chance of pulling off any kind of merger, you weren't really listening," he said finally. "Apparently, you don't realize how deeply we're in."

"That's not true—actually, my attempt to pull this thing off is due in large part to my knowing exactly just how deeply we are in," Morgan said emphatically, looking straight into Gino's troubled eyes. "Look, I recognized some time ago that the only way for us to play this was to go straight. That if we continued to keep things as status quo, CBN was going to be overrun with bureaucratic red tape sometime in the very near future—both you and I know that based on the past endeavors of the 'lettermen,' " Morgan offered, knowing that Gino would certainly recognize this as a genuine plea on his part for both their futures. "The FBI, ATF, NYPD, they're all in it together—lettermen to the last," he added in an attempt at disarming Gino with his humor. Apparently it went unnoticed because Gino did not laugh.

"Right, but what makes you think this is the definitive way to hold them off," he asked and Morgan realized two things. One that Gino, too was thinking about a way out. And he realized that Gino was scared. Of what Morgan was unsure, but he knew that fear was an immobilizing factor. It made you afraid of moving, of doing, of acting. Morgan realized that the only difference between him and his stepfather was that he was unafraid and willing to take a chance.

"Look, Gino, I never said it was the only way. I just think it's a pretty effective way." His emphasis was clearly on doing the thing that would lead to a successful outcome. "I don't want Mom and Gloria to get any more annoyed than they already are so let's adjourn this discussion for now. Can we sit down next week and go over the particulars though? You won't believe how this thing shakes out by just changing the overall shape of the ownership," Morgan stated excitely. "Remember that my major was business law and I haven't forgotten anything I learned in law school. Not to mention the fact that I have most certainly learned a few things since graduation," he added meaningfully.

"Okay, okay—now can we finish dinner in peace?" Gino held up his hand in resignation, clearly ready to change the subject.

Cora and Gloria returned to the table at that point, stepmother and daughter unified, at least, on this one issue. The remainder of the evening had been pleasant enough. As they were lingering over coffee and Tiramisu, the maitre d' approached their table.

"Excuse me, Mr. Sorrentino, but the gentleman at the table over there sends his regards and this bottle of Sambucca for your family's enjoyment," he said, gesturing to a small table in the corner. A man sat there alone, having coffee, his back to them.

Knowing that the after-dinner aperitif adorned with floating coffee beans was a highly acceptable way of extending oneself, Gino threw his hand up in acceptance and thanks to what appeared to be a total stranger. It wasn't until they were exiting the restaurant sometime later that he saw the face of his benefactor—Special Agent John Reid, Federal Bureau of Investigation–Northeast Division/NYC Bureau.

Ten

The phone rang once before it was abruptly picked up. "Reid," he barked into the mouthpiece loudly, his eyes never leaving the computer screen before him. Accessing the department's confidential files, even after more than fifteen years of service with the FBI still made him nervous, almost as if he were the one with something to hide. Whoever it was on the other line hung up quickly. Whether it was in response to the rudeness of his tone or perhaps a wrong number, he'd never know or care. What he did care about was his case—the one he'd been working on for the past seven years. The ongoing investigation of the Sorrentino crime family.

It was only now, when he seemed to be getting close to delivering the necessary evidence in support of new indictments that things seemed to be falling apart.

The case was complicated. Very complicated. And to make matters worse, previous attempts on the department's part to investigate and prosecute the lead suspects had run into the worst possible outcomes, especially for several potential witnesses.

He remembered, with a bitter taste in his mouth, the boldface headlines, "Federal Officials Unable to Nail Sorrentino Crime Family." The story had gone on to point out that federal officials had declined to reveal exactly which investigations had been compromised by the recent rash of bodies turning up without pulses, but it was apparent that it all centered around the Sorrentino family. And although at that time they actually had Gino Sorrentino in custody, he'd been released on one million dollars bail due to the lack of evidence and pressure on the federal prosecutor's office.

The entire chain of events had not only been frustrating, but downright embarrassing.

If the department's suspicions were even remotely close to being correct, Gino and his people were guilty of hundreds of counts of racketeering, securities fraud, money laundering, and possible FCC violation.

Looking at the computer screen, he scrolled down the list of names of investors in Cityscape Broadcast Network and realized that he'd have to get a subpoena issued for the records by Monday morning. If what he suspected was correct, CBN was also somehow connected to several other potential takeovers that Sorrentino and his associates had a history of initiating with less than scrupulous business tactics.

Picking up the phone, John dialed into central headquarters and asked for his ace in the hole, agent Brooke Warren.

"Yeah, Brooke, listen, I think it's time to move on our buddy, Sorrentino. I should have the paperwork ready in about two hours for the warrants. Can you see to it that we don't run into any snags on that end? I don't want this to take three days," he said without waiting for an answer. He knew his partner—had worked with her, driven with her, even made love with her for the past five years. She knew what to do and would carry out his every wish without question.

"Look, it's no problem for me to get the ball rolling here at Division Headquarters," she replied quickly into the phone. "Just make sure you have all the backup paperwork filed before it reaches the District Attorney's office. I don't have to tell you how it will roll if there's even a hint of your not following procedure to the letter," she reminded her husband.

"Yeah, I know. Hey, how'd you get so smart anyway?" he joked, mainly to lighten the tension. Inside, he realized that he felt more confident, more in control than he had in a long time. Especially after realizing that the dinner conversation he had overheard two nights ago was clearly a well-disguised "meeting." Employing recently developed equipment born of technological advances in digital sonar access, he'd not only been able to hear each word spoken by everyone at the table with crystal clarity, he'd also gotten the entire dinner conversation on tape. That tape was currently downstairs at the "audio lab" being transcribed and processed for future use as needed. It would be added to the thousands of hours of additional tapings that had been collected over the past five years. The volume of evidence now gathered in this case was reaching monumental proportions, but the Bureau knew its thoroughness would come in handy. The suspects involved in this case in particular were extremely resourceful and clearly possessed the financial stamina to engage only the best in legal representation. That made a tremendous difference in how the department had handled its proceedings—only now they felt they'd been overly cautious. That's why the special task force headed by John Reid, Special Investigator, had been created. Their mission was clear, although the means to the end held intricacies that made it unclear at times how it would all play out.

"Look, Brooke, I know you're not supposed to be working on this stuff now due to the reassignment, but just do me this one favor would you?" he asked quietly, knowing his butt would be on the line if any of his superiors got wind of his former partner's involvement in accumulating evidence on this case.

"John, don't worry about it. You know how I feel about the Bureau's decision to split us up anyway. It was bull—but it was their call. We may have to abide by it, but we don't have to like it," she ended succinctly. "I should be able to have those warrants sometime in the next thirty-six hours," she added.

"Okay, listen, I owe you one on this. Once we have the books on Sorrentino Waste Management and Sorrentino Construction Supplies, we'll be able to piece together how the broadcasting company ties in with everything," he explained.

Tension was clearly evident in his voice, but there was something else there, too. Victory . . . Special Agent John Reid felt sure he was very close to getting his man. It would mean seven years of work wrapped up in a neat little bundle if all went according to plan.

Now all he had to do was deliver the package. And the package was one Gino Sorrentino.

Eleven

Lauren backed out of her designated space, exited the garage and was greeted with gray skies, storm clouds and an overwhelming sense of gloom. Rain had dominated the forecast for the past three days with no immediate relief in sight. Autumn in New York was usually a blend of mild days and cool nights with an Indian summer bonus. The unseasonably dank weather could possibly be held responsible for a shift in the moods of many of the city's inhabitants. Lauren was not among the unaffected.

Although her dinner date with Michael nearly a week before had gone pleasantly, perhaps even taking them to a new level of understanding and awareness, she still had some reservations. Along with those reservations was the ever-growing feeling that she was quite possibly being unfair. After all, his behavior on their last date had been beyond reproach.

She'd accepted his invitation knowing full well that if things started to move in a direction that she found in any way uncomfortable or compromising, she'd bolt for the door instantaneously. But that had not been the case and after a while, after really allowing herself to relax, she'd begun to realize that she had perhaps miscalculated his motives.

The time she'd spent at the offices of WJZZ had not

only been a pleasant and insightful peek into Michael's world, it had served to elevate their relationship to another plateau. Somehow, she no longer thought of him as the world-traveling, music-spinning, woman chaser she'd initially pigeonholed him as.

If truth be told, she now held him in reasonably good standing as an extremely talented entrepreneur with whom she'd shared an earth-shattering first experience in lovemaking. What continued to plague Lauren was the realization that at some point during that day and into the evening, her mind seemed determined to focus on his arms, his lips, his chest and the rest of his body. Recurrent thoughts of their lovemaking were dominant as they shopped for groceries, prepared dinner side by side and, most of all, while they relaxed listening to music for more than two hours.

Lauren had tried to reason them away, tried to banish them from her waking thoughts and especially tried to overcome what had become a nightly pattern of dreams. She'd even discussed it in a surface way with Gloria the previous evening as a last resort, but only after she'd been backed into a corner by her roommate's perceptive nature. Gloria was extremely good at spotting her moods and drawing her out of them with a heart-to-heart chat.

"Lauren, you still haven't told me what is really going on with you and this guy, Michael Townsend. I know you've been out with him a couple of times and all that. I also know you, Lauren. Whenever you're worried or trying to think something through, you always go into a cleaning frenzy and you've cleaned, sanitized and organized every room in this apartment, save mine, in the past week. Talk to me, girlfriend. What the heck is going on?" she'd finally asked. Her green eyes had been luminous with exasperation and she'd stood her ground, unwilling to take anything less than the truth for an answer.

"God, sometimes I wish you didn't know me so well. But, honestly I don't know what to think about this situation I've gotten myself into," Lauren had answered, sitting down on the sofa, glass cleaner and newspaper still in her hands. She placed them both down beside the glass coffee table she'd just finished cleaning and put her hands above her head, clasping her palms together in a steeple-like fashion.

"Obviously, I like the guy. That goes without saying. And he seems to like me too, but I'm not sure if he's acting according to some master plan or if he's just playing it cool because of the night that we spent on his boat, *Megahertz*. Things moved to a different level so quickly, if you know what I mean." The concern written on her face told her roommate all she needed to know. Girlfriend was in deep and Gloria realized that it was probably the first time that Lauren had allowed herself to become emotionally involved.

"Well, how did you guys leave it the last time you went out—last week I guess?" Gloria could sense that Lauren was really going through her own private hell trying to sort out a relationship she had been blindsided by.

"See, that's the thing. Nothing happened that night although, honestly, I wanted it to. I don't know, it's like my body has become a traitor to my mind and all I can think about is going to bed with him again," Lauren said.

"Wow, I think you've got it bad and that ain't good," Gloria commented, trying not to smile until she could see Lauren's reaction to her prognosis. In fact, she now knew that the only thing that would really help Lauren's emotional stability would be to talk to the one person in her life who could really affect some change in her perception, her reactions and her motivations.

"Lauren, you know I love you like a sister. Probably more because I don't have one—just that crazy brother of mine, Morgan. I really think you should have a conversation about some of your reservations about love with your mother. I know how close you guys have always been and I also know what you told me about the divorce. Maybe she holds some of the answers."

"I don't want to upset her with my foolishness," Lauren said solemnly. "She's got enough of her own problems. I know she's still adjusting to the move—she bought a town house and moved to Laurel, Maryland about eight months ago. And although I helped her navigate some of that transition, I know it's been rough on her. She started working at an architectural firm recently. Maybe it is time for me to pay her a visit, see how she's doing and everything," she ended, now deep in thought.

"Good girl," Gloria said coming over to her and placing both hands on Lauren's shoulders. "I know that will make you feel better. Even if you guys don't talk specifically about Michael Townsend. Just the fact that you'll know that she's okay will set your mind at ease on some of the issues you probably don't even realize you're carrying around," Gloria added.

Lauren had called her mom in the next half-hour, made plans to drive to Maryland the following day and finished bringing the apartment to an acceptable level of cleanliness. By the time she went to bed that night, she was exhausted.

Now, as she approached the New Jersey Turnpike and the remaining drive south, she realized that this trip was long overdue. She wondered what her father would say if he learned that his daughter was falling in love. Sharing it with her mother was one thing. Lauren knew it would be sometime down the road, if at all, that she'd feel comfortable letting the colonel in on her private life.

Her parents had been extremely close, all for one—one for all. They'd shared many things for a very long time. That's why their divorce had come as such a shock—probably even to them. And that's what Lauren had to find out. For her own peace of mind, her own sanity, her own life going forward. What, in God's name, made people who obviously loved each other, relied on one another, trusted one another and most importantly, after vowing to spend their lives together, decide to divorce after almost three decades of complete cohesiveness? Not to mention all the stages of transition they'd weathered based on the many assignments customary to her father's military position.

Lauren arrived at her mother's complex just as dusk approached. Wingate Gardens Town Homes, located just east of Interstate Highway 95, was a gated community.

At least now I can stop worrying about safety issues regarding Mom's place, she thought as she pulled up in front of 49 Newbridge Court.

She immediately noted that her mom's Saab 9000CS was parked in the adjoining space and smiled.

"Like mother, like daughter," she murmured to herself, acknowledging that their taste in automobiles ran along the same vein. The Swedish automobile had become a family preference after their exposure to them in Germany where the roads were a driving enthusiast's dream. Noted for its "no speed limit" category, the Autobahn was an excellent testing ground for the German-made Mercedes Benz and Audi, as well as the Swedish-manufactured Volvo and Saab.

Lauren didn't get the opportunity to ring the doorbell as Eva Traynor had seen her daughter pull up as she watched from the bedroom window.

Opening the door wide, she exclaimed, "Hey, what took you so long, I was expecting you at least two hours ago." She threw her arms around Lauren's slender body.

"I know, I'm sorry but there was a lot of traffic on the New Jersey Turnpike," Lauren responded, laughing as she clutched her mother to her tightly. She suddenly realized just how much she'd missed her, the sound of her voice and the smell of her perfume.

"You always smell so good," she said, remembering the familiar fragrance of White Shoulders her mother had worn for the past twenty years.

"Thank you, sweetheart. You know it felt like I was waiting so long because I've really been waiting for you to come down for more than just the two hours," she admitted meaningfully. "Come on in and make yourself at home. Let me show you your room—I mean the guest room," she said, correcting herself carefully as she led the way down a tastefully decorated corridor lined with framed prints by Georgia O'Keefe. The exaggerated floral and desert-inspired art was totally appropriate as the entire town house was done in a Southwestern inspired design—from the stark-white fireplace and white upholstered furniture in the living room, to the pastel-colored accents used throughout. Eva Traynor had applied the use of her God-given talents. Design came naturally to her and it showed in her use of boldly colored accent pieces, stark neutrals for the larger pieces of furniture and richly textured items dispersed tastefully throughout each of the rooms.

Lauren gasped when she entered the guest bedroom. Painted a vibrant yet subtle shade of blue tinged with lavender, it held a double bed with an art deco brass headboard, a large oak armoire, and an antique oak dressing table with matching chair. The curtains and matching comforter had been done in a soft, but rich shade of asparagus green and the trim work on the doors and windows covered in a stark white. The carpet, thick and luxurious, was a soft, creamy shade of fern green, which accentuated the richness of the brass and oak furniture pieces in the room. A print by Roy Lichtenstein done in bold strokes of color including those on the walls and floor adorned one wall, framed in a complimentary oak.

"Mom, this room is beautiful," Lauren finally managed to utter, knowing that her mom's use of her favorite color combination, lavender and green, somehow signaled that this room held a special place not only in her mother's heart, but for who its designated occupant was to be. Sure it was a guest room, but Lauren recognized and responded to its colors as had been planned.

She crossed the room and hugged her mother once again. "Look at you. You're almost the same size as I am," she exclaimed, noting that her mother's figure, which had never been burdened by excess, was now substantially trimmer than the last time she'd seen her.

"I hoped you'd like the room, but I didn't think it would take you quite this long to get to see it," she said, smiling while admonishing her only daughter for taking much longer than expected in making her first trip to see her. It had been a little more than eight long months. "And yes, I've lost some weight. I joined the new workout center about two miles down from here. The complex also has a health club I use for swimming and a nice, relaxing massage at least once a week," she added.

"Well, it looks good on you, Mom. In fact, if I didn't know better, I'd say you look more relaxed and beautiful than ever. Is it possible that the divorce from Daddy is actually agreeing with you?" Lauren asked somewhat timidly, not really expecting an answer.

"I don't think agree is the exact word I'd use, but yes, I am beginning to adjust to the changes and actually have found some inner peace with my job, keeping busy during the week and decorating and furnishing this town house," Eva answered candidly. "Is that why you found it difficult to come down and visit? Did you think I was living the life of a miserable, divorced, unhappy woman?"

"No, Mom, and I apologize, but you know how I felt about the divorce," Lauren admitted slowly. "It's only now that I've come to realize just how complicated love really is," she added, looking into her mother's eyes and willing her to understand.

"Sweetheart, is anything wrong? You've had me a little worried since last night when you called and said you were coming today," her mother said.

"Actually, Mom, I'm not sure where I should begin, so let's wait until later. I should have come down much, much sooner and for that I am sorry. I guess I had to grow up a little before I was willing to recognize just what it was that you and Daddy were going through," Lauren said while starting to unpack her overnight case.

"Look, let's not talk about that now. Why don't you finish putting your things away and we'll have a nice dinner down at the Baltimore Inner Harbor—how about Maryland crab cakes?"

"That sounds great. Just let me get unpacked and freshen up a little bit," Lauren responded eagerly. "Oh, wait, I brought something for you," she added while rummaging frantically through her garment bag's many pocketed areas. "Here it is," she said finally, and pulled out a small green box wrapped with a twine bow. Her eyes sparkled with mischievous excitement.

Eva unwrapped it quickly, throwing the twine down

on the bed before settling herself like a young girl. Opening the box, she gasped and held one hand up to her chest in utter surprise. "Oh, Lauren, you shouldn't have," she said lifting the diamond pendant from the box. "Oh, it's beautiful," she gasped, tears springing to her eyes in an uncontrollable flood. The triangular-shaped pendant held a quarter-carat diamond in its center and was hung on a twenty-inch box link chain. Its sparkle against the black velvet interior of the box shone brilliantly and Lauren was glad she'd worked the overtime in order to be able to pay it off without committing it to a credit card.

"Mom, that's to let you know that I really appreciate all that you sacrificed while I was growing up and you were traipsing all over the world following Daddy and helping to keep our family together. I love you," she said and kissed her mother's cheek.

"You don't have to thank me for anything. I loved you and I loved your father. I still do. We are a family and that's what families do. Stay together—for as long as possible," she said pointedly. "Listen, get dressed and we'll talk this out over dinner. I'm going to get dressed myself. I have to put on something that will do justice to this beautiful necklace." Her voice was filled with pride as she held it up to her neckline.

Their conversation over dinner was filled with explanations, admissions, revelations, but more importantly, no recriminations. Lauren came to a new understanding of both her parents' motivations for the divorce through her mother's honest reflection concerning much of what had transpired throughout the years. That she had been fair and equitable in her recollection of the chain of events made Lauren love and respect her even more.

"So, talk to me about yourself, sweetheart. You've hardly said one word about the job, your apartment, your roommate, your friends. Are you dating any-one?" Eva asked suddenly, curiosity getting the better of her.

"Oh, the job is fine. I recently applied for a posi-tion with Worldwide's Charter Division so that I can fly less, but hopefully increase my salary. And my roommate, Gloria, is great. In fact, it was partly through her suggestion that I hightailed it down here to see you. She thought I should talk some of my fears over with you."

"Fears? Lauren, I've never known you to be afraid of anything," her mother responded, one eyebrow arched inquisitively. She sat forward as if attempting to coerce the explanation for her daughter's apparent need for consolation from her.

"Mom, listen, I don't think there's any easy way to say this, but I think I'm falling in love with someone. And I don't want to. I mean, I know it sounds ridiculous, but I don't think I'm ready to put myself on the line like that. And especially not after what I saw both you and Daddy go through in the past couple of years. After talking with you today I have a much clearer picture, but I'm still reluctant to enter that arena," she ended, looking into her half-filled wineglass as if it held a so-lution.

"I see. So, that's what all this is really about," Eva said, a smile playing about her lips. "Lauren," she said softly taking her daughter's hand in her own across the white of the tablecloth, "listen to me very carefully. You cannot hide yourself away and escape from the moon, the sun nor the tides that affect change in your life. The things we've just discussed give credence to just that. Life will unfold as it will. And if you've met some-one whom you feel is special and, apparently you have, you'll have to open yourself up to the experience with-out any guarantee of the outcome. That's what life is all about," she finished, looking into her daughter's eyes.

"I know you're right, Mom, but I don't think I have the courage to go through all the trials and tribulations that love seems to require. Why can't we just be friends and leave out all the emotional baggage that seems to accumulate?" she asked, hoping against hope that there was an acceptable answer somewhere in the cosmos to help her out of this emotional quandary.

"It would be too easy, too simple and not at all compelling," her mother answered succinctly. "You're a lot stronger than you take credit for. After all, you're my daughter not to mention your father's daughter. You come from extremely strong stock and I actually think that's what's working against you, young lady. You're stubborn and you want it your way. Well, you might as well get used to it. It may already be too late. It sounds like love has found you even though you're pushing against it with two hands and both feet—kicking and screaming all the way," she ended now laughing.

"Mom, you make it sound like I'm some kind of lunatic, but when you put it that way, I suppose I am being a bit dramatic," Lauren said, a smile playing around her mouth.

"Yes, I would say so. Just relax and let things unfold. Now that we have that settled it seems we have two things to celebrate before we leave." Eva then consulted the wine list, signaled the wine steward to the table and ordered a bottle of champagne.

"What exactly are we celebrating? I'm almost afraid to ask," Lauren whispered as her mother continued to wear a triumphant smile on her attractive face.

"Well, obviously one is your breakthrough to reality," she responded smiling with love and affection at her daughter's surprised look. "And the other is the promotion that I received two weeks ago. I am now head of the design department at the architectural firm of Donner and Warren, Inc," she added dramatically.

"Oh, Mom, that's terrific. I knew you'd been hired, but I didn't realize you were actually using the skills you'd acquired at the Parsons School of Design years ago."

"Well, I'd been assisting my boss for the past six months, mainly doing administrative assistant tasks, but then he asked me to fill in as a substitute for the designer who left to have a baby. I've been involved in the selection of fabrics for use in reception areas, conference rooms, general seating areas, and executive offices along with various other furniture used in the firm's corporate projects. Also, matching carpet swatches with other existing fabrics and textures to be used in a specific environment, and even choosing appropriate artwork for some of the finished projects. Anyway, it seemed that a couple of the projects I worked on resulted in the firm receiving additional assignments and my boss was impressed. Then about two weeks ago, he told me that the managing partners had discussed it and they wanted me to assume the position because they realized that I had an eye for it. It seems that the former design department head won't be returning after her maternity leave is over and they'd also noticed the Parsons School of Design on my resume."

"Mom, I am so proud of you. You've given me a tremendous amount of hope and inspiration just by example. I am thoroughly blown away by how you've been able to not only adjust, but rise well above, well," she faltered. "I'm speechless."

"Well, thank goodness, for once in your life you're

at a loss for words. Let's toast to love, life and happiness," Eva said, smiling indulgently and raised her glass.

"And to mothers and daughters with resilience," Lauren added laughing.

"Yes, that too. Now, tell me more about this intrepid young man who has boldly dared to threaten my daughter's safe, solid existence. I remember your being a tomboy in junior high, and swearing off boys for life. My, my, how things have changed," she said, laughing.

"I still think I had the right idea; it's just that something happened between high school and college that severely jeopardized my ability to keep them at bay—I grew up," she added laughing. "Michael, that's his name," she added, a smile lurking around her lips now, "is everything I've always fought against. Handsome, intelligent, smooth, accomplished, successful—in a word—a nightmare and it seems he's adopted me as his pet project. You know for years I didn't date, really. For some reason, I can't seem to say 'no' to him and it bothers me that he has this control over me."

"Well, it sounds as if you've met your match, darling, and as much as I'd like to tell you what to do, it's going to be your call all the way. Do you think you'll continue to see him?" she asked then.

"I have a date with him on Saturday evening. I was hesitant about going through with it, but after this conversation, I suppose the only thing to do is just go and see how things progress."

"Well, if it's any consolation to you, I'm happy that you've at least met someone who is a challenge to that stubborn nature of yours. Your father would be proud of the progress that you've made too. I know he worries about you in that big, cold, impersonal city."

"Thanks, Mom, for that vote of confidence. I plan

on writing to Daddy at his new base in Colorado when I get home. I can't tell you what it means to me to finally understand and accept you guys and your decision to split up."

They left the restaurant well after midnight. Two women with a clearer understanding of what it means to be a woman in a world of possibilities.

When Lauren left Maryland late the next afternoon and headed toward New York City, the sun shone brilliantly for the first time in four days.

Twelve

Michael, in response to Lauren's questions on what she should wear, had said to dress casually, be mindful of changing weather patterns, and to above all, be practical. Lauren decided that his idea of practicality was oftentimes off kilter, so she wore a long denim skirt, a white halter top, navy oversized cotton knit sweater and low sandals. She also threw her favorite sunglasses and a large silk scarf into her oversized straw bag.

That should do it, she thought as she also included a tube of sun block in her makeup pouch.

"Now, whatever he has in mind I should be ready for," she mused.

And although the date had originally been set for Saturday evening, he picked her up at the revised time of 3:00 P.M.

"What's the matter. Has someone been missed around here?" she asked teasingly as she entered the passenger side while he held the door for her entrance.

"No, I just thought it would be a shame to waste a beautiful day and especially what promises to be a wonderful sunset."

"Oh, so the sunset will be somehow visible from wherever we're going. Can't I have a little hint?" Lauren questioningly teased him. "You're not fair. You always have me at a disadvantage. I never know where we're headed," she said, pouting.

"And you have me at a disadvantage also. Your beauty is an unfair advantage no matter how you cut it. Stop complaining and fasten your seat belt." He smiled while leaning over to ruffle her hair playfully.

He'd dressed casually also—jeans, a gray v-neck pullover sweater and matching gray cowboy boots. He looked rugged, handsome and sexy, but not necessarily in that order.

Michael guided the car smoothly into the midtown traffic headed east of the city and traveled through the Midtown Tunnel toward the Long Island Expressway. Some hour and fifty-five minutes later they entered the town of Bayshore, Long Island and headed toward the Fire Island Ferry Terminal where they parked the Jaguar.

"I've heard a lot about the eastern end of Long Island but never really gotten a chance to explore it. Is Fire Island really lovely?" Lauren asked as they waited to board the next boat.

"I'm hoping you'll think so," he replied, putting one arm around her shoulder. "My parents always brought me out here in the summer to fish and a couple of times, we even rented a cottage. I love the shore, the sunsets, the surf, its so beautiful no matter what time of year. I just wanted to share some of that with you. Especially since I know your summers at the Jersey shore must have made you fond of beaches as well," he added.

The twenty-minute ferry ride was charming and refreshing. And although they were one of the few couples on board who had traveled light, carrying only that day's clothing and nothing else, they didn't feel at all out of place.

The tiny island was abuzz with activity. From the many couples with young children to the teenagers and slightly older adults who had found a haven for their love of the outdoors.

Michael and Lauren walked the beachfront area down to a local restaurant, which opened out onto Fire Island Bay and was accessible by boat. "You know we could have sailed here on *Megahertz,* but then I wouldn't have gotten the chance to snuggle with you during the entire ferry ride," he said, laughing as he kissed her softly on her lips. She turned into the kiss and responded hungrily, surprising herself at the naturalness she somehow felt with him.

"Hmm," he murmured against her cheek as he glided his lips across her soft, wind-blown face. "You smell like sea, salt and sunshine and I love sunshine," he said smiling down at her.

"You're just trying to impress me with your knowledge of the different ways to travel to new and exotic places," she accused teasingly.

Flynn's, one of three local restaurants situated on the bay side of the tiny island, was abuzz with a vibrant reggae band hashing out hit after hit from Caribbean artists like Bob Marley, Lauryn Hill and Beres Hammond. Families abounded, but there were plenty of young couples making up the complexion of the open-air forum and as they sat enjoying dinners consisting of crab cakes, sweet potato fries and green salads accompanied by a bottle of Chardonnay, the sun began to set. It was breathtaking. Lauren felt serene and relaxed as she enjoyed Michael's company and the overall atmosphere of the island restaurant.

"So, tell me about your visit with your mother. I know you said you stayed overnight. How did everything go?" he asked suddenly, looking into her amber eyes with concern.

"Actually, it was wonderful. All this time I had a lot of my facts sort of turned inside out and it was not only causing me grief in my own life, but causing me to think my mother was living a miserable existence. Now I've come to realize that things may change, but we grow to accept them, even rise above them," she said candidly looking at Michael with a new awareness.

"Is that so," he queried, smiling now with the sudden realization that she was finally opening herself up to him emotionally for the first time. He was pleasantly surprised. Actually, he was ecstatic.

"So you mean you're ready to admit that men are not the horrible, beastlike creatures that you'd made us out to be," he said, making a face that resembled a tortured gargoyle.

"Sort of," she responded laughing. "Stop making that face or I might have to change my mind. Honestly, I don't think Mom and I have had that kind of heart-to-heart talk since I was maybe twelve or so. You know, the dreaded one with your parents about the birds and bees. We've been close, but I guess there's been some distance there too," she admitted.

"Well, the important thing is that you guys were able to pull it together when it counted. You know I admire your parents for being honest and up front in their handling of their marriage. That's probably where you get your levelheadedness from."

"So, you think I smell of sunshine and that I'm level-headed. Wow, I'm starting to think you might just have a small place on your little dance card for me after all, Mr. Townsend," Lauren teased.

"Yeah, I suppose you could say you've wormed your way into my existence somewhat, but don't get too comfortable. I've been known to throw a damsel in distress overboard in a heated moment. Speaking of dancing, how about it?" He'd effectively changed the subject as he stood up and took her hand. Lauren faintly recognized the chords to, "Could You Be Loved," the hit song by reggae legend, Bob Marley, as they moved onto the dance floor, which was crowded with all manner of couples, families with children, teenagers and restaurant patrons.

They danced for what seemed like hours, one melody interwoven into the next, each springing up without a clear delineation of a change of tune.

When Michael gathered her close as the strains of "Wait in Vain" began, Lauren felt her pulse quicken. She could feel the rapid pounding of his heart against her chest. His arms, strong and taut, wrapped her in a cocoon of warmth and solidarity. His thighs, pressed intimately against hers, were firm and taut, muscular but lean. She knew that he wanted her and felt herself responding in turn. His lips, warm from the sun, the wine and the dancing, traveled along her jawline and kissed her softly on her cheek once before coming to rest briefly on her lips. Looking into her eyes, Michael gently lifted both her hands, one by one, from his back and placed them on his chest, never losing eye contact with her. He delivered tiny, soft, brief kisses along her lips, her face and her forehead. It was exquisitely sensual and left Lauren feeling lightheaded.

"You know it would have been pretty difficult to throw me overboard since we didn't sail *Megahertz* out. Perhaps next time?" she asked daringly with one eyebrow raised.

"Definitely, next time *Megahertz* it is, but only if you'll promise to act as my first mate. That's my one condition to your being allowed onboard," he stated officiously. They both laughed.

They stayed throughout the early evening, laughing, talking and dancing whenever the mood hit them. They watched the sun set slowly in the sky, an orange glow highlighting the entire palette. It was a beautiful setting and only enhanced the mood for them both. As the last strains of the Bob Marley hit "Jamming" ended, they walked from the dance floor, hands intertwined, and made their way to the table.

"Now, let's head back to the mainland before you dance me down to a splinter in my one peg leg, "he said laughing and pretending to limp as they gathered their belongings. The sun slowly burned its way into the recesses of what promised to be a beautifully clear, nighttime sky.

It was well past midnight when Michael and Lauren pulled into the parking space in front of her building.

"Would you like to come in for a cup of coffee?" she asked, leaning over to kiss his lips as she'd done many times throughout the day.

They were soft and warm, and she was not certain if her invitation for coffee actually included anything more substantial, but then, neither of them wanted any entanglements. They'd both made that perfectly clear from the very beginning and it didn't warrant further discussion. She thought frequently of the time they'd spent on *Megahertz* and the sensuous, terribly satisfying lovemaking that had ensued, but she wasn't sure she was ready to include more of the same into their relationship.

She especially was unsure if Michael was ready to enter into a committed relationship. Although they'd seen more of each other than she'd actually thought would come about, she believed that he probably still saw other people, perhaps even slept with them and she knew she wasn't ready for that reality.

"Actually, I do think I'd like to take a minute before I start the drive all the way into the city, and a cup of coffee sounds perfect," he admitted.

It had been a long day, and an especially pleasant

one. He found that when he was in Lauren's presence, things always seemed to go well. Inwardly, there was the almost imperceptible ring of a cautionary bell—then all was silent."Thanks, why don't you go on in and I'll park the car and be up in a minute," he said quickly.

"Great," she said, swinging her legs to the ground as she exited the car.

Gloria, as usual, was not at home and Lauren entered the apartment hoping that in addition to coffee, she would be able to find some kind of snack to serve. Searching the cabinets, she found several unopened boxes of Bretton whole wheat gourmet crackers.

"So much for non-carbohydrates," she said as she opened a box and spread the contents out across a cheese board. Shopping always produced several different kinds of cheeses since both she and Gloria had a preference for a particular brand and style. Gloria was especially fond of Jarlsberg and Lauren's favorite was Monterey Jack with jalapeno peppers or blue cheese. She was in luck. They had all three so she alternated the slices and cut a wedge of blue. She then alternated the slices creating an alternating pattern of light and dark creaminess. Then she put the coffee on to brew.

Entering her bedroom, she removed her navy blue sweater and skirt, leaving the white halter top intact. She then pulled on a pair of black body-shaper leotards. The buzzer sounded just as she was spraying a light dusting of Gucci Rush on her elbows and wrists.

"Wow, something smells great," Michael said minutes later, entering the apartment. "Is that you or the coffee or both?" he teased, realizing it was the first time that they'd been together alone in her apartment—on her turf, so to speak.

"Probably both," she responded, laughing too. "But we do subscribe to a gourmet coffee service. I thought you might like to try the hazelnut," she said, showing him into the living room.

"Great. Hey, in the five minutes it took me to park the car you've transformed yourself into an incredibly sexy little black kitten," he murmured appreciatively, his eyes hungrily taking in the unobstructed view of curves facing him. The tight black leotard pants molded to Lauren's slim curves as if made for her; her long legs seemed to go on forever. The white halter top, covered most of the day by the navy blue sweater, enhanced and outlined the curves of her breasts alluringly, leaving her shoulders and back bare to his gaze. The golden almond of her skin shone in stark contrast against the white of the halter top as Michael felt his composure begin to slip. He took a deep breath. He wanted coffee, only coffee, for now.

"You know, this apartment is exceptional. I didn't really get the chance to appreciate it the night of the party. I think this is the first time I've seen the furniture in its rightful place and all that," he said.

Glancing around the earth-toned environment, he realized someone had a real gift. Or they'd hired an interior decorator. An L-shaped sectional covered in warm beige velour constituted the seating environment. The walls were painted a subtle shade of pale coral. It was dramatic, but extremely effective in making a statement. Feminine, bold yet conventional, as nothing was too austere or ultra modern. The carpet was a plush oatmeal-colored pile and touches of warm bronze, coral and stark-white accent pieces were strategically placed throughout. The unusually low coffee table was a large square slab of oatmeal-colored marble on which sat several Japanese bonsai trees in separate rock gardens.

Half-moon wall sconces adorned each wall, creating ambient lighting with just the right tone and hue. The effect was warm, tranquil and thoroughly functional.

"Gloria and I did it together, but she trusted my judgment on a lot of it—I guess I picked up a little from my mom. She's a design school graduate. I remember growing up, our house, no matter where we were stationed, was always filled with unique pieces from whatever part of the world we'd most recently lived in," she said, smiling at the memory.

"Come on into the dining area and we can have our coffee," she said, moving to turn on the CD player. The sounds of Seal's "A Little Crazy" began to float out, its funky uplifting Euro-beat sounding almost out of place in an environment that for the most part, appeared to be provincial and cozy.

"So, that's what you listen to when I'm not around," Michael teased as she began to set out the cheese and crackers, adding two large clusters of red seedless grapes to the platter.

"I can see that having grown up and been exposed to Europe obviously did influence your musical tastes. Wow, what an advantage," he observed with a small degree of envy. His knowledge and appreciation of music were inbred, enhanced by his exposure at Northwestern, and nurtured by his responsibility to the station, but he'd always known that Europe's contribution to the world beat was more than substantial.

"Well, my dad's favorite thing to do was blow his tenor saxophone—it was more of a hobby than anything else. 'Earl' as he named it, went anywhere we did. I remember one night when we were stationed in Germany, we went to a small guesthouse where they serve beer and wienerschnitzel, to listen to a band play. Dad hadn't told Mom or myself that he was going to join them on stage, but he did. We were blown away by how good he was and how much he loved doing it," she said smiling at the recollection. He was incredible—I remember he was the only black guy on the stage and when he started blowing on that saxophone, all the attention seemed to hone right in on him. Afterward, people came up to our table, shaking his hand, telling him he was going to be the next Grover Washington Jr. and whatever. I'll bet he still has Earl," she murmured softly.

"I think that's the first time I've ever heard you talk about your dad," Michael observed, noting that she had done so with obvious pride.

"Yeah, well that's because I was pretty angry with him about the divorce and all that stuff. I promised my mom I would write to him, though. Anyway, yeah, I love Sting, Peter Gabriel, Julia Fordham, all that stuff. And of course, I love jazz, but there doesn't seem to be anyone making music for my generation anymore," she offered.

"That's an interesting comment," he said, pouring them each a cup from the carafe she'd brought to the table as she served the other items onto sandwich plates.

"I knew a lot of older people felt that way. I don't think I realized that perhaps some of the people in your age group would feel like that too," he admitted.

"Oh, definitely. Gloria and I talk all the time about the fact that, musically, we feel as if we belong to the generation before us. Rap music and the hip-hop era somehow don't begin to express us or our vision of what it's all about," she added.

"Well, market analyses bear out your contention. There's a whole generation of demographics out there that's not being tapped. I personally think that the lack of a solid core in R & B as well as popular music is one of the greatest contributors for why the station has been doing so well. People don't know—don't hear anything else to listen to. Jazz is the last great bastion of incredible music. And I predict that even the hip-hop generation is going to turn to jazz in about a minute to start sampling for their next contingency of music," he ended.

"I really like hearing you talk about music," Lauren said, looking at him in wonderment. "You become so animated."

"Well, I enjoy talking about music, too and you're a very good listener—as a matter of fact, you're great to talk to," he said, reaching across the table to wipe a crumb from the side of her mouth. The contact was electric and they both felt it.

They continued talking, eating and listening to CDs by Simply Red and Julia Fordham, unaware of the passing time. When Lauren finally glanced at the oval clock overlooking the dining room table, she gasped, realizing it was nearing 3:00 A.M.

"Would you like me to help you clean up?" he asked, rising from the table as he collected their plates.

"No, but thank you. I'll just load the dishwasher. The rest can wait until tomorrow," she said, removing the remaining items and placing them on the kitchen counter.

She turned then and as Michael put the dishes he was holding on the countertop, he leaned over and kissed her. She hesitated but for a moment, then stepped into the kiss and felt herself tremble ever so slightly. Or was it him. She didn't know and didn't care. She moved into his arms and it felt as if she had been born there.

"I've wanted to do this all day," he said, trailing kisses from her lips to her jawline, down her neck while inhaling her fragrance.

"But you did kiss me today," she protested through a haze of desire as she ran her hands slowly along his finely chiseled back, noting the contour and definition as if committing them to memory.

"Not like I wanted to," he said as he once again kissed

her hungrily, shutting off the flow of any words. He thrust his tongue into her mouth languidly, drawing her engagement by merely coaxing. And she in turn responded with her own exploration of the inner recesses of his warm, increasingly familiar terrain. They played with each other, much like dolphins teasing, performing a mating dance within the surf. Leisurely stroking, molding and heightening—their desire building to a fever pitch in the one room of a house created to withstand temperatures of extreme heat.

Michael lifted Lauren, placing her on the countertop, his hands finding their way underneath the halter top and coming to rest on the smooth expanse of skin on her back. They were both breathing rapidly and he moved into the inner circle of her legs on either side of him. The now differing angles of their respective heights added a unique vantage point and Michel continued to drink from her mouth as if he were a man recently marooned on a desert island without water. She could feel the power of his passion pressing into the crevice between her legs as she also became acutely aware of her body's own response. Michael's hand traveled in a slow, circular pattern on her breasts as he continued to kiss her and she knew desire so sweet, so intense, that it created an ache deep within her.

His thumb circled her breast in a tantalizing dance and it immediately peaked, impudently seeming to beg for more. He repeated his action on the other side and the response was the same. He now had his hands full, his mouth fully engaged and his senses assailed by the nearness, the feel and the pure essence of Lauren.

Lauren could feel the evidence of his desire between her outstretched legs. She suddenly shifted, slid down the countertop placing her feet on the floor with Michael still standing before her, his legs now straddling her body. The contact, full body, frontal and extremely intimate, was the final straw for him. He tore his mouth from hers and gasped out harshly.

"Lauren, unless you want me to make love to you I think I should leave now," he said pointedly. "Look, I know you got spooked last time and I don't want to rush anything, that's why I haven't let things get out of hand again. But this was unplanned, I really just wanted a cup of coffee," he said, looking into her eyes which were clear, trusting and waiting for him to make his point.

"I can't promise you I won't get spooked again, Michael," she answered honestly. "I will tell you that I do want to make love to you. You must think I'm awful to admit that to you," she said, looking away shyly.

"Lauren, look at me, sweetheart," he said, taking her chin in his hand. "Knowing that you want to make love with me as much as I do is all I need to know and actually I think that answers my question," he added. He moved back then, pulled her halter top back into place before kissing her chastely on the tip of her nose.

"It's not time yet," he said, running his fingers through his hair as he attempted to compose himself. He took several deep breaths, all the while looking into her eyes. She smiled up at him, shyly, passion still plainly etched on her face.

"I'll call you sometime during next week," he said, picking his keys up from the living room table. "Maybe we can take *Megahertz* out on the weekend," he said as she walked him to the door.

Lauren felt unsure of herself. She knew she wanted him. She'd surprised herself at the depth of passion she'd not only displayed, but felt. But she also knew that he was probably right. Time was on their side.

"Great, I'd love it," she said as she turned to him at the door.

"Fine, then it's a date. Just let me check the weekend

weather. Oh, also, I think we're just about ready to seal the merger so perhaps there'll be something to celebrate," he announced excitedly.

"That's great, Michael. I'll look forward to it."

"So will I. By the way, that was great coffee," Michael said, smiling as he made his way to the elevator.

Thirteen

The intercom on Michael's desk flashed once and was silent. He looked up. Reluctantly, he tore his eyes away from the report he was reading, and hit the button impatiently.

"Yeah," he practically growled.

"Are you reading this thing the same way I am?" Duke asked increduously.

"Yeah, I think I am. I'm almost finished—look, why don't we sit down together in my office in about fifteen minutes—we can compare notes."

"Fine, I'll bring the coffee."

Some fifteen minutes later, Duke, true to his word, walked in with two Starbucks cups in hand and sat in one of the chairs facing Michael's desk.

"Here, the regular is for you," he said pushing one container toward Michael.

"Hey, thanks, man. I needed this about an hour ago when I got here, but I didn't feel like stopping."

"Yeah, well I just sent my assistant out. She's addicted to their double lattes. I just offer to pay for hers and it's a done deal." Duke laughed.

"What can I say, dude—you're a smooth operator. But obviously not as smooth as our friends. Not by the sound of this report," Michael said bringing the conversation around to the subject at hand.

The advisory report from Burns, Eden and Glick-stein, the consulting firm they'd come to rely on when-ever any issue of compliance, acquisition or possible merger was under consideration, had done their jobs prudently. They possessed, among the various partners and associates affiliated with the firm, over thirty-five years of experience in the communications industry. Their reputation impeccable, their research infallible, they'd issued a report that was unquestionably dubious.

"Look, the numbers bear out everything that Morgan said at our initial meeting, but the numbers are not the real problem are they?" Michael's rhetorical question hung heavily in the air as both men considered the im-plication.

"Right. The problems comes in with the connections these guys have into other avenues of business—like waste management and construction supplies. Did you notice the affiliates listed with those firms?" Duke re-sponded, clearly concerned.

"Not only did I notice, but I'm trying to put someone on to it for me as we speak. That's why I asked you to give me another fifteen minutes. The only way we're gonna know exactly what the deal is with this situation is to have insider information. That means 'delving deep' my partner, and the most effective way to do that is to go undercover," Michael stated with certainty.

"I hear you and I agree." Duke knew his partner, knew his capabilities and had one hundred percent con-fidence in his ability to ferret out enough information to help them resolve this dilemma. He also knew Mi-chael had valuable connections with the NYPD.

"Look, as it stands now, time is on our side anyway because B,E and G came in with the report ahead of schedule. That bought us some additional time to do our own due diligence," Duke pointed out.

"Right, so let's see what else we can dig up. Hopefully

we'll be able to get the real story by the time our next meeting is scheduled with Morgan. But guess what, if the deadline approaches and we're still not totally sure of what this is—you know the duck theory—looks like a duck, sounds like a duck, it probably is a duck. If this thing still looks like a duck, then we'll at least know what's quacking by the time we go into that meeting," Michael said pointedly.

"Okay, that sounds about right. Look, if there's anything you need from me in terms of furthering our insight into this thing, don't hesitate to let me know. I realize you have your own sources," he said smiling, "but just know that I'm in this thing too right up to my beard," Duke ended as he smoothed his face to emphasize his point.

"Hey, I've got this covered, but thanks anyway. I figure we should know something pretty soon. You know another thing that struck me is that, on paper at least, Cityscape Broadcasting Network is rock-solid. The first half of the report reads like an investor's dream. Impeccable track record, solid gains over the past five years and growth potential through the roof. The real concerns didn't start to surface until I got to the subsidiaries and management teams listed. That's when the red flag went up. Obviously the same was true for our cracker-jack consulting team because that's the one flaw they pointed out in the final analysis of the report," Michael said closing his copy.

"I know. And although I'm not thrilled at the prospect of what their involvement with that element probably signifies, you have to admit that it's ingenious. You saw the numbers. The profit center of the entire organization is centralized through some of those smaller, non-communication related firms. That's where a good deal of their extensive cash flow comes from. With that kind of profit center, CBN doesn't even have to hit a high margin of profit. They can be as much of a cash cow as they want. They're fully funded through their subsidiaries," Duke offered.

"Yeah, and that brings us to another unanswered question. They obviously don't need us to merge with them from a financial standpoint, so what's in it for them?" Michael asked. "I mean, I realize that our numbers for the NYC/NJ/Connecticut market share are attractive—very attractive. But I'm really curious now just how focused these guys are in terms of radio as an entity. From the revenues derived from their other business holdings, radio clearly is not their ace in the hole," he added.

"You know, you're probably right about that, but Morgan seemed to be dead set on doing this deal and that has to mean something. He obviously, for whatever the reason, is serious about joining forces with us and increasing that market share. Maybe he's realized that it's important for them going forward to create a dominant presence in the local markets as well as their existing stations in the metropolitan area."

"Okay, that might wash. You know, Lauren tried to warn me about CBN and its murky reputation, but I brushed her off thinking she might have been overreacting to her roommate's obvious affluence. As it stands now, she was probably more on target than I'd like to admit."

"Well, it certainly seems that you and Lauren have made some headway since we last spoke of her. At that time, she wasn't returning your calls if I remember correctly," Duke said, the beginnings of a smile lurking around his mouth. He was enjoying seeing his usually carefree partner enter a realm of obvious attachment and attention to another human being. He didn't know if it was time yet to say "I told you so" but he'd certainly be there to deliver the line when and if it was appropriate.

"Oh, I see. So, you think this is some kind of joke, don't you. Well, she's not giving me a hard time after all; in fact we have another date for the weekend. I'm taking her out on *Megahertz*, weather permitting." Michael's voice held a triumph he didn't altogether feel, but he didn't dare let his partner in on his uncertainties.

"Great. Look, I think it's interesting that she said anything to you at all. That must have been awkward for her with the roommate thing and all," Duke said earnestly. "She must really like you after all," he added.

"Well, if she does, she'll never admit it. I told you she's stubborn, willful, and extremely beautiful. Bad combination, good genes. I still don't know exactly what I'm going to do about her, but she's fun to be around. Anyway, I promised her we'd do the boat thing so I guess I have to live up to it."

"Oh spare me, don't sound like you're pressed. This is me, Mike—I know you. If you didn't want to be bothered with Miss Good Genes, she'd be history. You're only hanging around for one thing my brother and you and I both know what that is."

"You're wrong, Duke, I'm not sleeping with her lately. We've been out at least twice in the past three weeks and I haven't laid a hand on her. Well, maybe a hand, but I have not taken her to bed," he admitted.

Duke narrowed his eyes then, looking at his partner with a new respect and something else—curiosity. "Are you attracted to this woman physically?" he asked then.

"God, if I was any more attracted to her, there would be a law against it. It's just that something happened on our first date that really scared her and blew me out of the water. Since then, we've been taking things real slow. You know, one day at a time so to speak," he said resolutely.

"Okay, well it sounds like you know what you're doing. Look, you've never had any problems with the ladies. Not even in college and, I suspect, since well before. Just handle your business," Duke said encouragingly.

"I'm not saying she's a problem. In fact, she's a very sweet, very attractive, truly remarkable woman. It's just that I'm used to dealing in another way and she doesn't fit the format," he said then, using an industry term in the hopes of making his partner understand his dilemma.

"So, get rid of her," Duke said, inwardly cringing at his callousness. But if what he suspected was correct, that statement could be the catalyst his partner needed to come to terms with his true feelings.

Michael sat back in his chair, deep in thought for what seemed like an eternity.

"I suppose that's the answer right there in front of my face all along," he said solemnly. "You know, you're right. I don't have time to play these games," he added as if trying to convince himself.

"Hey, you know I'm the last person to give advice to the lovelorn; after all my track record stinks—0 for 0," Duke said, referring to his former marriage which had resulted in divorce after only six months.

"Whatever you do, get your head straight because we have a lot of work ahead of us in the coming year, merger or no merger," he added.

"Yeah, I know. Listen, don't worry, I'll can handle it. And I'll let you know as soon as I get anything solid on CBN," he promised as Duke stood up to leave his office.

"Great. Don't forget, if you need my help or input on any of this, don't hesitate to give me a holler. This stuff is nerve-wracking," Duke threw over his shoulder as he left Michael's office.

"That, my friend, is an understatement," Michael

said under his breath as he returned his attention to the paperwork on his desk. His reference included much more than the proposed merger.

"Detective First Grade Walter Townsend, please," Michael said into the speakerphone on his desk, one hand still on the report's highlighted pages.

"One moment please," the NYPD operator said authoritatively into the phone. Thirty seconds later, he was connected.

"Detective Townsend."

"Hey, Dad, how are you?" Michael asked quickly.

"Fine, Michael, I'm fine. And you?" his father asked, his voice solid and deep, reminding Michael of his childhood. He'd always liked his dad's voice and felt that his genes for being able to transcend to radio had been passed on from him.

"Did you get a message about two hours ago? I left it with our usual code reference so you'd know it was business related," Michael asked.

"Yeah, the trouble is I was out on a call. My investigative unit just undertook a new assignment and I just got back. Haven't even had a chance to sit down yet. What's up, son?" his father asked then, realizing that Michael did not call often and especially almost never deigned to use their code reference "Bridgetown" which held a special significance for them both. Barbados had been the birthplace of Maria Townsend's father. Although Michael's mother had been gone from the earth for some time now, he and his dad never forgot her. Her love, her generosity, her spirit were with them for all time.

Walter Townsend had never remarried. He didn't date and didn't socialize much. His work as a detective with the New York City Police Department was his life.

He and his only son, Michael were as close as two men with equally demanding mistresses could be. They got together several times a year, holidays, birthdays and occasionally a hastily arranged dinner at a Manhattan restaurant so that each could get caught up on the other's current life condition.

He hadn't received a call from Michael using the code name "Bridgetown" for many years. Established when he was in college and used in the vein of disguising the frequency of his calls for the things kids in college usually call home for, it was Michael's way of not being ribbed by his dad for calling so often. He figured if he didn't leave his real name, no one but his dad would ever know it was him. What he didn't know was that his father had issued a proclamation to everyone in his office that if any calls came in from "Bridgetown," he was to be told immediately. That those calls, in particular, were of a priority nature.

"Okay, look, Dad, there's no other way to say this, but I need a huge favor from you. Nothing like a parking ticket or anything, this is more in line with public records research. But look, I don't want to impose on you or anything. You just took on another assignment. Do you think you'll have the time to look into something for me?"

"Look, Michael, you're my son and anything you need in terms of information I'd feel almost compelled to gather for you. Don't worry about my time frame. There's always another investigation where New York City is concerned. Just tell me what's going on with you? What kind of information are you looking for?"

"Okay, Dad, here's the deal. There's a firm—Cityscape Broadcasting Network who is interested in merging with WJZZ. They've made us a very attractive offer. The problem is that they have several subsidiaries that my partner and I both think are questionable. I know that if there's any scuttlebutt on these firms within the department, you'll be able to uncover it and let me know the lowdown."

"I see. Okay, give me the names and locations of all the companies you're interested in and I'll personally look into each one. Why are you and Duke even considering merging with these characters if you're having second thoughts about their legitimacy?" he asked then, all five senses of his detective's body coming to attention.

"Because the merger would mean a tremendous amount to us as entrepreneurs, as communications experts, and on the whole, as two guys who want to be able to garner as much of the market as we possibly can. Our goal has always been to reach the top and this deal would signify our arrival so to speak. We just have to be very careful that everything is legitimate and that's where you come in."

"Well, thanks for the vote of confidence. Coming from you it means a lot," his father said jokingly. "Fax that stuff over to me in the next five minutes—no cover note. I'll work on it and have something back to you as soon as I can," he added.

"Great, and thanks, Dad. Look, why don't we do dinner in a week or so. Whatever night you're free during the week is good for me," Michael said, thumbing through his calendar.

"Sure thing. Okay, send the stuff so I can work on it. I'll talk to you in a few days."

"Right, and thanks again, Dad."

They both hung up at the same time. Another click, faint though distinct, was heard two seconds later.

Fourteen

Gino Sorrentino was living in torment. Tormented by conflict, tormented by loyalties and, most of all, tormented by his commitment to his colleagues. It was a commitment he no longer felt compelled to uphold, but the alternative was unthinkable. Not to mention unhealthy. He had no grand illusions as to the amount of effort it would take for this dilemma to be resolved. He'd wrestled with the situation for the past couple of years, with the additional pressure of Morgan's recent input only adding more pressure to the load. And although he'd admired, respected and even come to love Morgan who'd grown into a remarkable man, the decisions to be made going forward were so critically important that he couldn't let his emotional ties, even of a family nature, prejudice him in any way.

Even the love he had for his wife, Cora, couldn't be allowed to interfere with what he knew had to be done. She'd fascinated him from the first time he'd spotted her in a florist shop on Columbus Avenue. Striking black hair, green eyes and a carriage born of royalty. Even the wedding band she'd worn around her neck on a chain hadn't put him off. It had served to intrigue him all the more when he realized that it probably symbolized a marriage that had somehow been interrupted. Why else would she wear it around her neck instead of

on the third finger of her left hand. His thoughts were
that if she was his wife, she'd definitely wear the ring
in its proper place and sport a personal bodyguard during daylight hours too. Nights, he figured, he could take
care of.

It had taken four visits to the shop for him to get his
nerve up to even ask her a direct question. Six months
later, they were an item and, within that same year, they
were Mr. and Mrs. Sorrentino. She'd been widowed only
two years before, but Gino considered it his lucky day
when he'd entered "Floral Equations" on that cold
January day. The fact that she owned it had been inci-
dental. That she also had a son who was attending law
school had been uncanny. He too had been left with a
child to raise, a daughter who was then fifteen, beautiful, and distinctly difficult. He definitely considered it
his fate to have spotted, met and married Cora Isabel
and that was one of the most difficult aspects of his
decision-making process going forward. She'd been
widowed once already. He couldn't bear the thought of
her having to go through that again. Gino knew that
there was a distinct possibility that something unexpected could very well happen to him if he didn't make
the right decision.

Gino also knew, only too well, that his current position as CEO of Cityscape Broadcast Network was crucial
to his colleagues. He realized they'd leave no stone unturned when it came to uncovering any information on
what was taking place in anything they had invested in
and still had major control over. He knew them too
well. He himself came from a long line of "wiseguys"
who'd always found a way to make things happen.

His great-grandfather, Giovanni Sorrentino, who'd
migrated from Sicily in the early 1920s to the streets of
lower Manhattan, had been a member of the Black
Hand. And his grandfather, Carlo Sorrentino, who'd

also lived and died in the same neighborhood, had been part of La Cosa Nostra. Passed on from generation to generation, his father, Anthony Sorrentino, had been destined to inherit the legacy.

"Little Italy" as it was now called, had seen many generations of racketeering, bootlegging and muscling in on small business owners for protection. In the 1920s, when alcohol was declared to be illegal, the Mafia really gained a foothold as prohibition took center stage. People like Bugsy Siegel, Vito Genovese, Arnold Rothstein, Lucky Luciano, Frank Costello, Albert Anastasia and Dutch Schultz became the known members of organized crime, "gangsters" or "mobsters." The roaring twenties rolled its way into the depression of the thirties and mobsters were the only ones with any money. They also had cohesion, discipline and organization and were known for violence and intimidation, their reputations far outlasting their actual longevity.

War for the control of the underworld took place in 1931 and after much bloodshed, the "Five Families" were formed. They controlled much of what was done in New York City at that time, including nightclubs and their performers like Duke Ellington, writers or columnists like Damon Runyon and Walter Winchell. Even the FBI's J. Edgar Hoover, was reportedly controlled through fear of a leakage of his true sexual orientation which allegedly included cross-dressing and such. High-class nightclubs such as the Stork Club and the Copa Cabana were frequented by Mafia members on a regular basis. The mob established a history of paying off crooked cops, lawyers and judges. Even government officials were reportedly on the "take."

In the 1930s, they controlled the docks with infinite precision and even the establishment in 1936 of the International Longshoreman's Association or ILA couldn't stop the Mafia's airtight control over who could load and unload the multitudes of huge containers coming into and leaving the Port of New York.

Even sports was not immune to the long reaching tentacles of the mob. In the 1940s, boxing was the enterprise they set their sights on. At Madison Square Garden, the location of Friday night bouts, there was major mobster influence on not only who fought, but who won and who lost for many years. Gambling and prostitution had also become big business with drugs making an entrance later in the sixties.

Gino considered himself lucky. Incredibly lucky. Former investigative efforts by the Grand Jury led by both the FBI and the NYPD had been unsuccessful in their attempt to convict him of any wrongdoing. But he also knew they could be relentless. That was why the deal that Morgan was so eager to put together worried him more than he cared to admit. It only served to increase the visibility of Cityscape and that was something he was inherently trying to avoid. The lower the profile, the longer he could remain in obscurity. Hence the longer he could enjoy anonymity. There was something else he couldn't seem to shake from his repertoire of recurring thoughts of late. It was something he couldn't share with anyone, not even his beloved wife and confidant. She'd become a part of him in the last ten years. He shared most of his thoughts with her, even the ones concerning the business although he knew it was highly unorthodox for a "member" to take his wife into his confidence. He trusted Cora like he'd trusted no other human being on the face of the planet.

He couldn't trust her with this though. Hell, he didn't even trust himself with these thoughts. Lately, thoughts of Joseph Volacci had become prominent in his mind. He didn't know if it was his watching of the television series *The Sopranos* and the storyline of one of the mobsters going undercover for the Feds, or if it was his memory of his father's anger and reaction to the announcement of the actual case. Whatever it was, it was causing him the loss of many a night's sleep. Gino recalled that his father had said it all started with Volacci being sent to federal prison on charges of drug trafficking. While imprisoned, he learned that a hit had been put out on him by his own people in an effort to silence him and he turned to the authorities for protection. He, in fact, became the first bona fide member of the Mafia to turn state's evidence hence creating "The Volacci Papers." His testimony sent several important "family" members to prison for many years and it was never forgotten.

Years later, Henry Hill, another prominent member of the family, also turned states evidence after his involvement with the infamous "Brinks robbery" at New York City's John F. Kennedy Airport. More prominent Mafia members went to prison.

Gino was experiencing nightly cold sweats because he knew that the Feds weren't finished with him. He'd been able to slip through their last investigation with the help of his colleagues and their less than traditional persuasion tactics, but he wasn't convinced that he'd be fortunate enough to endure the same fate twice. He also realized that if the Feds approached him with a deal, he wasn't one hundred percent sure of his response. Although the thought of going totally legitimate held its own features of attraction, Gino tried not to kid himself. To do that and cut all ties with the "family" would include its own built-in self-destruct mechanism. After all, the motto of the family was "forever—until death do us part." There was no resignation, no retirement, no cancellation possible.

Seeing Special Agent John Reid at Fiorello's the week before had shaken him. It was like a wake-up call. They wanted him to know they were around and that could only mean one thing. They must be getting close again, close to either reopening their investigation or worse yet, close to indictment.

Gino picked up the phone and pressed the speed dial # two.

"Hey—how about 2 P.M. today?" he said brusquely into the receiver.

"Fine—I'm glad you changed your mind," Morgan said at the other end.

"Don't assume anything. I'll see you in a couple of hours," he said abruptly, placing the receiver into the cradle.

Morgan was prepared to pull out all the stops in convincing Gino of the absolute necessity in going forward with the acquisition of station WJZZ. He was actually looking forward to the opportunity to display the knowledge that he'd gathered, the research that had been done and the results they'd come up with which did, in fact, confirm that an acquisition of this kind would mean more to CBN going forward than he'd actually realized. There were some things, unfortunately, that he'd neglected to take into consideration.

"Look, the stats you have here on paper hold out— that much is definitely true Morgan, but that's not really the problem," Gino pointed out.

"Well, for God's sake tell me what the problem is. You've been pussyfooting around this deal for the past two weeks, and I know you couldn't get into anything heavy with Mom and Gloria present, but it's just us now, so come clean, Gino," Morgan rallied, obviously impatient to get to the bottom of things.

"Remember a few years ago when the Feds held me for a couple of days then had to let me go for a lack of evidence?" Gino asked quietly, never taking his eyes off Morgan's face.

"Sure, how could I forget that. It was a law student's worse nightmare. A family member in custody—not to mention the publicity," Morgan stated, clearly still bitter at the obvious embarrassment it had caused.

"Yeah, well that little episode may not be totally over. The other night when we left the restaurant I saw someone who could very well be ready to start up that entire episode again. You know the Feds never wrapped that case and they don't let things like that go," Gino reminded him.

"Yeah, but you were against this deal even before the other night. What gives with you, Gino? Come on, level with me."

"Look, Morgan, what I'm trying to tell you is that any high-profile move like an acquisition, a merger, any spike in holdings, etc., could bring unwanted attention. You know publicity or attention from our enemies is something we just don't want right now. Until the threat of this thing is over, I'd just as soon that CBN remain as the status quo. Even though the deal looks sweet on paper and those guys would be a definite asset, I just can't chance what it might mean in terms of publicity right now," he ended.

"Okay, I think I see what you mean. Let me ask you a question though. Without the threat of your being indicted on whatever it is that the Feds think they have on you, can CBN stand the inquiries that have to take place if an acquisition or merger is to take place? I guess what I'm saying is that from a corporate standpoint, are we clean?" Morgan held his breath as Gino's answer held the key to his future.

"Well, it sort of depends. Cityscape as an entity unto itself is definitely clean. We didn't want to put anything in place that the FCC could slam us for so we were more than diligent about keeping everything well above board. It gets a little more complicated though when you take into consideration that CBN also has subsidiaries or holding companies that turn a very nifty profit each month, some of which may not be as spic and span as the communications end. Don't forget we have the waste management companies throughout about thirty-five states as well as the construction supply firms. A lot of intricate business is done through the guise of both those operations," Gino ended, without having to deliver a statement of personal indictment.

Morgan had suspected as much, but he'd never put his stepfather on the line to confirm or deny the existence of just such a network of business enterprises. The fact that he'd admitted just where the line was drawn was invaluable. Now Morgan knew that even if he had to pull the plug on the initial deal he'd constructed with WJZZ, at some future time, after careful revision, it was entirely possible to reconstruct it with provisions in place to separate the waste management and construction supply portions.

"Gino, I appreciate your coming clean with me about all of this. It was driving me crazy because I knew that acquisition was the rightful next step so to speak and I couldn't for the life of me figure out why you were so resistant to it."

"Well, now you know, so just sit tight. My seat on the board of CBN is the key to a large part of the federal investigation. I'm glad we made the initial decision to leave you off early on when you first came on board. Your title of Chief Operations Officer allows you to function in my capacity whenever I need it, but allows you to be exempt from the Board's directives. It was a stroke of genius, and I owe you a great deal of thanks for coming up with that," Gino said, genuinely extending gratitude to his stepson, business partner, and collaborator on many levels.

"No thanks necessary. I had to find a way to pay you

back for taking care of my educational expenses anyway. I'd consider us even at this point," Morgan said, laughing.

"Well, even is stretching it a bit far, but you've definitely repaid more than a good portion of the debt. It was worth it. I always wanted to have a son. A son in law school was definitely a bonus," he said.

"Speaking of sons and daughters, your daughter is pretty upset with you about the other night. I spoke with Gloria this morning and she's vowed to not attend the next family dinner. She's spoiled rotten, Gino, and it's your fault, although my mom didn't do much to squelch that behavior either," Morgan offered.

"Gloria is still behaving like the fourteen-year-old she was when her mother died. I know it's been rough on her; hell, it's been rough on me too but I was lucky. I found your mother. Gloria is so busy flying all around the country, buying clothes and attending parties, she doesn't have time to settle down, find a husband, have a couple of kids. Then she wouldn't be so unpleasant when things don't exactly go her way," Gino stated with finality.

Morgan laughed at the thought of his kid sister married with children. "I don't think you're going to see that for quite some time. She's not interested in dating anyone right now," he added, though for the life of him he couldn't understand why. She was definitely attractive. She was intelligent and she traveled often, meeting lots of people on a regular basis. That she often chose to hang out with him could be seen as an asset. He made sure she stayed out of trouble, didn't hang with the wrong crowd and kept her nose clean. He actually enjoyed her company, most times preferring it to some blind date or bimbo he'd have to explain every minute detail of the evening to.

"Don't worry about your sister, she'll turn around.

Look, I'd better get going because I promised your mother I'd get back and we'd catch a movie at the Cineplex this evening."

"Okay, thanks again for clearing all that up. I'll have to think of something by way of explanation for retracting the offer," Morgan said, walking Gino toward the reception area.

"Yeah, well you attorneys are usually pretty good at putting on a show," Gino said.

"Sure, sure, blame it on the attorneys. They always do," Morgan responded with a shake of his head. Inwardly, he cringed knowing that this was a deal he'd had his heart and his professional soul set on. And although he fully realized the ramifications Gino had outlined to him, he also knew great disappointment that he'd have to somehow finagle himself out of an acquisition that he'd not only worked hard to pull together, but one that would have effectively moved CBN into bona fide legitimacy.

Fifteen

Lauren's week sped by, starting with a trip to Los Angeles, which included an overnighter and the return flight stopping in Chicago for a full two-hour layover. She'd then flown to Atlanta on another overnighter, then direct back to New York. By the time she walked into her apartment on Thursday afternoon, she was exhausted. Checking the answering machine, she noticed there was one message from her mom, one from Michael, and one from Worldwide Airlines Administration. She looked at her watch and noted it was well past six P.M. *Worldwide's administrative offices would be closed now,* she thought.

After unpacking her suitcase and carryall and changing into a comfortable terry-cloth jumpsuit, she sorted through the mail. Nothing unusual. Just the normal bills, notices and magazines. There was also a Worldwide Airlines envelope addressed to her. She tore it open quickly, curiosity getting the better of her.

She'd been assigned the position she had requested as senior flight attendant on their Charter Service Division. The letter instructed her to call their headquarter's office as soon as possible to receive instruction on further training and her new assignment.

Wow, that was really fast, she thought. She'd only applied three months prior, but word of mouth had been that the division was actively looking to recruit top-notch flight attendants. Lauren had sent her resume and credentials into the division almost immediately. Well, it had paid off and she would soon be flying charter flights, domestic and international, something she'd always wanted to do. She couldn't wait to tell Michael. She knew he would be proud of her and hoped it would make him happy to know that she was doing something she'd always wanted to.

She also was looking forward to telling her roommate. Although Gloria had no desire to move out of the ranks of standard air passenger service, she was always a solid supporter of anyone else's endeavors to move into something new. Lauren was sure this would be no different. After all, their existing schedules were often at odds. They very rarely spent more than a day together in the apartment in the expanse of one month at times. Then sometimes as fate would have it, they'd wind up having a chain of days off at the same time and would get to enjoy each other's company.

Lauren quickly dialed Michael's number at the station, glancing at her watch and noting the lateness of the hour. "I hope he's still there," she prayed realizing that he did oftentimes work well past 7:00 P.M.

"Townsend," he answered on the third ring, sounding preoccupied.

"Well, hello, Mr. Townsend, this is your friend in Cobble Hill," she said coyly into the receiver.

"Hey, kitten, it took you long enough to return my call. What are you, on some kind of time warp anyway?" he teased. "I called you on Tuesday and Wednesday. Don't you check your messages while you're away?" he asked more earnestly this time.

"Actually, I do check them, Michael, but sometimes between trips and flights, it's so hectic that I can't get a handle on them. I'm sorry. I promise that whenever

I pull messages off my machine, if I have anything at all from you, I'll call you back right away. Okay?" she asked sincerely.

"Yeah, well that's what I would expect of you, Lauren. Flying around all over the place, nobody knows where you are at any God-given hour, I mean sometimes it's unnerving. What if I need to speak with you right away?" he said then, obviously still upset.

"Well, I guess I never gave you my worldwide pager number. Listen, it's good throughout the continental United States. It's the number that my parents and my roommate have just in case of emergency. I'll give it to you also, okay," she added, feeling a genuine need to offer him the solace that he seemed to require as to her whereabouts. It was funny, this was the first time he had displayed anything more than a casual interest in what she did when she was not with him and instead of annoying or frightening her, it actually made her feel protected and needed, almost cherished.

"Look, no pressure or anything, Lauren. If you feel that you want to share that connection with me, fine. I was just a little worried about you this week when I didn't receive a return phone call."

He neglected to add that he'd been unable to get a decent night's sleep on at least a couple of those nights with thoughts of her alone, in a strange city encountering all kinds of obstacles, both man-made and man-inspired, without the necessary tools of defense.

"Anyway, the reason I was calling you was to confirm this weekend. The weather is going to be fine, seventy-five degrees, sunny with winds coming out of the southeast at ten miles per hour so it'll be great sailing weather. I was hoping we could leave on Saturday morning about ten A.M. and sail all day. Is there any conflict with your schedule?" he asked.

"No, it's fine because I don't have another trip until Monday afternoon. But I do have some exciting news to share with you," she said. "I'll save it until I see you though."

"Sure, now that you have my curiosity aroused. Okay, look, I'll pick you up on Saturday morning around ten o'clock. Dress for the sea, the sun and dinner, okay?"

"Sure thing, I mean aye, aye, captain." She laughed as she hung up.

The weather on Saturday proved to be a gift from God. Blue skies, calm winds and not a cloud in sight. Lauren dressed in a pale gray velour jogging suit, sneakers and a baseball cap. She'd put on an orange bathing suit under her sweat suit, just in case. After all, they would be on the water, and a bathing suit was certainly apro-pos. A soft knit black-and-beige striped dress with matching cardigan, black sling back pumps and the requisite change of underwear with an extra T-shirt just in case were also thrown into her canvas bag.

That should do it, she thought, mentally trying to cover any and all circumstances.

Michael picked her up just after ten as promised. He was dressed in khaki Dockers, Top-Siders and a blue-and-white striped T-shirt. He looked virile, handsome and sexy. Lauren couldn't take her eyes off him as he loaded her things into the trunk.

"Is something wrong? I mean do I have my shirt on backwards or something?" he asked, noticing her pro-longed stare at one point as he stopped at a red light.

"No, not at all. I was actually just thinking how handsome you are," she admitted candidly. It was the first time she'd admitted it to herself or to him.

"Well, thank you very much. You don't look half bad yourself," he returned. He thought that she looked incredibly sexy, the cap turned backwards on her head, ponytail hanging down her back. The velour texture of the jogging suit only served to enhance what he already knew was smooth-as-velvet skin. The orange of the bathing suit accentuated the glow of her apricot-colored skin. He took a couple of deep breaths, realizing that at some point during this date, he'd have to make a decision. He couldn't keep, would not keep, torturing himself with the question of whether Lauren Traynor belonged in his life. Duke had put the right spin on it the other day. If she was going to be a problem, she would have to be eliminated. Looking across at her, her eyes hidden behind sunglasses, he suddenly realized that it was a lot easier said than done. Somewhere along the line, she'd gotten into his gut—something he'd promised himself not to allow any female access to.

"You're quiet this morning, Michael. Anything wrong?" Lauren asked then, sensing Michael's deep concentration.

"No, not at all. Actually, I was thinking ahead to the day I have planned. I had Hank stock *Megahertz* early this morning with everything we'll need for a full day of whatever we want to make of it," he added.

"Wow, that sounds like an adventure if I ever heard one," Lauren said, laughing at Michael's obvious enthusiasm. "Where exactly are we sailing to?" she asked, her curiosity getting the better of her as he guided them smoothly onto I-95 North.

"Well, I thought we'd idly sail up the Hudson until we reached West Point and then there's a really great old restaurant at the Thayer Hotel. We'll probably dock there for dinner. And although the river is probably a little too chilly for you to take a swim, there's always the Jacuzzi on board," he ended, smiling suggestively.

Lauren chose to ignore his insinuation and instead, snuggled down into her seat.

"That's right. You know last time I didn't have a suit with me so I didn't even attempt to use it. It sounds heavenly though." Lauren smiled, glad she had worn the suit after all.

At 11:30 they reached the dock where *Megahertz* was moored, pulled up anchor after loading some additional items from Michael's car, and headed out into the Bay immediately. The sun shone brilliantly on the water, casting a perfect balance to a day filled with promise.

While Lauren went below to stow her things, Michael concentrated on setting their course. It was a run he and Hank had made many times, but today, he'd chosen to skipper the boat alone, just he and Lauren.

"Hey, would you like something to drink, Michael?" she called from the galley.

"Sure, orange juice would be fine," he responded, his concentration still on navigating his way through the inner sanctum of the harbor area. Until they were out on the open ranks of the river itself, where boating traffic was less congested, he'd operate the vessel manually.

"Coming right up," Lauren responded gaily, liking the responsibility of taking care of the skipper of this craft. The kitchen area, or galley, as it was called on a boat of this size, was well stocked. Hank had done his job well. Fruits, vegetables, juices, coffee, even champagne and wine were loaded into the cabinets and refrigerated areas. There were several containers of prepared salads, including tuna, chicken and potato. Two crusty loaves of French bread lay atop the counter, blue cheese and a round of brie were stowed inside the small refrigerator.

"Hey, looks like we're going to be out here for quite a while by the stash of goodies inside," Lauren commented as she handed Michael his orange juice.

"Hank knows one of the first rules of the sea is to make sure you have more than enough provisions," Michael said, seriousness in his voice. "You never want to be on board without something you might need. There's no Gristedes out on the ocean, nor Rite Aid, or the equivalent," he added.

"Got ya," Lauren responded. "Need any help navigating?" she asked suddenly, one arm raised in an effort to ward off the direct sunlight. She'd left her sunglasses below while getting their refreshments.

"No, I'm fine. You can make yourself comfortable and I should be able to join you in about five minutes. I just want to make sure we're clear of our closest neighbors," he indicated, motioning to the other nearby boats.

The day passed smoothly as they enjoyed each other's company more than they were willing to admit. When the sun was high in the sky and the temperature reached a balmy seventy-nine degrees, Lauren braved the heated Jacuzzi with Michael vowing that it was still too cold for him. But after hearing her purring, cooing and sounds of joy for more than ten minutes, he relented stripping down to a pair of shorts he had inside the cabin.

The spa was just large enough to accommodate them both comfortably and Michael was once again glad that he'd chosen *Megahertz* complete with all of the specifications he'd wanted.

Lauren's thighs felt like silk underneath the jet-propelled water. Her breasts rose against the orange fabric of her bathing suit top temptingly. Michael wasn't sure if it was more torturous to have stayed on deck watching her frolic in the frothing waters, or to have joined her. She laughed then, at something totally inane, and he pulled her to him, kissing her on her still-open mouth. She wound her arms around his neck, her thighs almost automatically wrapping themselves around his torso. It was exquisitely sensual, the swirling water around them, the heat of their bodies accentuated by the eighty-five-degree water of the Jacuzzi. Their mouths moved against each other's, each attempting to get the better fit. Their tongues caressed, teased, and tortured, not able to get enough of whatever it was that each sought. So intent were they on the passion that had spontaneously erupted, neither realized they were suddenly both underwater. Abruptly, they came up for air, then laughed at their passion.

"Wow, you're getting to be something else, Miss Traynor," Michael teased, pushing her head underwater again for a split second. She came up sputtering.

"Don't you even try it, Michael. I didn't do anything; as a matter of fact, I was minding my own business trying to enjoy a relaxing occasion in the Jacuzzi. You started up," she said with exaggerated disdain.

"Well, if you want me to leave," he said and turned to lift himself out of the water.

"No, that's all right, I'm not selfish. I know how to share, but you have to promise to behave yourself," she said smiling now.

"Or what?" he asked mischievously, knowing that she would not be at all happy if he kept his hands to himself.

"Or pay the penalty of all pirates who trespass while at sea," she answered with challenge, mystery and intrigue filling her voice as she raised one eyebrow.

Michael laughed then. "You know, you're a whacko. A gorgeous whacko. Okay, I'm keeping my distance because I don't know what you're capable of."

Lauren crossed the short distance between them and kissed him softly on his lips, placing both hands on his bare chest. She could feel the strong beat of his heart and knew that it mirrored hers. "You know what I'm capable of better than anybody in the world," she said, looking intently into his eyes.

Michael felt the blood coursing hotly through his body. He knew she was issuing a challenge to him at that moment. The last time they'd been on board *Megahertz* they'd made love all night long and well into the next day. And although she'd started out a virgin that night, her inexperience had quickly shed itself as layers and layers of more sensitivity and passion had unfolded each time they'd made love. That's why it had come as a complete surprise to him when she'd failed to return any of his phone calls. He'd realized then that her response to him had been unexpected on her part. Now, it had taken him the better part of six weeks to realign their relationship from the ground up. Friends first, companions first, and all that comes before lovers. He recognized that it wasn't his usual modus operandi. But Lauren wasn't the usual woman. For the first time in his life, he realized that he cared about another human beyond what his own personal needs and wants were.

"Sure, Captain Hook. Stay in as long as you want. I'm going to check our navigational components like a good captain should," he said kissing her soundly on her lips as he lifted himself out of the spa. He'd dropped anchor earlier after deciding to join Lauren.

"Hey, how about some lunch. I'm starving while you're turning yourself into a well-preserved prune danish," he called out to her over the drone of the restarted engines.

"Okay, I get the hint," Lauren replied as she stepped out of the warmth of the water, wrapping herself in a huge terry-cloth bath towel.

She dried herself brusquely, noting the temperature change. Hurrying below deck, she quickly stripped off the wet bathing suit and replaced it with her warm terry-cloth jogging suit. Thankful that she had had the presence of mind to bring along the right clothing, she entered the galley to begin searching for luncheon fare. She found a platter and filled it with scoops of various salads, fruits and bread and cheese. Next, she prepared a pot of coffee, placing a carafe of pineapple juice alongside.

"Captain, lunch is served," she called out in less than ten minutes due to the well thought out preparations of Hank. She'd try to remember to thank him the next time she saw him. She was starving and Michael was ravenous.

"Wow, I never seem to realize how hungry the open air of the sea makes you until I'm on board *Megahertz,*" he exclaimed as he filled his plate with the assorted salads and accompanying fare Lauren had set out in the dining area. The window seat was done in all glass, offering a panoramic view of the Hudson River in all her majesty. Michael had once again turned off the engines, dropping anchor for this lunchtime interlude. Golden's Bridge in Dutchess County was now only visible briefly in glimpses to the south of them, while the cliffs of the Palisades of New Jersey majestically lined one shore, the grand beauty of upstate New York on the other.

"This is so beautiful," Lauren marveled, taking small bites of her lunch.

"I know. No matter what the season, the beauty of the open sea is unrivaled," Michael said.

"Well put, Captain," Lauren said then. "By the way, remember I told you I had something to share with you? Well, I got the assignment with Worldwide Charter Administration. I actually start in two weeks."

"Well, congratulations. Well done. I knew you'd get it. We'll have to celebrate over dinner, okay?" he asked, genuinely pleased and excited by her good news.

"Sure, by the way how're things with the merger?"

she asked, suddenly remembering that he too might have something to celebrate.

"Actually, there are a couple of kinks in the deal. Right now, Duke and I are having our people do some more in-depth research and then we'll have to see. There's a great deal of positive attributes to it, though, which is why we're even taking the time to dig a little deeper," he added.

"I see. Was any of what I told you a couple of weeks ago helpful? I mean, was I even close to being right about their being less than up-front?" she asked carefully.

"Actually, Lauren, you have been great about all of this. I don't imagine that it's easy sort of feeling that you're somewhere in the middle of a major financial decision that involves two major communications entities and on the brink of establishing an emotional relationship at the same time. I actually give you a lot of credit. You've got a lot of guts," he said earnestly.

Lauren didn't know how to respond. He'd just voiced the very real concerns she'd struggled with in the past weeks, and was only now coming to terms with. He was either extremely good at dishonesty or he was actually telling the truth in terms of where he stood. She'd have to make a determination as to which was which at some point. But not now.

"Thank you," she murmured softly.

"Need some help cleaning up?"

"No, you can return to your captain-like duties," she said laughing. "I think I'll join you up top so you can teach me more about the ship's navigational system. Just let me finish cleaning this stuff up," she added.

"Great. Your first lesson in boating will take place in exactly fifteen minutes. All hands on deck at three-thirty," he said checking his watch.

"Fine. I'll meet you there."

The remainder of the afternoon passed effortlessly. And as the sun began its slow, yet still magnificent decent in the sky, Michael pulled into the waterfront wharf for the Thayer Hotel at West Point. A historical landmark of architectural delight, its lighted interior seemed to beckon to all who passed. They'd both changed clothes for dinner. Michael wore a pair of charcoal gray slacks, a white business shirt casually opened at the neck, and a navy blue blazer. Lauren had donned her tiger-striped dress tying the cardigan casually over her shoulders, pulled her hair up into a French twist, and looked relaxed, yet elegant.

Michael, in keeping with his earlier promise to celebrate her new appointment, immediately ordered a bottle of champagne. Throughout dinner, they toasted inane things like her having learned the names of most of the navigational elements on the boat that day and such. By the time dinner was over, it was well past eleven P.M.

As they headed back toward *Megahertz*, hand in hand, Lauren stifled a yawn.

"Tired?" he asked.

"I think it's the sea air. Either that or the Jacuzzi today really relaxed me more than I'd realized," she responded.

"Well, you can take a nap if you like while I head back. I'm pretty wired from the coffee I just drank."

"You mean you really don't mind if I sort of shut down on you for about an hour? I don't want you to think I'm a terrible cocaptain."

"Not at all. In fact, I insist. Don't worry, I'll wake you as we approach the harbor in Greenwich."

Lauren felt as if her head had just hit the pillow when she first realized Michael was calling her name. She'd removed her dress, crawled beneath the layers of warm comforter and sheets, and apparently passed out. She realized, too, that the engines were no longer turning.

"Where are we?" she asked sleepily, trying to get her bearings all at once.

"We've pulled into the harbor. I know I promised I'd wake you on approach, but you were really out. Man, you're no sailor," he said.

Her hair had come down from the French twist she'd fashioned earlier and as she sat up, unaware of her disheveled state, the comforter fell away from her body, revealing her lacy black brassiere, her breasts rising full and flush against the fit of the cups.

Michael took a deep breath, but it did nothing to quell the rise of his desire. He looked into her eyes and knew that she saw and shared the battle he fought. They moved toward each other then. He kissed her hotly, mindful that if she rebuffed him this time, he'd probably never get over it—but Lauren had her own struggles to overcome. Waking up in his bed with him standing over her, looking devastatingly handsome, the dark curls of his hair all tousled by the wind as he'd powered and manned the vessel that had carried them safely home, had a powerful affect on her. This was a man—tried and true and there was nothing about him that was to be short-changed.

She pulled him down toward her then, no words necessary. He held her to him, savoring the warmth of her body, the smell of her still-fragrant perfume, and the fact that she wore nothing but two pieces of scanty underwear.

This had been the scene of the first crime. *Megahertz* seemed to hold a cache of answers for them. There'd be no regrets this time.

Michael continued to kiss her, savoring the warm cavern of her mouth, the silky feel of her hair and the fit of her in his arms. He eased the tiny straps down her arms, then reached in back of her to unhook the skimpy garment. He then tore his shirt off, while she looked on with hunger in her eyes. Her breasts rose and fell with each breath as he deliberately held her in his gaze while he removed his trousers.

His passion was evident as Lauren reached out both arms to him, beckoning him to join her in bed.

"Whatever happened to the modest little virgin I met a couple of months ago?" He laughed, realizing that they had both passed several critical milestones in recent weeks.

"I'll discuss that with you later," Lauren responded as he once again took her in his arms. Their passion was like a fire too long held back and each felt the power of its heat. He kissed his way down her neck, his mouth an insatiable oven of heat and when his lips found her breasts, she moaned wantonly. His tongue circled her breasts teasingly, her nipples rising in response as her hands found their way to the flat planes of his chest and stomach. She felt the sharp intake of his breath as her hands found him and she released him from the boxer shorts he still wore. He felt so silky, so smooth yet equally so strong in her hands.

Michael kissed her lips again, his hands now peeling the scanty underpants down her silken thighs. He called her name softly once, then twice. "Lauren, look at me," he coaxed and she opened her eyes. The penetrating gray of his stare held her as she felt him touch the core of her, realizing that her readiness was evident by the flood of moisture present. As he continued to touch her, stroke her, she felt tension begin to gather in her belly. Each tug of his mouth on her breasts caused a surge of feeling deep in her womb. His hands knew their way well and she knew the sweet response of release then. It came in waves so pure, so delightful that Lauren had forgotten just how overwhelming it could be. She then helped him out of his last restraint, their mutual eagerness evident by the hurriedness of their hands, their lips, their tongues. Michael reached over to a side drawer of the bed and, without breaking his contact with Lauren, took out a tiny packet. Carefully, and slowly, he applied the sheath, remembering the first time and not wanting to make the same mistake twice.

When he entered her, it was like her world had been completed. Their fit was perfection, and he knew he never wanted to be anywhere else. All the restraint they'd exercised in the most recent weeks had served only to create an increasingly growing hunger. That hunger was now being expressed. She sheathed him like a hot, wet glove and Michael felt himself going over the edge. He mentally controlled himself and hovered there, waiting for Lauren. He built their passion much like he'd built their love—bit by bit, element by element, strategy by strategy. He did not have to wait long. The ripples of response he knew her capable of gripped him spasmodically, creating an avalanche that threatened to overtake them both. Afterward, breathless, yet beaming with satisfaction, he gathered her into his arms, nestling her for a long quiet moment. "You are one quick study—I'm almost afraid of what you'll be like if this keeps up." He laughed as his mind recounted what had taken place only minutes before. "Wow," he said, laughing to himself much like a man who had found gold where all others had failed.

Lauren giggled, too, then. "Who me, the virgin?" She then playfully slapped him on his trim rump, shocking him even further.

Sixteen

The first frost of the season threatened to descend on the city early one evening as throngs of office workers spilled out onto the streets of lower Manhattan. Having been confined to the interiors of the gray concrete structures they now exited since well before 8 A.M., their eagerness to move on to the next stage of their routine day was evident in the brisk pace of their stride.

Walter Townsend, whose day had also begun well before dawn, walked among them. The report he held under one arm weighed heavily on that side of his body, serving to keep him mindful of its presence. It also weighed heavily on his mind. The contents were damning.

In the past week, he'd checked NYPD records for any and all histories of each of the entities contained on the list Michael had faxed to him after their brief conversation.

Initially, he'd thought of his son's skepticism as the normal reticence exhibited by any businessman where a major corporate merger was concerned. But after completing a thorough search of past and current records, including any possible on-going investigations, he'd actually been offended by the sheer volume of evidence currently stacking up against Michael's potential business partners. That they felt secure enough to even suggest any type of merger or acquisition was, quite frankly, laughable. But Walter Townsend was not in a laughing mood and as he hailed a cab which would take him to the restaurant where he was meeting his son for dinner, his face showed visible signs of strain.

"Fifty-second Street," he said to the driver as they headed uptown. He leaned back into the well-worn leather interior and shut his eyes briefly. It had been a long day and an especially long week. It had taken him only minutes of researching the department's archives to come up with the first investigation which had taken place some six years earlier. And although a joint task force consisting of the NYPD and the FBI, who had been more interested in the interstate commerce aspects of the operation had been formed, neither had been able to make the charges stick.

Michael, who was waiting inside the lobby of "Joe's Pier 52" saw his dad exit the cab and knew from the lines on his face that he was worried about something. The two men hugged briefly, each not wanting to say more than was absolutely necessary before the time was right.

"Dad, I'm really glad we got to do dinner. Let's not allow so much time to lapse next time," Michael urged, knowing that their busy schedules contributed to their allowing months to go by without their getting together. But he sometimes missed the closeness they shared, recognizing that his father was not getting any younger.

"Yeah, tell me about it. Don't we say that each time and still another two months will pass before we'll do something about it. Don't worry, Michael, I know you're busy, but I also know that you would rather have dinner with me than anybody else on the planet," his father kidded, knowing that the joke would get him to relax and put an end to whatever feelings of guilt he was heaping upon himself.

"Dad, you're something else," Michael said, laughing in spite of himself. "What are you gonna have to drink? Maybe we should order a bottle of wine," he said suddenly, thinking it would do them both good to relax and unwind.

"Sure, why not. I'm not on duty again until tomorrow afternoon. How about a nice bottle of Merlot?"

"Sure. Does that mean we're ordering steaks?" Michael suggested, intuitively knowing that his dad loved nothing better than the steak au poivre they served. He'd had it the last time they had eaten at Joe's Pier 52 and raved about it for weeks.

"Yeah, although you can stick with the seafood. Specialty of the house as I recall is your favorite," Walter answered, laughing at his son's obvious familiarity with the menu.

Their food, which arrived sometime later, was excellent and as they continued to enjoy the meal, the wine and, in particular, each other's company, some of the tension brought on by the discussion each knew must take place, dissipated.

"I don't have especially good news to relate so I hope you're still thinking of this thing with a totally open mind," his dad said, abruptly setting his wineglass on the table.

"Don't sugarcoat it. Duke and I knew from our consultant's findings that there were problems. That's why you got the call. We just want to know how deep it goes," Michael offered.

"Very. There was a very thorough investigation started about six years ago which turned up all kinds of evidence against one guy in particular, Gino Sorrentino. Unfortunately, although it was a joint effort concerning the FBI and NYPD, they were unable to make the charges stick. It even received a small amount of negative publicity, which sort of left both departments with mud on their faces. As a result, these guys have been kept under scrutiny it seems. The buzz in the house is that it won't be long before they're gonna take another fall. This time, it'll be a lot harder for them to get up from it. It's all documented here," he said, pushing the heavy manila envelope toward Michael.

"We noticed that there was a pretty clear separation of business assets when it came to the network of radio stations and the subsidiary companies. Does that effect any of this in a positive way?" Michael asked, clearly hoping for some small shred of assurance that the deal was not altogether without merit.

"Somewhat. Actually, if they were to separate the two entities, it might not be so bad because the heads of departments on those subsidiaries are really the guys who were under investigation. And Gino Sorrentino. The remaining members of the radio network, CBN, wasn't it, looked fairly legitimate," he added.

"Dad, I can't thank you enough for handling this for me. We still have some decisions to make, but having this information makes it a hell of a lot easier."

"Don't mention it. I would have been insulted if you had gone ahead with a deal of this magnitude without any input from your own private investigator," he added laughing.

They continued to enjoy the meal and didn't leave the restaurant for another two hours.

John Reid, the Special Task Force formed to investigate and bring about the indictment of Gino Sorrentino, and the United States Government were almost ready. Code named "Operation Showtime," the eight officers assigned to back him up had been gathering evidence for the past several years. There would be no mistakes this time, there would be no second, no third chance. It was either now or never.

They had covered all their bases. They'd even placed a mole in the NYPD's investigative unit, which had been one of the sources of leakage last time. They were taking no chances this trip and by placing someone deep undercover within the city agency, it acted as an added "insurance policy" that very little could or would go wrong.

That's where we neglected to cover our bases the first time, John mused as he surveyed the warrants in front of him, mentally ticking off each and every member of the Sorrentino crime family he'd vowed to take off the streets.

Aside from Gino Sorrentino, who was the head of the powerful family and thereby, the most coveted, there were two other factions that ran their subsidiary businesses. Anthony Sorrentino, a second cousin of Gino's, ran the successful and very lucrative waste management companies that operated along the eastern seaboard. Sorrentino Waste Management, Inc. had been formed years earlier, but had grown tremendously in the past two years and now posted revenues well above the national average for a company of its size. There were also the revenues that did not make it to posting. That was yet another aspect of this operation that Special Agent John Reid knew made it all the more compelling to shut them down. He'd let the Internal Revenue Service handle their business when the time came.

Duane Caparelli, godson to Gino, headed "Sorrentino Construction Supplies," which was a smoothly run, solid profit center that wholesaled and distributed heavy-duty construction items throughout the United States. Most of the business was centralized through an intricate web of union stewards, local shops and construction foreman. Every once in a while, there would be some noise made by someone trying to infiltrate one of the unions, or a group who claimed to be left out of the employment end, but it all fell on deaf ears. The construction jobs, along with the workers routinely chosen to work the high-paying, though dangerous construction sites, were chosen well in advance.

John Reid's purpose, in a word, was to put an end to the systematic corrosion of everything that the Sorrentino name labeled. The waste management company, the construction supply wholesale network and, most importantly, the man himself. He now had the necessary tools in hand. The warrants had been issued. He had a twenty-four-hour window of opportunity that he knew was crucial to the case he was still building.

He had the hundreds of hours of corroborative tapes that the "audio unit" had successfully uncovered producing several new points of indictment. He had the financial records for the past four years on all three companies, including Cityscape Broadcast Network. Unfortunately, their records, standing alone, were not a problem, but the subsidiary companies, Sorrentino Waste Management and Sorrentino Construction Supplies, Inc., were another story altogether.

Not only were their books doctored, but the companies themselves indicated serious manifestations of financial malfeasance. It spelled money-laundering. And that could only mean one thing—drugs, prostitution, racketeering, etc.

The phone rang and he picked it up still deep in thought. "Reid here," he said, rubbing his eyes wearily.

"The war room is yours for 4 P.M. Everybody from your team has been notified so you're on for tomorrow morning—6:00 A.M.," Brooke said quickly.

"Thanks. The orientation will be short and sweet. Everybody on the team knows exactly what we're gonna have to do—lock and load," he recited.

"Okay. See you at home," she said then and hung up.

The fifteen-minute briefing which took place promptly at 4:00 P.M. was attended by all seven agents who comprised the special task force dubbed "Operation Showtime." Each possessed a special quality or trait that made him irreplaceable on the team. Five men, two women, and Special Agent John Reid all went over, very carefully, each and every nuance of the next morning's exercise. Nothing was left to chance. Contingency plans were discussed, revamped and then re-discussed until it was all down to a science.

Now all they had to worry about was Murphy's Law.

Seventeen

The enticing aroma of basil, thyme, oregano and a slowly simmering spaghetti sauce greeted Lauren's nostrils as she entered the apartment. Gloria was preparing dinner.

"Hey there," she called out as she stuck her head into the kitchen.

"Hey there yourself," Gloria responded continuing to chop red onion, zucchini, carrots, yellow and red peppers, as well as several other vegetables on the cutting board in front of her. Her hair was covered by a red bandana. The blue denim oversized shirt she wore over jeans was covered with splotches of the ingredients she'd used in preparing the sauce.

"Wow, you look really domesticated." Lauren laughed as she entered her bedroom to place the dry cleaning she'd just picked up on her closet door.

"Well, lucky for you that I was of a mind to do some cooking," Gloria responded while lifting the pot cover on her sauce to stir and add additional spices.

"I guess you're right. Take-out gets downright boring sometimes. Do you need any help?" she asked, walking to the sink to wash her hands.

"Actually, yeah, you can prepare the salad if you want to. Everything is in the refrigerator," Gloria added.

"So tell me what brought on this bout of domesticity," Lauren asked, knowing that anytime Gloria started cooking, she most probably had something on her mind.

"Oh, so you think you know me like that," she laughed and then paused.

"In all honesty, I am a little concerned about Morgan and my dad. You know, even though they put on this macho front, both of them are really quite vulnerable. I mean Gino has his people and all, but Morgan really doesn't hold with that end of it and sometimes, like the other night, when they both go at it, it just goes all through me. I guess what I'm really trying to say is that my family is really screwed up," she ended, placing both hands on her hips to emphasize her point.

"Hey, don't feel bad. Every family has its skeletons in the closet. You should be happy that at least Morgan isn't in on all that goes on in your father's world. Imagine what it might feel like if they were both involved in that stuff," Lauren said in an attempt to lift Gloria's spirits. She did, however, believe in her statement. The fact that Morgan might be above some of Gino's tactics should be seen as a saving grace.

"Yeah, well you haven't ever been present when those two start to go at each other. It's like neither one will budge an inch for the other's side. Even my stepmother, Cora gets annoyed. And Morgan is her son so you know it must bother her."

"So, what is it that happened that was so terrible?" Lauren asked as she began washing the lettuce, tomatoes, cucumber, and mushrooms for the salad.

"Just the fact that they were trying to have a business discussion at our family dinner was annoying. Then Morgan has been trying to convince Gino to handle things a little differently and they apparently disagree on that point so it became an argument. Trust me, if it hadn't been for the fact that Gino can really get crazy about family get-togethers, I would have blown out of there. As it was, they finally pulled it together after my stepmom and I made a stand," she added.

"Wow, that's really something. You shouldn't have had to go there," Lauren said, realizing her roommate's frustration and giving her ample room to vent.

"Tell me about it. Anyway, it all turned out okay. I spoke with Morgan this afternoon and he said he and Gino straightened out a few things last week at the office so I guess all's well that ends well," she said. She then began adding the vegetables to the simmering sauce, turning the fire down to a low heat.

"I'll put the pasta on if you want," Lauren offered, having sliced all the salad ingredients and assembled it into one large glass bowl.

"Great. How about angel hair? That way the pasta primavera will really be light in calories," Gloria responded.

"Fine," Lauren said looking into the overhead cabinet where they kept the packages of pasta, boxed cereals, and other dry goods.

Gloria walked into the living room, turning on the CD player. The melodic strains of Sting's "Englishman in New York" now filled the apartment.

The telephone rang. Lauren answered, hoping that it wouldn't be the airline calling about scheduling. She was all set to begin working with the Charter Division and knew that they would quite possibly call at anytime to give her lines for the upcoming month.

"Hey, Morgan, it's Lauren. How are you?" she asked quickly.

"I'm good and yourself?"

"Fine, I'm doing good," she responded, hoping Gloria would take the phone from her before she had to prolong the conversation any further. She'd always felt mildly uncomfortable with Morgan.

"Is Gloria there?" he asked then.

"Sure. I'll put her on," Lauren responded quickly.

Gloria had overheard the exchange and now walked toward her bedroom. "I'll take it in here," she said over her shoulder.

Lauren pulled out a two-and-a-half-quart stock pot, filled it half-full with water, added a pinch of salt and waited for it to boil. She also poured a capful of olive oil to add just as it reached the boiling point. That would prevent the strands of pasta from clumping together even as it cooled.

Gloria reentered the kitchen several minutes later.

"I hope you don't mind, but Morgan wasn't doing anything so I invited him over to join us for dinner," she said casually while checking the sauce for flavor and the right balance of vegetables.

"No, not at all," Lauren responded, masking her slight reluctance to this unexpected turn of events. After all, if her roommate's brother wanted to drop by, who was she to express any dissatisfaction. She'd just make an early exit.

"Okay. I'm going to take a quick shower and put on something else. I look like a student from the New York Restaurant School." Gloria laughed, noting the mosaic of sauce, vegetable and other stains branding her attire.

"Sure, go on ahead. I'll finish up with the pasta and set the table," Lauren offered. "How about some garlic bread?" she asked.

"That sounds great," Gloria responded while putting a bottle of red Zinfandel on the table. If Morgan was joining them for dinner, wine would be a safe addition to the meal as that was one area that he and Gino agreed upon. Wine with meals was a must for them both.

While Gloria showered and dressed, Lauren called her mom and they caught up on the past week's developments, covering work issues first. Lauren quickly told her mom of her newest appointment with Worldwide Charter Division.

"And how about your job. Has the promotion kicked in yet?" Lauren asked.

"Oh, yeah—and so have all the accompanying head-aches, but I do enjoy the field of design," she added. "We just started a really large project for MCI Worldcom whose new headquarters in Hunt Valley are not too far from the office." She added, "But enough about work. How was the date with your gentleman?" Eva asked cautiously.

Lauren took a breath and then laughed. "Actually, it was fine. I mean it was wonderful." She blushed. She was infinitely glad that her mother was not able to see the expression on her face as the memory of everything that had transpired during that day and into the evening came vividly back to her. "I had an absolutely wonderful time. We went out on his boat, sailed north of the city all the way to West Point and had dinner at a restaurant that's been there since the early 1900s," she ended.

"Sounds lovely, and I take it that you're not feeling as if you now have to break off contact with him just to establish your independence?" her mother asked intuitively.

"No, not exactly. It's kind of hard to explain, but I think I've got it under control," she responded.

"Okay, just remember what we talked about a couple of weeks ago. Nothing ventured, nothing gained," her mother reminded her.

"Right. Okay, Mom. I'll probably call you again in a week or so. Take good care of yourself."

"I will. You take care, too, darling and go out with him again soon, dear," she said.

"Love you, Mom," Lauren said.

"I love you too, dear," her mother responded.

They both hung up as the bell rang. Morgan had arrived.

He was still wearing a suit and tie, having only just come from the office. Gloria had changed into a pair of dark brown slacks, a light green sleeveless turtleneck sweater, and brushed her hair down around her shoulders. The navy blue of his suit, picked up the deep tones of burgundy in his tie and even though the lines on his face signaled fatigue, you could also see something else registering just below the surface—excitement.

"I brought a bottle of wine just in case," Morgan offered as he loosened his tie before sitting at their dining room table.

"Thanks, Morgan, we do have wine here you know," Gloria responded, a bit disappointed that he would think them so lacking in rudimentary household items.

"Well, I just wanted to make sure. You know it's not a meal without an accompanying bottle of wine," he said smugly.

"Now you're starting to sound like Gino and I know you're not trying to go there," Gloria reminded him with an arched eyebrow as she began to place the bowls of steaming food on the table.

Lauren took the garlic bread from the oven, and began to slice it.

"So, Lauren, you're awfully quiet. What've you been up to?" Morgan asked, watching her work quietly, yet efficiently at the chopping block. He'd always been aware of her good looks, yet there was something about her that made him think of her as off limits. Perhaps it was that he realized she was slightly afraid of him and that was a turn-off.

"Not a thing. Just working and trying to stay out of

trouble," Lauren answered carefully. She had never felt comfortable around Gloria's brother and tonight was no exception. She was never really quite sure of where he stood on so many issues.

"Sounds like something I wouldn't wish on my worst enemy. You must do something for fun sometime," he responded.

"Can we have a peaceful dinner without you giving everybody in attendance the third degree," Gloria interjected.

"Yeah, here, let me open the wine for you ladies," he offered, reaching for the corkscrew on the countertop. "I promise to be nothing less than charming for the remainder of the evening," Morgan said, pouring the wine graciously. And he kept his promise.

The dinner, a study in simplicity, was excellent. The pasta was served al dente. The sauce, a rich, thick primavera, was enhanced by the parmesan and romano cheeses and fresh vegetables Gloria had added as it simmered. And the accompanying salad and garlic bread only served to enhance the meal.

The company, on the other hand, was another matter. Although Morgan had promised to be charming throughout and had in fact kept that promise, both women recognized, without acknowledging it, the effort it was obviously taking for him to remain thus so. Neither was surprised therefore when he broke with his own self-proclaimed edict.

"So, Lauren, tell me, are you still dating Michael Townsend?" he asked as he poured himself a cup of coffee, which Gloria had just brewed.

"Morgan, you're out of line. Who and when Lauren dates is none of your damned business," Gloria said, anger written all over her face as she looked at her stepbrother as if he'd just been categorized as an emerging sub-species.

"It's okay, Gloria. I don't mind talking about it with Morgan. After all, if it wasn't for that dinner party, I probably wouldn't ever have seen Michael again. And to answer your question, yes, I have continued to go out with him. I think he's pretty cool actually," Lauren admitted, surprising even herself with the candor with which she spoke.

"Great. I'm glad to hear that. He and his partner Duke are very interested in becoming partners with CBN; we're just finalizing some of the details. Our legal department has to okay everything before we can give the deal a green light," he added.

"I see. Well, Michael doesn't go into any great detail when it comes to his business plans but I'm sure if it's meant to be, it will," Lauren responded as she began clearing the dishes from the table.

"Can we please change the subject?" Gloria interjected.

"Sure, sis. Listen, why don't you ladies allow me to load some CDs into the system and we can continue our evening in the living room where we can relax," he suggested, obviously in no hurry for the evening to end.

"I'm going to pass on that if you don't mind, Morgan. I need to catch up on my laundry, not to mention that I have an early-morning flight to Florida," Lauren explained.

"Oh, don't tell me that you're gonna run off now that we've just finished dinner. I thought we'd all get a chance to sort of hang out," he said.

"Morgan, you can program whatever you like for a short time. I'll join you in the living room in a minute," Gloria added as she finished restoring the kitchen to order and turned the dishwasher on. She liked having her brother around—to a degree. It allowed them to catch up on each other's lives without the pressure of their parents being present. She'd been pleasantly surprised when he'd called and asked to stop by this evening—that was not his norm. She suspected he was trying to cut ties with his usual cronies—some of whom were affiliated with Gino's world. That's why she'd practically welcomed him with open arms. If he was trying to establish a new set of friends, a new way of life, she was all for it and would help in any way possible.

Lauren said, "Thanks for a wonderful dinner you guys—really," and walked into her bedroom knowing the laundry had given her a well-justified excuse out of the evening's possibilities. And she did have an early-morning flight to Florida, which meant the usual routine of packing, hair, nails, etc.

"Come on, big brother, fill me in on what the latest gossip is in radio," Gloria joked as she joined him in the living room, but was interrupted by the telephone's ring.

She picked it up, listened for a moment, a look of increasing worry and concern casting a shadow on her face.

"Oh, no," she cried looking at Morgan with panic and grief just as she dropped the phone from her hands. "It's Gino. Oh my god," she cried. Morgan sprung up and ran to the phone, taking the receiver from her hands.

"Hello, yes, hello, Mom. What's the matter?" he asked, his voice rising frantically.

He listened for a moment, his brow wrinkling with worry.

"Oh no. Mom, take it easy. We'll be there in a half hour." He motioned silently to Gloria to start moving as she stared at him aghast, her mouth trembling.

She ran to the bedroom, grabbed her purse and was at his side instantly.

"Let's go," he said as he picked up his suit jacket and car keys.

Gino had suffered a massive heart attack. His condition was serious. He'd been admitted to the intensive care unit at St. Francis Hospital in Roslyn, Long Island, which specialized in open heart surgery and reportedly was one of the finest medical facilities in New York, cardiac care its specialization.

They arrived at the hospital one hour later, but it was too late. Gino Sorrentino was dead. Cora was inconsolable and almost incoherent with grief. They had been working on their patio repotting several of the many azalea plants housed in large terra cotta pots which lined the walkway. It had been a hobby of Cora's, born of her love of flowers. She'd never forgotten the small florist shop she'd owned many years before Gino had come into her life. Sometimes, he'd help her tend to them, and that day had been one of those special times with the warmth of the sun seeming to call all who enjoyed the outdoors. They'd only been working for what seemed like an hour when Gino had complained of not feeling well so they had gone inside to have something cool to drink. He'd then lain down and taken a nap from which he awoke feeling worse.

Cora had called his doctor who, after listening intently to the description of his symptoms, urged them to meet him at the hospital immediately. They'd arrived a short time later, but Gino's condition had worsened. Now sweating profusely, with noticeable pain in his arm and shoulder, fear was written on his face. Cora had never seen her husband exhibit fear—she had not known that he was capable of experiencing it. And in the last moments of his life, when she realized the depth of his pain, knew that he was as vulnerable as the next man, she also came to the realization that they had shared a very special relationship.

He died before they were able to perform the open heart surgery his condition would have required. He died before either Morgan or Gloria reached the hospital. And he died before he was able to tell his wife, Cora, how very much he loved her, loved their life together and loved the ground she walked on. But he hoped she'd read it in his eyes as he took his final breath with her holding on to his hand for dear life as she kissed him softly, tears streaming down her beautiful face.

Special Agent John Reid was notified within minutes of their arrival at St. Francis. His people had kept their prime subject under surveillance for the past several months as they gathered the last shreds of evidence.

Members of the NYPD task force, which had been assembled to both assist and pull together their own special brand of evidence were also notified immediately of the condition of one of their most elusive suspects in recent history.

Some members, upon hearing the untimely, if not unfortunate, news shook their heads in amazement.

"That Gino was one slick S.O.B. He must have smelled indictment in the air and chose to go the other way," one agent said, expressing his exasperation at having been involved in gathering a mountain of evidence for the past seven years, only to have it all become a moot point due to the death of the suspect.

"If it wasn't so tragic it would be laughable," he added, shaking his head in frustration.

Special Agent John Reid had a decision to make, a very important one. He could move forward with the serving of the remaining warrants and at least recoup some of the losses or he could put everything on hold, wait until the funeral was held for Sorrentino and then see how things looked. This was the one contingency they had not been able to prepare for. After careful consideration, as well as much heated conversation with both his superiors as well as the more senior members of his investigative team, the decision was made to move forward with what they had.

Although Gino Sorrentino had been their number one target for most of the investigation, both Anthony Sorrentino and Duane Caparelli were now also prime suspects and the amount of evidence they had been able to gather against each was both solid and damaging, to say the least. The arrests would be paralyzing, ruthless and all the more powerful because of the death of their head kingpin, but so be it. Too much time, effort, and unrelenting concentration had gone into gathering the resources necessary to reach this point.

Fate had dealt an unprecedented hand in the death of Gino Sorrentino on the eve of his destruction. But the hands of justice would, nonetheless, continue to move forward in its efforts to thwart organized crime at its best.

Eighteen

Amid muffled sobs, tears and gulps of panic, Gloria told Lauren of her father's death in a hastily made phone call later that evening. Lauren immediately canceled her early morning flight knowing her roommate would need her throughout the next twenty-four hours and, perhaps, beyond.

Gloria and Morgan did not return to the apartment until nearly 2:00 A.M.; neither of them was in good condition. Morgan was dropping Gloria off before he joined his mother at the home she shared with Gino on the North Shore of Long Island. He tried to put up a stoic front, but tension, pain, and grief were clearly evident on his face.

"Listen, Gloria, get some rest and I'll call you later. We'll have to begin making the arrangements today so I'll send a car for you sometime this afternoon. I'll call you first so you can be ready, okay?" he asked with concern clearly etched on his face.

"Sure, but Morgan, why don't I just come out with you now? That would save you the trouble of sending the car and all that," she offered thoughtfully.

"Because you're beat and if you come out to the house now, you won't get any rest because you'll be trying to do any and everything you can. Trust me. Stay here, get a couple hours of shut-eye and then come on out. It's bound to be pure pandemonium anyway once you get there. I wish I didn't have to delve right in, but I do. I can't let my mother bear the brunt of the tidal wave that's about to come over her," he said then, thinking of all the different factions of Gino's empire that would have to be notified, mollified and pacified over the course of the next few days.

"Okay, big brother, I trust your judgment," Gloria said then, her voice cracking just a little as her eyes misted over, thinking of her father and how vulnerable he'd looked against the white of the hospital bed.

Lauren, who'd gone into the kitchen after hugging Gloria tightly when she first entered the apartment, now approached with a cup of tea in hand.

"Here, drink this. It's herbal and will help you relax some," she said. She'd already offered her condolences, but somehow, it hadn't seemed like enough. How do you offer someone your sorrow for a loss that's got to be overwhelmingly devastating to them? She'd never understood that and always hated funerals, memorial services and the like for that very reason.

"Thanks, you're a sweetheart," Gloria said as she pulled out a chair and dropped into it. She hadn't realized how tired she was until just now. Morgan moved quickly to the door knowing he had over an hour's drive ahead of him. He also planned to stop in at his own apartment first to change clothes and put a couple of things into an overnight bag. He knew the next few days would be hectic, filled with unexpected developments and the like and just wanted to be prepared if he had to remain by his mother's side overnight.

"I'll call you later. Get some rest until then though; you're gonna need it," he warned.

"I will. Go on, get out of here," Gloria said, knowing he was worried sick about his mom and how she'd make out when she had to enter alone the home she'd shared with her husband of almost ten years for the very first time.

"Don't worry about her. I'll be here," Lauren said as she walked Morgan to the door.

"Thanks, Lauren. I appreciate it," he responded with a half smile on his face.

"Morgan, you don't have to thank me. Gloria is my friend and whatever she needs, I am only too happy to provide her with. I feel terrible that this happened. I mean, it's all so unexpected," she said then, searching for the right thing to say.

"Yeah, I know. It sort of hits you like a ton of bricks," he responded as he rang for the elevator.

Morgan arrived at the Long Island home in record time. But he'd been unable to beat the vultures. Several different news teams had arrived and greeted Cora Sorrentino as she'd returned to the home she had shared with her husband. Accompanied by Gino's right-hand man, Reggie, who had driven them to the hospital, Cora was somehow able to successfully duck into the house without answering any of the rapid-fire questions which were put before them by the eager correspondents looking to gather information for the early morning news broadcasts. As Morgan drove his Lexus into the driveway, they once again descended, all asking questions at the same time, each trying to throw his or her voice over the cacophony of sound being bandied about.

"What were Gino's last words?"

"Who's next in line for the Sorrentino empire?"

"Is it true that the Feds were only minutes away from serving an arrest warrant against the Sorrentino crime family?"

"Will you testify before the grand jury?"

Morgan reacted at that point, his anger overcoming his grief and his judgment.

"Don't you people have anything else to do? We're in mourning here. Show some respect," he threw over his shoulder, making his way quickly to the front entrance of the home. Inwardly, he wondered what the heck was going on. It was as if all hell had broken loose and he was on the inside track. He'd turned his pager and cell phone off since the events of early last evening, not wanting to have to concentrate on anything but the situation at hand. Now, he wondered if he'd missed some very important occurrence.

Once inside, he was not at all pleased to see his mother glued to the television set.

"Mom, I thought I told you to get into bed and get some rest," he said softly, knowing that to chastise her at this point was ludicrous.

"Morgan, have you seen the morning news yet? Look at this," she said in a horrified voice.

He walked into the great room which housed a built-in sixty-inch screen, fireplace, and wraparound sofa and dropped himself onto it. He was bone-tired, but knew that rest, as well as his feelings about Gino's death, would have to be dealt with at another time. He looked in amazement at the screen then.

Apparently, several members of the Sorrentino business empire had been arrested on charges of money laundering, racketeering, and interstate commerce violations just that morning. Both Anthony Sorrentino and Duane Caparelli, heads of two of their more lucrative divisions, had been served with arrest warrants and taken out in handcuffs. The books of Sorrentino Waste Management as well as Sorrentino Construction Supplies, Inc. were now under the scrutiny of the Feds. Both business enterprises had also been put on official "lock down" as well, padlocks and all.

"Shit, that's what those reporters outside were talking about," he mumbled under his breath. What a nightmare! Gino had just missed this, he was sure. Talk about timing. He also wondered what effect this would have on the remaining business holdings, especially CBN. Morgan was not naive enough to believe the company would be unaffected by these latest developments. He also knew that Gino had assured him that CBN was a separate faction and that he'd kept it that way for a reason. It could and would remain the one entity amidst their holdings which was clean and above board.

"Mom, please, you have to turn this stuff off and get some rest. I insist," he said over her protests as he turned the set off and ushered her upstairs to her bedroom.

"I don't think I can sleep, Morgan. All I keep thinking about is how we were just going to repot some plants. Now Gino is gone and this," she added, pointing to the now-blank television screen, her voice cracking as tears slipped silently down her cheeks.

"Listen, Mom, I know this is hard for you, but I'm here for you. And for God's sake, don't worry about that stuff on television. You know Gino provided for anything the Feds could have cooked up. Can I get you anything before you go up? How about some tea or something?" he asked as she began to climb the stairs.

"No, I don't want anything right now. Thank you, dear, I'm just going to try and get some rest," she said then, her voice sounding heavy with grief.

The remainder of the day passed like a blur with relatives, friends, business associates and lawyers coming in and out of the house much like a conference was being held. Cora rested for a short while, then found her way back downstairs and into Gino's office where she began trying to put things in order.

Morgan continued to meet with the business associates, lawyers and colleagues who dropped by in a steady stream and Gloria, who arrived sometime in the early afternoon, kept the relatives supplied with food, drinks and a ready supply of tissues.

Lauren had remained at the apartment at Gloria's insistence, answering the never-ending telephone callers who seemed to have been tele-conferenced of Gino's recent death. She'd been directed to forward those who were relatives or close friends to the Long Island number, and take messages from those who seemed distant or mere acquaintances.

She was surprised when the phone rang and Michael's secretary came on the line, asking for her. He only did that when he was either very busy or not expecting her to answer.

"Hi . . . I didn't really expect you to be there. Weren't you scheduled to fly today?" he asked.

"Yeah, but I canceled due to an emergency. Have you heard about Gloria's dad?" she asked.

"As a matter of fact, I have. It's been on all the news wires. That's why I called. I was actually going to leave a message for you to call me."

"I see. Gloria left for their home on Long Island to join her stepmother and Morgan and I promised to stick around here until about five o'clock, then I'm taking the train out there also. I feel so badly for her. You know she was very close to her father, although she definitely tried not to show it," she added.

"Yeah, well now she'll have to come to terms with some of that," Michael said quickly. "Listen, do you want me to stop over there? Are you all right? You sound kind of funny," he added.

"No, no, I'm all right. Just a little shook up from all the excitement," she answered, wondering why she felt she needed to avoid seeing him.

"Okay. Listen, call me tomorrow or so. I worry about you when I don't hear from you," he said earnestly.

"I will, and thanks for calling. I'll give Gloria and Morgan your condolences," she responded then.

"Okay. You be careful, too," he said quickly before hanging up.

The next few days passed so quickly and in such a frenzied fashion that it all seemed surreal. The funeral, which was attended by a cross-section of close relatives, friends, business associates, "family" members, New York's underworld kingpins, and even some curiosity seekers, was a whirlwind of activity. The press was effectively held at bay by several family-related security members, but were still able to get photographs of the arrival and departure of several noteworthy individuals. Their reports also centered on the most recent arrests of several key members of the Sorrentino family and how the deceased had narrowly missed being named in the same set of indictment papers.

Morgan and Gloria remained by the side of Cora Sorrentino constantly, shielding her from anyone and anything which would make this most difficult time harder for her to endure.

Lauren, as a supportive friend, helped out at the house, attended the services and became increasingly aware of the overwhelming responsibilities associated with the death of a loved one. She also became increasingly aware of her own reluctance to let her guard down and admit her feelings for Michael and move forward with their relationship. Something about the reality of death as a possibility shook her from the moment she'd received the call from Gloria at twelve midnight some days before. It had unsettled her in an unexpected way, causing her to want to avoid seeing and or talking with

Michael. Yet she knew within the confines of her being that he, above all, was the one person who would understand what she was really feeling.

He and his partner had shown up at the wake for Gino Sorrentino on the evening before the funeral and burial. And although Lauren had been polite, even pleasant when she'd talked with him after the service, she'd avoided him when refreshments were being served, purposely keeping busy with others who'd arrived to show their respects.

Michael, not wanting to intrude on what he felt was a natural obligation and responsibility to her friendship with Gloria hadn't wanted to seem intrusive, but Lauren's sudden lack of enthusiasm had not been lost on him. She'd turned him down when he'd suggested they take off together briefly to have a cup of coffee, and she'd neglected to return any of his phone calls.

Now, exactly one full week after Gloria's world had shifted, Lauren too felt as if she was totally unsettled and did not know what her exact response should be to many things.

She did know one thing, though. She would be happy to get back to work. Work always solidified things for her. A schedule, a program, a dictum gave her the normalcy which she'd come to associate with order. Right now, her world felt as if it was out of order and she attributed that to Michael. The time they'd recently spent on board *Megahertz* had spun her world out of control. She didn't try to deny the pure, unadulterated passion they'd shared, the pleasure they'd enjoyed, or the emotions which they'd obviously both experienced, however, her reasoning told her that any and all of these entities spelled trouble. Big trouble for her and she only knew one way to avoid trouble. Remove yourself from the vicinity.

Lauren called Worldwide scheduling and requested

back-to-back flights for the following two weeks. She was happy to find that because she'd recently transferred to the Charter Division that they did, in fact, have the slots open to accommodate her. And although she did consider giving Michael a call to notify him that she'd in fact be out of town for the next couple of weeks, something stopped her from dialing.

I know he'll start asking me a lot of questions and I just don't want to deal with that pressure right now, she told herself, effectively justifying her rationale. *Besides, with the death of Gino Sorrentino and all that's transpired with the arrests and such, the deal that he had on the table with CBN and his station is probably dead. Now, I don't have to worry about coming into contact with him through Morgan or anything,* she thought to herself. *That chapter is closed,* she reasoned.

Inwardly, Lauren knew that she would have to close more than a chapter of herself to forget all that had transpired between herself and Michael Townsend. The evenings they'd shared, the laughter they'd inspired, the nights she'd spent on his boat, the passion and love-making they'd enjoyed. It would take some time, some distance and lots of control, but she would do it. She had to face the possibility that she had opened herself up to the ultimate in vulnerability. And although she kept hearing the calm, sage advice that her mother had given her during their most intimate of talks, it still frightened her more than she dared to acknowledge. The pain of losing someone whom you were so connected to was to be avoided at all costs. Nothing ventured, nothing gained. You couldn't lose what you did not have.

Lauren set about convincing herself that she was opening a new chapter in her life, one that did not include Michael Townsend or any man for that matter. She had her work, which she enjoyed immensely. She had both her parents whom she cherished even if it was at somewhat of a distance. And she had her life. She'd concentrate on those things for the time being and hopefully effectively block out any thoughts and or memories of the most recent past.

Just to make sure that she didn't waver in any part of her decision, Lauren also decided to begin expanding the amount of time she traveled for personal pleasure. She'd always loved seeing new and exotic places. Now would be a most excellent time to explore some of the places she'd read about, dreamed about, but never had the opportunity to experience. In between traveling for work, she'd be sure to book out-of-town trips, even if they were only for a couple of days at a time, in all the ports of call she'd always wanted to visit. The far reaches of the United States, the Caribbean, Mexico, Canada, even Europe if time permitted. Worldwide had access to lines which reached into each of these destinations so that the only consideration would be the time element. Perhaps Gloria would join her on some of the trips. It would be good for her to get away too, Lauren reasoned. By the time her head hit the pillow that evening after preparing for her early morning trip to Los Angeles, she was actually excited at the prospect of her new plans. She'd effectively pushed all thoughts of Michael Townsend to the far corners of her mind. Or so she told herself.

Nineteen

In the weeks following the burial of Gino Sorrentino, Morgan was inundated with legal as well as business fallout surrounding the indictments of the heads of Sorrentino Waste Management and Sorrentino Construction Supplies, Inc. The indictments included seventeen charges of racketeering, interstate commerce violations, fraud, misrepresentation, money laundering, etc.

The legal representation alone could amount to a fortune and, although the financial repercussions had most certainly been prepared for, Morgan knew that this time it would be infinitely more difficult to mount an effective defense. He, better than anyone else in their organization, knew just how long and hard the Federal prosecutor's office had been working on the case. And his in-depth knowledge of the intricacies of law told him that they had only moved in only when they had an insurmountable amount of evidence. And not one moment before.

Morgan was also somewhat intrigued that CBN had not been named as yet in any separate, or connected indictment and suspected, correctly, that the reason behind it was Gino's death. They couldn't prosecute a corpse. And CBN itself, was clean.

In addition to the mounting legal defense of the subsidiary companies and their heads, Morgan also had his business consultants going over the original proposal for the merger/acquisition of WJZZ. He reasoned that the death of Gino Sorrentino freed CBN up for structural realignment. If they could effectively strategize a way to separate CBN's holdings of the waste management and construction supply companies, there was the distinct possibility that the deal could still go through. He'd already gotten the unofficial word back from eyes and ears he had in place at Burns, Eden and Glickstein that their feelings had been positive to CBN, but negative to the other holding companies. Morgan, a shrewd negotiator and effective businessman since before graduating from New York University School of Law, still smelled a winning team in acquiring WJZZ and he was determined to pull the merger off.

Remembering Gino's initial response to the proposed merger/acquisition, Morgan also now realized that those reasons had since lost their validity. If he were to effectively separate the companies before the merger, there would be no spillover of negatives if and when the other Sorrentino companies went down. In fact, Morgan realized that Gino would be proud to have found a way around the Feds in this one regard. And he had most definitely cheated them out of the little tea party they'd planned on his behalf.

Gino must be laughing his ass off, Morgan thought as he sat going over the stacks of paperwork on his normally uncluttered desk. He'd thought of his stepfather often in the weeks since his death. And although he'd be the last to admit it to anyone, he not only missed him, but had come to the realization that some of his business practices actually had multilevel advantages. But Morgan's intimate knowledge of the legal system kept him firmly entrenched on the right side of the law. He'd never venture too far to the left. His thoughts were interrupted by the buzz of his intercom. He'd asked his secretary to hold all calls except from his mom or Gloria.

"Yeah," he said into the phone, picking it up instantly.

"Hi, Morgan. Are you busy?" Gloria asked, her voice seeming to come from far away.

"No, not really. What's the matter, you sound funny," he said wondering if she had been crying.

"Nothing. I mean I was just sitting here thinking of some stuff and wondered what you were doing," she said too quickly.

"Well, honestly I'm up to my eyeballs in sorting out tons of paperwork. You wouldn't believe the stuff I now have to put my signature on for approvals," he admitted.

"Yeah, I guess now it puts you in charge of most of the corporate decisions," she said, suddenly realizing the magnitude of Morgan's responsibilities for the first time since her father's death.

"Hey, it's a lot, but it's not anything I can't handle. Don't worry about me—what's going on with you? When are you scheduled to return to work?" he asked.

"Actually, I fly for the first time tomorrow. It feels like months have passed since I've been at work, though I know it's only been close to three weeks. Lauren's on back-to-back assignments. I haven't seen her in more than a week," she added, sounding lonely and depressed.

"Look, Gloria, I'd ask you to do something with me later tonight, but I have to meet with the guys from CBN to sort out some things. When do you get back from your trip?"

"Not until three days from now. And I'm only at home for one day then I turn around and fly back to the West Coast for a two-day layover," she added.

"Well, if you don't mind sitting through a boring business discussion that will include dinner, you can join us. We're meeting at the Shark Bar on Amsterdam and Seventy-fourth at eight."

"Morgan, do you think it would be okay?" she asked, unable to mask the rise in her voice which gave clue to her obvious excitement.

"Sure it'll be okay. I mean, how many business meetings have you sat through with us in the past? Gino would probably be pleased to see you mature into a young woman capable of handling social as well as business obligations simultaneously," Morgan added, knowing it would please Gloria to think of Gino looking favorably on something she had done.

"Great. Now, what should I wear?" she asked, sounding as if she were all of sixteen going out on her first date.

"Something elegant, chic and fairly conservative. After all, this is a business meeting combined with dinner," Morgan answered easily.

"Okay. I think I know how to handle it," she responded.

"Look, I'll pick you up around seven-thirty, so be ready. Hang up and let me get some work done," he added before placing the receiver back into its cradle.

Michael and Duke arrived at the restaurant at seven twenty-five and were seated at the table being held in reserve for the Pryor party. They were curious, to say the least, at what Morgan had termed the latest developments concerning the merger/acquisition proposal. After attending the wake for Gino Sorrentino, they'd discussed the current status of what they believed was a dead deal with each coming to the conclusion that although unfortunate, it was sometimes the way the cards were dealt. They'd also seen the television news, read the headlines and heard the industry gossip concerning the arrests of several of the Sorrentino top managerial components and realized that they had been right on target in their assessment of their subsidiary companies. What was most difficult for them to acknowledge now was the fact that had it not been for the untimely death of Gino Sorrentino and the ensuing arrests, they might have very well gone ahead with the deal in its original state. The report that Michael's father had delivered was both scathing and thorough in its description of the New York City Police Department's vast knowledge of indictable crimes committed by these same individuals. If anything, it was that final piece of the puzzle which had put the brakes, so to speak, on the deal for both Michael and Duke.

They'd both been mildly surprised when they'd received a call from Morgan less than two weeks after the funeral to suggest they meet and talk over dinner. Not wanting to come across as judgmental or biased, they'd agreed to hear him out. After all, with the developments which had most recently occurred, the landscape of the deal had changed dramatically. Even their consultants at Burns, Eden and Glickstein, whom they'd spoken with briefly during the course of the past week, suggested there might be something salvageable if structured properly.

Morgan arrived with Gloria in tow some fifteen minutes late. Traffic coming across the Manhattan Bridge leading into the FDR Drive North had been totally congested and they'd moved at a snail's pace until hitting 14th Street heading uptown.

Morgan made introductions all around, forgetting that Gloria had met Michael on at least two other occasions. Duke, who'd only seem glimpses of her briefly at the wake was instantly mesmerized. He remembered telling Michael that he'd heard this sister of Morgan's was a knockout, but he hadn't really taken a good look at her when he'd seen her.

Her hair, a rich, glossy black, hung just below her shoulders and shone brilliantly, even in the dimly lit interior of the restaurant. She'd worn a black suit, her only jewelry a gold and onyx pin in the shape of a triangle which adorned her left lapel. She looked very chic, very elegant, and very much in mourning. Duke was attracted immediately to the simplicity which she displayed. And although he realized she was, in fact, the daughter of a deceased Mafia kingpin, he also recognized a vulnerability she herself wasn't even aware of.

"So, guys, sorry to have kept you waiting, but traffic was a bear. What are we drinking?" Morgan asked, picking up the wine list.

"Nothing for me," Duke responded, holding up a glass which contained soda water with a twist of lime and a splash of bitters.

"I'm good," Michael said still nursing a half-filled glass of vodka and orange juice.

"Okay, I guess it's on us. Gloria, what would you like?" Morgan asked, scanning the list.

"Whatever you choose is fine," she answered, feeling somewhat intimidated by all the masculinity present at the table. Although she'd remembered that Michael Townsend was devastatingly handsome, his partner, Duke Hayes was incredibly sexy. The beard, the salt and pepper hair pulled back into a ponytail and the physique all spelled rebel which she'd always found attractive, but she knew this was not the time nor the place to flirt.

"Morgan, how about a nice bottle of Cabernet Sauvignon?" she suggested, thinking it would go nicely with whatever was ordered at dinner.

"Good suggestion. They have a 1997 here from the

Sonoma Valley. We'll take a bottle of this one," he pointed out to the waiter.

"Okay, gentlemen, well I guess you could say I brought my secret weapon," he teased, referring to Gloria's unexpected presence. "Actually, my younger sister has a vested interest in any business transactions which will take place going forward and I really just wanted to begin including her in the flow of information," Morgan said then quite truthfully.

"Well, there's nothing wrong with that," Duke said, smiling as Michael nodded in agreement.

"We were surprised when we received your call. With all that's transpired in the past three weeks, we didn't think you'd be up to talking business right now," Michael interjected. "You mentioned some changes that may be on the horizon," he added.

"Yeah, I know you both realize that with the death of Gino Sorrentino comes a difference in the way our corporate structure rolls out. I've been in consultation with our attorneys and business advisors and they've informed me that a minor reorganization is in order. With that in place, CBN will stand on its own as a corporate entity. Now, what that means to you is the subsidiary companies like Sorrentino Waste Management and Sorrentino Construction Supply, Inc. will no longer be linked. Do you get my meaning?" Morgan asked then.

Duke was the first to respond. "Yeah, if I get your meaning, it realigns the structure of CBN so that it stands alone which is one of the things our consulting team suggested was the more favorable scenario for the merger/acquisition to take place."

"Right. I knew that if your people were sharp, they'd be advising you to hold off for a while until things either cooled down or blew up at CBN," Morgan said.

"How long will it take for this reorganization or restructuring to take place?" Michael asked then, knowing that time was on their side.

"It's actually being done as we speak. Our financial people, our legal people and our executive management team which, by the way, is headed by me, are slated to work on this goal for the next month to bring about all the changes we'll need in the next thirty days. That's why I wanted to meet with you guys so soon. I didn't want to let any substantial lapse of time occur where the deal could lose its momentum for either side," Morgan added.

Their orders were taken then, the wine served and they all breathed a little easier, relaxing now that the cards were on the table. Gloria and Duke avoided making direct eye contact, but were very much aware of the existence of each other though they tried not to show it. Each engaged the party they'd arrived with in conversation, but neglected to reach across the table conversationally to each other.

"So you both agree to give it the thirty days so that we can restructure and resubmit the proposal based on CBN as a separate entity?" Morgan asked then, clarifying the main objective of the dinner's conversation.

"Yes, as long as we are able to once again have our people perform the necessary and required due diligence based on your revised format," Michael responded with Duke's agreement clearly in tow.

"We actually like the idea of this pared down concept," Duke said, acknowledging something he and Michael had discussed on previous occasions while dissecting the original proposal.

"Great—it sounds like we have a winner on the table," Morgan said then. "Let's drink a toast to a deal that can be done," he added. He then signaled the waiter to bring another bottle of Cabernet Sauvignon to the table.

After each was poured a glass of the deeply rich, fragrant wine, Morgan held up his glass.

"Here's to the new version of CBN and WJZZ," he recited as they all clinked glasses.

Gloria, who had been extremely quiet up to this point said, "And here's to our newest partners in radio," as she'd once held her glass up in tribute to their proposed merger. Duke was the first to clink her glass.

Michael, who had been calmly wading through dinner thinking only of the business at hand, suddenly remembered that this was Lauren's roommate sitting across from him. The same Lauren who had ignored his phone calls of late, who had practically given him the brush-off when he'd seen her at the wake and the same Lauren who had made passionate love with him on his boat some three and a half weeks ago. It seemed like an eternity. And though he didn't want to admit it, even to himself, he wondered what was going through her mind. What would make her cut herself off from him after all that they had shared in the past months. He was growing weary of the unanswered questions he constantly had to ask of himself. They'd been through this before and come out of it okay, or so he'd thought. He'd thought it was all over with and now this. His pride would not allow him to ask for her. Hell, Gloria might not even be aware of Lauren's little games, he acknowledged to himself. But he couldn't help wondering just how much she knew.

As they prepared to leave the restaurant, he and Morgan became engaged in conversation about an advertising agency they'd each used in the past. High personnel turnover had always been one of their problems and the discussion centered on whether or not it affected productivity and service.

"I've always believed that was their way of keeping overhead costs down. You know, hire them young, inexperienced but talented and you can pay them at the lower end of the spectrum," Michael said expressing his philosophy on the agency's probable causes.

"Yeah, but at what cost," Morgan responded nodding in agreement at Michael's assessment of the situation. They continued to discuss industry gossip, related protocol and the latest developments in high-tech digital equipment.

Duke took the opportunity to induce Gloria into telling him more about herself.

"How long have you been flying with Worldwide Airlines and is that something you think you'll want to do for the long haul?" he asked conversationally.

"Well, it's been three years now, but I don't think I'll be doing it twenty years from now if that's what you mean. It's a living that also affords you the luxury of unlimited travel and that's why so many people love it," she explained.

"So, how often are you in the city for a few days at a time? Or are you always out of town?" he asked.

"Actually, I'm here quite often. More often than I'd like to be sometimes. My roommate flies a lot of long layover flights and is out of town a lot," she said.

"Well, maybe I can call you sometime. Perhaps we can have dinner and I can find out more about you. You were awfully quiet all throughout dinner," he said.

"Yeah, well that's because I knew this was a business meeting so I didn't think it appropriate to offer small talk," she said candidly.

He liked that.

They shook hands all around, preparing to leave the restaurant.

"Good night, and it was really nice meeting you," Duke said as he shook Gloria's hand. It fit into his nicely, securely, but definitely a firm handshake.

He liked that too.

Michael and Duke walked to the parking lot where Michael had parked his Jaguar in silence.

Duke spoke first as they awaited the attendant's return with the car.

"So what did you think of the proposal, in all honesty? Do you think we should have given him the additional time?" he asked.

"Sure. Look, we always said the deal held some really positive attributes, but the negatives were those subsidiaries. Now, without them and all that they represent, the deal really can be sweet. It's like we're getting rid of the fat which is bad for you and carving out the filet mignon," Michael said.

"Okay, that's what I'm thinking too. Boy, did you see his sister? I'd heard she was gorgeous," Duke said then.

"Oh, Gloria, yeah, she's attractive all right. Was that the first time you'd seen her?" he asked then, surprised by the animated look on Duke's normally serious face.

"Well, when we went to the wake I did see her, but she was so busy doing things, I never got introduced to her. Then tonight when she showed up with Morgan, damn, I mean she is gorgeous," he exclaimed.

Michael looked over at him, realizing that his partner had been bitten, and laughed.

"Look, I am not going to even get into this with you. I am so into my own stuff with her roommate that I am the last, the absolute last person to talk to about a woman. Man, she is pulling my guts out and she doesn't even know it," he said, the emotions surfacing in unrelenting waves as he spoke.

Duke looked over at his partner.

"Man, I thought you were going to stop seeing her if she didn't get her stuff together," he said.

"Yeah, the problem is that I thought she had herself together. We went out together about a week before Gino Sorrentino died. I took her out on *Megahertz*, we had a fantastic day, night and an even lovelier morning. When I dropped her off at her apartment, she was purring like a kitten, man, a kitten. But that's when she gets scared—every time we become close—really close, she shuts down, closes up and turns off. I spoke with her twice after that and then wham. She shut the communication lines down. She won't return my phone calls and I don't even know what state she is in because she's probably flying all over the freaking country to avoid seeing me," he ended, anger, frustration and something else registering in his voice. Pain.

"Wow, that's really rough, man. I don't even know what to say. Did you think of saying anything to her roommate about it tonight?" he asked.

"Naw. I'm going to leave it alone. Until I figure out exactly what I want to do, Miss Traynor can continue running, hiding and closing herself off from me and any other human being she comes into emotional contact with. Sooner or later, she will run out of places to run to. I'm beat—emotionally drained. When I saw her at the Sorrentino wake, she avoided me like the plague. I kind of noticed that she was acting a little funny so I suggested we go for a cup of coffee somewhere close. She turned me down. I knew then that we were in trouble again because that's her modus operandi," he ended, shaking his head.

"Damn, and here I am thinking of my next move on Morgan's sister. I don't know if I should even tackle that now after what you're telling me," Morgan said.

"Hey, don't let my situation spoil your thing—go for it. After all, they're just roommates, not clones," Michael said as he headed toward the east side to drop Duke off at the station where his car was parked.

"Well, at least it looks like the deal we wanted is still on the table. That's something to be thankful for," Duke reminded his partner, partly to take his mind off his current problems and partly because he believed it to be true.

"Yeah—that's something all right," Michael responded as they arrived at the garage.

"Look, I'll see you in the morning. Get a good night's rest," Duke offered as he got out of the car.

"Yeah, you too. See you tomorrow," Michael said.

It was a long drive home, but Michael resolved to do two very important things by the time he pulled into his garage. Putting Lauren Traynor out of his mind was the first order of business. The second would come with time but it was concerning the upcoming merger. He'd throw himself 100 percent into this new business venture if it came through. That way, not only would it be thoroughly successful, it would be thoroughly his. Oh, Duke would be involved too, but he needed to be a part of something larger than himself at this point. He needed to become merged with something which he could identify with. CBN/WJZZ would be his new identity, his new mistress, his new lady.

For the first time in three weeks, he slept like a baby.

Twenty

Lauren quickly discovered that working with the charter division of Worldwide was a blessing in disguise. She was learning all the nuances of handling a smaller, more detailed passenger list. She was getting used to the more compact equipment, although she had been trained thoroughly on the DC 707 aircraft models during her most recent orientation. And she was attempting to adjust to the latest restrictions she had placed on herself concerning Michael.

The captain and first officer were busy doing preflight checks as she boarded the forty-eight-passenger aircraft and proceeded to stow her belongings in the designated storage area. Lauren glanced at her wristwatch, noting the full half-hour before their scheduled passengers would begin boarding. Today's flight consisted of the members of the New York Yankees baseball team who were headed from New York to Atlanta to play the Atlanta Braves at their home stadium. The Peachtree State would host the designated game the next evening at seven o'clock. The team would return to New York the day after with the same crew and comparable equipment.

That meant a full day and a half layover for Lauren in Atlanta. She was already looking forward to the shopping she would do at the Lenox Square Mall in Buckhead and planned to visit the Martin Luther King Museum as well. Having never had the time to really explore some of America's great cities, Lauren was looking forward to many such long layovers in the popular cities of the south, the sunbelt, even as far west as Seattle and, of course, California.

She approached the small cockpit area now, thinking it would be good to find out if there was anything she could get early on for the captain or first officer.

"Can I get you guys anything before takeoff?" she asked.

"Yeah, you can get me something for a whopper of a headache," Captain Pearson answered quickly. His normally ruddy coloring, topped off by a thatch of reddish-brown hair and blue eyes, was a tad shy of its usual brilliance. If truth be told, he looked a little green around the gills, his hands unsteady as they went about the routine tasks he performed prior to takeoff as part of the standard pre-flight check.

"Sounds like somebody had a heck of a night in Dallas," the first officer said, laughing as he continued to complete the required inspection of the instrumentation panel.

"You should talk. My mistake was in switching from bourbon. If I hadn't started drinking draft beers, I don't think I'd have this monster running around in my head right now," the captain said.

"You're probably right—hindsight being twenty-twenty. I'll take you up on that offer by way of a Coke myself," First Officer Camden replied.

"Great—I'll be back in a jiffy," Lauren responded, turning to leave the cockpit.

She was glad she had offered to be of service. Both men sounded as if the hub city of Dallas, Texas, had shown them one good ole time from which they were still recovering.

The limited space of the galley restricted the fare available on charter flights, however, there were some amenities afforded. Lauren removed a bottle of Perrier water and a can of Coke, while she scanned the emergency medical kit for a packet of pain relievers. Finding several varieties, she chose Advil and Motrin. They always seemed to work for her. As a matter of fact, lately she'd had several slight headaches on days that had been particularly long. She was also experiencing mild fatigue which she quickly associated with her new and until now, unfamiliar schedule.

"It's just nerves and the unfamiliarity of the routine," she told herself whenever the thought crossed her mind.

She dismissed, wholeheartedly, any notion that recurrent thoughts of Michael, the difficulties she'd experienced sometimes sleeping at night, as well as the momentary flashbacks she fought off during each day, were in anyway related to her abrupt interruption in the relationship they'd previously shared.

Although she also realized that it had probably been somewhat unfair, marginally selfish, and ultimately final, Lauren still felt as if she'd done the right thing in cutting all ties. He'd tried to reach her several times in the early weeks following Gino Sorrentino's death and funeral. She'd almost been tempted to give in at least once, but she'd resisted successfully, putting herself closer to believing that she was "over" Michael Townsend once and for all.

Lauren had, throughout this same period, been extremely sensitive to her roommate's loss of her father. And although Gloria had never professed to be close to the well-connected, oftentimes distant, Gino, Lauren had recently come to realize that a great deal of her attitude had been a defensive mechanism. Obviously the death of Gloria's natural mother many years before,

Gino's subsequent marriage to Morgan's mother and the changes to the ensuing family structure had taken a toll on the relationship. Building an emotionally protective wall around herself had been Gloria's response to the unacceptable set of circumstances she'd found herself in as a young woman losing her mother and father seemingly, all at once.

Lauren recognized and understood all that and, as a result, did her best to console Gloria through a grieving process that was not at all easy to define. She was there for her without criticism or question. Lauren's acceptance of Gloria on her own terms also served a dual purpose. It effectively cautioned Gloria from questioning Lauren's motives wherein Michael was concerned. And although her total allegiance to Gloria certainly held no "pre-existing clauses," she realized that the current climate of their relationship would act as a buffer when it came to any future discussions of her previous relationship.

Lauren brought the refreshments and pain relievers to the cockpit, returned to the cabin area and began preparation for the upcoming flight, her thoughts seeming to come from far, far away. She was tired and the flight hadn't even begun. But she was also excited at the prospect of more than twenty-four hours in an "unexplored" state, so she forced her mind to focus on the day ahead of her.

The passengers boarded, were seated and prepared for takeoff. They were ruggedly handsome, physically superior, award-winning, professional baseball players. At least seventy-five percent of the team was on board, along with their manager Joe Torre, who looked exactly like he did on television. Some of the other players, Derek Jeter, in particular, looked even better than he did on TV.

Lauren made it a point to handle the section that he

was not seated in. She didn't trust herself to look into his gray eyes, react nonchalantly and still be able to retain her professional composure. Something about him bothered her and thoughts of Michael bombarded her during the entire flight. She could see his eyes, dark gray and brooding, looking deeply into hers, asking unspoken questions. She could hear his voice, somehow commanding her to stop and remember the feel of his hands touching her, his arms holding her. Lauren could almost feel his lips on hers, softly coaxing the responses she'd come to know and enjoy. She remembered, only too well, the passion they'd shared. But she also was achingly aware of the hurt and pain one suffered when that same pleasure was abruptly interrupted and that was what she was trying to avoid.

Being proactive had its advantages—you were the one in control, calling the shots rather than someone else pulling the rug out from under you unexpectedly.

"Excuse me, but it's time for us to prepare for landing. Would you help me with this?" Lauren was shocked to realize that the other flight attendant on board, Melanie Newport, had been speaking to her. She realized that she had obviously been daydreaming and a flush of pure embarrassment flooded her face.

"Certainly," Lauren responded, securing the beverage cart into its position so that they could begin preparing the cabin for their upcoming landing at Atlanta's Hartsfield International Airport.

"Great. Whew, I'm beat. I can't wait to get to the hotel, take a hot bath and retire for the evening," Melanie responded as she, too, began completing the routine tasks associated with FAA safety precautions.

"Well, thank goodness it's not just me," Lauren laughed, breathing a sigh of relief. She'd thought she was the only one experiencing feelings of energy loss.

The entire Worldwide Airlines crew, consisting of

Captain Pearson, First Officer Camden, Flight Attendant Newport, and Lauren all arrived at the Swisshotel in Buckhead sometime after seven that evening. Not scheduled to fly again until the early-morning hours some thirty-six hours later, they checked in. Melanie and Lauren promised to see each other early the next morning at the hotel's fitness center for aerobics and the sauna.

Lauren, whose daily exercise routine had been somewhat disrupted with all the developments at home of late, attributed her recent low energy to insufficient exercise. She inwardly vowed to make the necessary changes, include some weight training also, and to additionally improve her current eating habits.

Exhausted, she removed her uniform, unpacked her toiletries and overnight bag and took a quick shower. She recognized she was hungry, but the tiredness she felt compelled her to take a quick nap. Lauren quickly slipped into a deep, but restless slumber with thoughts of dark gray eyes and firm, soft lips filling her mind.

"What took you so long to call me?" he asked, threading long fingers through her mane of hair. She'd left it down after shampooing and blow-drying it and it hung loosely, softly to her shoulders. The conditioner she'd used smelled of peaches and the scent reached Michael's nostrils in waves, inciting his passion just as much as the feel of her in his arms.

"I only called to let you know I was all right—your messages sounded urgent—almost to the point of desperation," she said defiantly, though the rapid pounding of her heart, each time he stroked the length of her back, belied her nonchalant stance.

"Desperate," he laughed, his gray eyes mocking her, yet issuing their own challenge. "You've got to stop running away, Lauren," he murmured against her mouth, beginning his quest for the response he knew she was capable of giving.

He molded his mouth to hers then, slowly entering that cavern of sweetness, and Lauren found herself unable to hold back. Her arms wound themselves around his neck, her mouth opened of its own accord, and her hips molded themselves to the man who stood before her. His arousal was evident, but he would take his time. This time, he would have her in his own good measure—and she would know when it was over who was in control.

Slowly, ever so slowly, he continued to kiss her, allowing the passion to build in tiny increments until they were both breathless and standing on knees too weak to support their bodies. He eased the tiny straps of the T-shirt down one arm, kissing her shoulders softly, allowing the tip of his tongue to burn a firebranding trail down the length of one arm. His kisses continued onto her breast, the natural firmness enhanced by the lacy white bra she was wearing. The tips of her nipples were barely evident, but Michael's mouth found them easily, lowering the straps of the bra easily and slowly down her arms. He reached around her back, unhooked the unnecessary barrier to his exploration, and continued his attentions. Lauren's breathing increased as he took the entire nipple into his mouth, loving it with his tongue until it reached a crescent peak. Her head thrown back, she could feel a throbbing in her womb which accompanied each tug of his tongue and the warm flow of moisture in her loins was like an internal flow of lava.

Michael continued to find himself caught up in the warmth, the softness, the responsiveness of her breasts, but when he felt Lauren's hand touch the front of his trousers, he almost exploded with desire.

"Sweet, sweet, kitten," he murmured into her mouth as she continued to fondle, mold and glory in the male hardness she was confronted with. She then slowly slid the zipper down, reached inside and boldly took hold of the length of him. Michael's sharp intake of breath told her everything she wanted to know. They moved as one toward the bed, not once losing

contact with each other as they removed clothing in between kisses, caresses and appreciative sighs.

"I love you, Lauren," he whispered, as he slowly entered her. Smoothing back the hair from her face, he kissed her softly as he began making love to her. The words he'd whispered hung in the air for a brief moment before Lauren, caught up in the passion, the heat, the intimacy of the moment found herself unable to hold back and whispered softly, very softly, "I love you too, Michael."

Lauren awoke then. She was startled to find that it was dark. She rubbed her eyes, looked at the clock and stared in disbelief. It was nine-thirty already. She had slept for a full two hours. And the dream she'd had troubled her. She wanted no more thoughts, no more dreams, no more entanglements with Michael Townsend. The fact that she was unable to control her unconscious mind was frustrating, to say the least, to her. It meant that no matter what she thought or did not think during her conscious hours, sleep presented an uncontrollable arena for her.

She swung her legs to the floor, realizing she had not eaten anything since early afternoon. *I guess I'll order room service,* she thought, but at the same time, a wave of nausea overcame her. Lauren headed quickly toward the bathroom where she threw up the remnants of her last meal.

Feeling weak, faint and more than a little surprised, she immersed a facecloth in cold water, placed it over her forehead and lay across the bed.

Now I know that I did not eat anything that could have caused this, she thought, mentally recalling everything she'd consumed that day as well as the day before. Yogurt, grapes, and a hard-boiled egg had been her breakfast. And the night before dinner had consisted of a grilled chicken breast over Caesar salad. *Perhaps the dressing on the salad. Maybe I'm coming down with a stomach virus,* she thought.

Lauren drifted off for a few moments while her stomach settled. She pulled herself together, noting the clock now read 10:03 P.M. and decided to order a ginger ale to settle her stomach. She also realized, surprisingly, that she was absolutely famished and overcome with the urge to have a pizza, something she didn't ordinarily eat.

"Room service? Yes, please send up a small vegetable pizza. Mushrooms, broccoli, green peppers, and anchovies on that. Oh yeah, and a large ginger ale please," she said quickly. "Room 138—thank you," she added and hung up.

Lauren devoured the pizza, surprising herself at the extent of her appetite. *Wow, I must have been really hungry,* she thought as she finished the bottle of ginger ale also. Feeling unusually content, she climbed back into bed, surfed channels until she found something mildly entertaining, and proceeded to allow the evening to unfold.

The morning's rays shone brightly when Lauren awoke. It was 7:45 and she quickly showered and pulled on a pair of black tights, oversized sweatshirt, sneakers and pulled her hair back into a ponytail. When she entered the exercise room some minutes later, Melanie was already on one of the spinning machines with a towel around her neck. Lauren joined her and they each worked out for the next hour.

Shopping was next. The Swisshotel at which they were staying was within the same complex as the highly regarded Lenox Square Mall, one of Atlanta's most recently developed, and creatively designed malls. It was also the place to be seen, attracting Atlanta's upscale residents, local celebrities and A grade tourists. And although Lauren lived in New York, one of the nation's finest retail hubs, she still found herself fascinated by the sheer abundance and variety of things available. Unable to stop herself, she bought two pairs of jeans at the Eddie Bauer outlet, then purchased a pair of low-heeled lace-up boots at Nine West.

Melanie, who lived just outside New York in Northern New Jersey, also was mesmerized by the multitude of stores at their disposal. She purchased a handbag at the Coach store and couldn't pass up a pair of matching shoes at Nine West also.

They decided to take a taxi across town and have lunch at Houston's Grill where they each ordered salads.

"You wouldn't believe the pizza I ordered from room service and ate last night," Lauren told Melanie over lunch. "It was huge, but I managed to eat the entire thing—something I've never done before," she added, her voice sounding disappointed.

"Well, with what you just put away I'd say your appetite is healthy by any standard," Melanie laughed.

"I'd better watch it though because the last thing I want to do is start gaining weight—then I have to really work it off by dieting and exercising my butt off."

"Tell me about it. The last time I gained eight pounds, it took me about a month and a half to really get it off and my boyfriend was on my back the entire time," Melanie added.

"You mean he didn't subscribe to the 'there's more of you to love' theory," Lauren asked, laughing.

"Not at all. He's a fitness fanatic and sees fat as the enemy. He even went so far as to issue a challenge to me. Thank God I was able to meet and surpass it. He said if I could lose the weight in no more than six weeks, he'd take me to Bermuda to show off my newly reinstated body."

"Wow, he's intense. So did you get to Bermuda?"

"Definitely. I actually lost the weight in about five and a half weeks, but it definitely was not easy and that's why I monitor what I eat like a hawk. I don't want to have it to lose again," Melanie said.

"Well, I've never had any problems with weight gain or anything. I don't even really like pizza so I don't know why I wanted that last night, but one night of pizza should not do that much damage. Anyway though, I'm definitely going to watch my next meals just to be on the safe side," Lauren said. The entire airline industry had strict regulations concerning its in-flight personnel. Their weights directly affected the aircraft's ability to hold additional passengers, cargo and luggage. As a result, each employee was painfully aware of the ramifications of any significant weight gain. Lauren normally weighed herself every morning just after showering.

In the most recent weeks, however, with all the changes in schedule based on the funeral and her new assignments, she'd neglected to do so. She reminded herself to be more diligent when she returned home.

They remained at Lenox Square Mall for several hours, walking, browsing and marveling at the variety of retail outlets. By the time they returned to the hotel, it was dark.

"Why don't we have dinner together at one of the hotel's restaurants," Melanie suggested as they approached the elevators.

"Great—how about The Palm restaurant?" Lauren asked. "About an hour should do it for us to get ready, right?" she asked as they entered and pressed their floor numbers.

"Sure. I'll call down and make a reservation for eight P.M. If there's any change, I'll call your room and let you know. Otherwise, let's meet there."

"Okay. I think I'll change clothes. I did bring a skirt that goes nicely with the boots I got today," Lauren said.

"That's perfect. I have some nice dress pants and a great sweater I've been dying to wear. See you later," Melanie said as she exited the elevator at her floor.

An hour and a half later, they met at the entrance to The Palm, an elegant steakhouse whose menu boasted some of the finest beef and chops Atlanta had to offer.

The Palm also had a long-standing reputation for offering some of the most delectable seafood combinations available in central Atlanta and both Lauren and Melanie chose a dish featuring shrimp, lobster and crab as the primary ingredients. Lauren had passed on ordering a glass of wine, ordering ginger ale instead. Melanie ordered a glass of Zinfandel as they shared an appetizer of grilled vegetables.

Halfway through dinner, a party of five businessmen from Chicago were seated at the table to their left. Obviously out to have a good time at their company's expense, they spared nothing when it came to ordering, having two bottles of wine brought to the table immediately. In no short order, they proceeded to loudly discuss what appeared to be the highly successful campaign that had netted them significantly profitable gains within their industry, as well as having earned substantial merits within their own corporate structure. Toast after toast was made to each individual present. It was actually quite a sight to behold. After their appetizers were served, they quieted down a bit, each man tackling the delicious fare put before him.

Lauren, wearing an ankle-length black skirt topped off by a gray angora sweater, looked somewhat surprised when the maitre'd arrived at their table with a bottle of wine, with a note of explanation reading *Please excuse our loudness as well as the interruption of your quiet, dignified dinner, but we just closed a $50,000,000 deal!* And Melanie, dressed in an apricot-colored turtleneck sweater, which only served to highlight and intensify her reddish-auburn hair was also quite flattered by the attention of the men present at the next table.

"Oh, please extend our thank you and congratulations to them. They didn't have to do that," Lauren exclaimed to the maitre d', laughing at the thought of Melanie drinking the entire bottle of Zinfandel and what it would do to her.

"Come on, Lauren, you have to help me. I cannot do this all by myself." She laughed as the bottle was opened at their table. Melanie was now pleading with her.

"Naw, I'm afraid you're on your own. I don't want to take the chance of my stomach rebelling on me again. I'll tell you what. I'll order another ginger ale and put a little of the wine into it—a wine spritzer, okay?" she said, offering the only compromise she felt would be acceptable to her stomach.

"Deal. That way they'll never know I drank almost the entire bottle by myself," Melanie rationalized.

The two tables continued to co-exist harmoniously until Christian James, the vice president of Public Relations decided perhaps they should extend an invitation to the two attractive young women who'd so graciously accepted their peace offering.

He approached their table. "We're celebrating the close of a really big deal and just thought it might be more fun if you joined us for dessert," he explained. He stood 6'1" but appeared taller due to the athletic cut of his suit and the fact that his frame held no excess flesh. He was lean and fine and both women knew it.

Lauren, sensing her friend's uncertainty, took the reins and politely declined the offer.

"Thank you so much, but we're both kind of tired and have an early morning flight back to New York," she explained. What she really wanted to say was, "I already have a pair of gray eyes that I cannot seem to forget, a knowledge of passion so thorough it's haunting and a lingering uncertainty that I cannot shake. No, I don't think it would be helpful or wise to join you and your clearly successful, fine as wine, upwardly mobile friends."

"But thanks again for the wine. We really enjoyed it," Melanie was able to add as Christian accepted their declination graciously.

"If either or both of you change your mind, just signal and come on over," he added as he crossed the room to rejoin his comrades.

The remainder of the evening was uneventful and in short order, Lauren and Melanie decided to call it a night. Their neighbors called to them as they rose, complimenting them on having been good sports to put up with all their noise even if it was a celebration. It was after 11:00 when they finally exited the restaurant and made their way to their rooms. They'd left an early morning wake-up call for 6:30 A.M. with the front desk as their shuttle was scheduled to leave for the airport at 7:25.

The next morning, Lauren once again experienced a bout of nausea. She was beginning to be a little concerned. She made a mental note to schedule an appointment with her doctor upon her return to New York. She consumed a container of vanilla yogurt purchased at one of the airport concessions and then went on about the business of the day.

The trip back to New York was short and sweet and Lauren was glad for that. Their passengers were in especially good spirits having beaten the Braves by a score of seven to four in only nine innings the night before.

She walked into her apartment feeling a little tired, looking forward to a hot shower and a quiet evening.

There were three messages on her answering machine—one from her mom, one from Gloria and one from her dentist reminding her of a appointment on Tuesday afternoon. And although she told herself she was glad there were not any additional messages from Michael Townsend, why did it feel as if her world were growing smaller and smaller. And more importantly, why should that matter? After all, she had things set up exactly the way she wanted them. No entanglements, no complications, no commitments. No Michael.

Twenty-one

Michael and Duke were ecstatic. It had taken an additional six weeks of research, filings and manpower, but as it now stood, the deal with CBN was in the go position once more.

Morgan Pryor had not only come back with a restructured proposal in the thirty days he'd promised, but according to Burns, Eden and Glickstein, the current deal was far sweeter than the original package.

Gone were the entanglements of both Sorrentino companies—Sorrentino Waste Management and Sorrentino Construction Supplies, Inc. In the past thirty days, they'd been restructured to stand alone without the tie-in to Cityscape Broadcast Network. That, and the fact that Gino Sorrentino was no longer an issue made the merger/acquisition palatable, even attractive by any industry standards used to measure a deal of this calibre.

"I can't believe it only took Burns, Eden and Glickstein ten business days to get back to us on this. They must've really burned the midnight oil to go over this stuff," Duke said as he and Michael conferred in his office one evening.

"Yeah and that included giving us a full financial status report on CBN too—something we only had a portion of the first time. Well, partner, I suppose this

means we can move forward and tie up any loose ends,"
Michael said continuing to read the documents before
him.

"How soon do you think we ought to let Morgan
Pryor know we're ready to move forward? We don't
want to look too eager," Duke said.

"Let's get back to him in a couple of days. After
all, we had to wait a full thirty days before his people
could give us the revisions. Fair is fair—we'll take the
full two weeks to come back at them. This is really
great though," Michael added enthusiastically.

"You know the night we met with Morgan and he
brought his sister along was a pivotal moment I think.
That gesture seemed to show his total commitment to
us as an entity. I don't think he would have done that
with just any set of potential partners."

"You might be right. I know he made a couple of
comments about my relationship with his sister's roommate. It didn't seem to bother him as long as we were
potential partners. Boy, was he wrong. I wonder how he
would react if he found out she dumped me."

"Mike, she didn't dump you, man, she did you a favor.
Obviously, the broad has some problems and you're better off without her. What you need to do is go out and
have yourself a blast. Consult your little black book, pick
the name with the wildest time attached to it and go
for yours. Don't even give miss high and mighty another
thought," Duke advised calmly.

"Hey—I'm not sweating it okay. I'm so over that
whole scene I cannot even begin to tell you. And as far
as miss high and mighty is concerned, it's her loss,"
Michael fired back.

He'd been so consumed by work lately that he hadn't
really had the time to contemplate dating. Thoughts of
Lauren occasionally surfaced, but he pushed them to
the back of his mind each and every time. He missed

her. He missed her like hell, but he'd never admit it. Not to Duke or to himself.

"Hey listen, with the holidays approaching there'll be lots of parties, gatherings and get-togethers. We'll do the whole circuit just like we always have and you know we always meet plenty of women. There's certainly no shortage of available, young, beautiful and intelligent women in New York City," Duke added.

"The holidays aside, I'm not up for any of it this time. I mean, I'll go to a couple of the mandatory show ups, but for the most part I'm satisfied to keep a low profile right now." He didn't want to add that the thought of meeting someone else, starting over, and that whole scene was just not on his list of things to do right now.

"Suit yourself, my man. I know you're still brooding over Laura, or whatever her name is, but I'm telling you the best way to deal with this is to get right back on the horse—you know what I mean."

"I do, but I disagree with you. I didn't fall off a horse—I fell in love and there is a vast difference in the recovery technique. Hey, I'll get over it and move on eventually, but right now my work is my methodology to recovery so let's just move forward with the paperwork, forward it to Morgan and his people and take this operation to the next level," Michael said with conviction.

"Mike my man—you're a powerful dude and I for one am awfully glad that you're my partner. You're absolutely right."

"Okay, I'm glad that we agree on something cause we definitely have a totally different approach when it comes to affairs of the heart. It's a good thing that sister of Morgan's didn't give you the time of day when you met her. I'd hate to see what kind of mess you two would have created."

"Oh, now you're gonna try and come off like some

kind of expert in the field of romance. Don't even try it, Mike," Duke said laughing. "It's funny that you brought that up because I had thought about asking Gloria out. I just didn't want to confuse issues by doing it before anything on the pending deal was finalized," he added.

"Well, just be careful. You don't want to mess up anything to do with what we have going on with Morgan and that is definitely his baby sister."

"Some baby. That was a fine-looking woman if you didn't notice my friend. "I thought about asking her out that very same night, but figured it would have seemed a little out of place to bring it up during a business meeting."

"Well, once again I caution you, Duke. Not based on anything that I've gone through, but simply because I'm sure Morgan is very protective of her and somehow I just don't think he'd be too thrilled with the thought of his sister going out with his newest business partner."

"You're probably right. I'll think about it. She seemed to like me and I definitely liked her," Duke said, realizing that he'd be treading on thin ice if anything went wrong in that arena. He also realized that it could very well be the danger that was attracting him to the situation. He dismissed that idea quickly though. He'd always been practical in his social life, except the one time when he'd felt compelled to tie the knot. That had resulted in an unqualified mess which lasted all of six months. Now, some years later, he felt he'd grown, matured and was more ready to approach a solid relationship with someone of a similar mindset.

Both Duke and Michael signed the necessary affidavits in the presence of their attorneys, who then notarized everything, certifying the entire package. It was then forwarded by hand carrier two days later to Morgan Pryor at his Madison Avenue office.

* * *

"This calls for a celebration. Jennifer, get me Duke Hayes and Michael Townsend over at WJZZ," Morgan said into the intercom on his desk. He'd received the signed documents, presented them to his legal team and received word that all systems were go. He couldn't be happier. CBN would thrive under this new agreement, expansion into additional markets would be made all the more possible and the principal partners would all benefit handsomely in the coming months and years.

Morgan realized that none of this would have been possible save the death of Gino Sorrentino and it saddened him. He realized that Gino had meant more to him than he'd ever realized and that even in death, he had commanded respect and genuine affection.

"Morgan, I have WJZZ on the line—both parties are on," his secretary announced a few minutes later.

"Hey you two. I think congratulations all around are in order," he said excitedly into the phone.

"Yeah, it certainly seems that way," Duke added from his line.

"We're looking forward to a long and profitable association," Michael threw in, knowing that it was exactly the way both he and Duke felt.

"Listen, guys, I'm thinking that we should celebrate this merger in a big way so I've already spoken to a couple of people and we're throwing a small but lively party to announce the merger. It's still in the planning stages, but let me know if you have any conflict with November fifteenth, okay?" Morgan asked enthusiastically.

"No, the fifteenth looks like it's okay on my calendar. What about you, Mike?" Duke inquired.

"Yeah, the fifteenth is fine. That's a Friday evening. What time are you shooting for?" Michael inquired.

"I figure we'll cordon off one of my favorite haunts for a few hours, have the entire thing handled by the restaurant staff and maybe include a cocktail hour, dinner and a little music and dancing, say beginning at seven for the cocktail hour," Morgan said.

"Wow, that sounds great—especially the music and dancing. So, you're going all out," Duke asked laughing.

"Hey—it's not every day the industry is able to pull off a merger of this kind. We're really excited at the prospect of acquiring talent in the calibre of you two and I'm not just saying that to gas you up."

"Well, we're excited too and this is something we've been interested in structuring for quite some time also. We're looking forward to working with CBN and you, Morgan," Michael said, earnestly.

"Look guys, why don't we sit down at my office early next week, say Tuesday at ten-thirty or so to finalize all the finer points and logistics. The FCC approvals should be in soon and we can begin merging all the necessary elements so that we'll have a smooth transition. We'll put something into the mail for the dinner party so that we can send it to several key players and get them into the action too. You know, almost like a coming-out party for us as a merged entity," Morgan stated.

"That's a great idea. Do we have a budget for this?" Duke asked, forever the financial scorekeeper.

"Don't worry. This one is on CBN totally. Going forward we'll create some form of a joint financial entity for publicity and marketing—pretty much the way it was outlined in the proposal. You guys should put together a list of industry types you think you'd want to be there too."

"Sounds great. We're looking forward to meeting you next week at ten-thirty on Tuesday too," Michael said.

"Yeah, Tuesday's fine. See you then, Morgan," Duke added.

"Right, and before I forget, the annual Radio Engineering Convention and Golf Tournament is scheduled for early December at Wyndham Resorts in Miami. We usually charter a flight and go down for two days of pure heaven. You both might want to include that on your calendar of upcoming events," Morgan advised.

"Point taken. We'd actually gotten the invitations, but were undecided. I guess we'll count on being there," Duke said quickly.

"Great. Okay, I'll catch you guys next week," Morgan said, hanging up.

"Hey, stop in for a minute will you, Mike," Duke said before Michael could hang up.

"Sure thing."

"Well, he didn't waste any time getting things started now did he," Duke commented as Michael entered his office moments later.

"No, but that's an extremely good sign. I think his personality is the perfect fit for our business attitude. We're all three take-charge guys. We don't let any time or space interfere with whatever we're currently engaged in. We just move forward."

"No doubt, and that little coming-out party he's planning will be a huge boost to the ratings in terms of our stock in the industry. You just know he's going to invite all the movers and shakers in the communications industry."

"Well, if the small dinner party he threw at his sister's apartment back in the summer was any indication of his entertainment values, you're right on target. Everybody who was anybody was there. I even ran into Danton Arias there and you know that dude gets around."

"You didn't tell me Danton was there. Man, what a character. I remember him from our days back at college—he was Mr. Soave Bolla even then. What's this I hear about him and a European collection?" Duke asked, sounding genuinely interested in what their former classmate was up to.

"Hey, he's doing very well with his collection. I understand his designs made the cover of *Vogue* magazine several times in the last two years. That is certainly a pivotal accomplishment for any designer," Michael said.

"Well, I am definitely looking forward to this party. It's only three weeks from now so I guess we'd better work on our portion of the guest list soon."

"Yeah, if you want to go over it now we can. That way we can give it to Morgan when we meet him at his office on Tuesday morning."

Their list was short, but extremely sweet. Vice presidents/general managers of CBS Radio, ABC Radio, Time Warner, etc. They also included the program directors from local stations like WQCD 101.9, KISS 98.7, WBLS 107.5 and WLIB. It was going be one hell of a party.

Twenty-two

Zanzibar, located in the middle of midtown Manhattan's west side, played host to the coming-out party of CBN's newest acquisition on a wet, cold and windy Friday night. That didn't stop anyone who was anybody in the industry from being there.

The guest list aside, the restaurant/club/bar was filled with people, some whom had indeed been invited, others who were somehow industry-related, but had just shown up for a chance to rub elbows and be in the company of those who were involved.

Duke and Michael showed up promptly at ten past seven, entered the large cocktail area and were immediately inundated with congratulations from their peers, colleagues and members of their newly acquired staff.

Morgan, who'd been in deep conversation with the general manager of a sister station quickly came over to them both.

"Now the party can officially begin," he said, smiling as he shook the hands of both his new partners.

"Hey, Morgan, this is quite an interesting place," Duke noted as he looked around the dimly lit Manhattan enclave.

"Well, our first choice backed out on us due to the date and time constraints, but the food they'll serve us here is excellent. I had it catered by Fiorello's at Lincoln Center."

"Wow, you really went all out for this, Morgan. I'm impressed," Michael added as he signaled the waiter who was patrolling with a tray hot of hors d'oeuvres. Mini quiches, stuffed mushrooms and fried zucchini sticks were in abundance and both Duke and Michael helped themselves as they headed toward the bar.

The back room of the restaurant had been set up with ten round tables, each holding six dining places. The dinner hour wouldn't begin until 8:00 with music and dancing at 9:00 P.M.

Drinks in hand, Michael and Duke separated and began circulating within the confines of the gathering, joining cluster after cluster of their industry counterparts.

Michael, who was discussing recent changes in radio format with two executives from WABC Radio, was somewhat surprised when he spotted Lauren and Gloria entering the restaurant. He hadn't expected that they would attend. Momentarily caught off guard, he realized at that moment that he had mixed feelings. He inwardly made the decision to be calm, businesslike and above all, not to allow the evening to be at all affected by whatever his relationship had been with Lauren Traynor. This evening and all that it signified was too important to be influenced by a relationship that had fizzled so quickly.

Lauren and Gloria made their way slowly into the crowded room. Morgan spotted them from where he stood at the end of the bar and quickly called to Gloria, happy and surprised that she'd decided to attend. He'd had to go to great lengths to convince her to come.

"Hey, I'm really glad you made it," he said, wrapping her in a bear hug that was filled with unexpressed emotion.

"I am too. You see I brought my sidekick with me," she responded, indicating Lauren.

Morgan gave Lauren a brief hug in greeting and noticed that she looked somehow different. He somehow couldn't put his finger on exactly what it was though.

"Listen, let me get you both something to drink. What are you having?" he asked.

"I'll have champagne. Isn't this a celebration?" Gloria asked, laughing.

Morgan had wanted his mother to be there also, but she'd declined saying that cocktail parties were for young people. He'd realized then that she was still getting used to the fact that Gino was no longer around and probably felt uncomfortable in social settings that would have normally included the presence of both of them.

"Okay, champagne it is. Now how about you, Lauren?" he asked, turning to her laughing.

"I'll have a wine spritzer for starters," she said, smiling at his obvious enthusiasm.

"Great—I'll get those and you two can start to mingle. There's lots of people here that you already know from that first dinner party and lots of people you can get to know," he added smoothly.

Although the interior of the establishment was somewhat dark, faces that were familiar stood out extremely well in the dimly lit enclave. Gloria took Lauren by the arm and they approached a couple who Gloria recognized immediately.

"Danton and Susan—how nice to see you both again," Gloria exclaimed as they were greeted, air-kissed and held at arm's length for inspection.

"You both look great," Danton exclaimed, noting their trim figures, their fashionable hairstyles and, most of all, their attire. His designer's eye didn't miss a beat.

Gloria was wearing a black leather skirt, matching boots and a white silk shirt with silver rhinestones on one side of the collar. Large silver hoops adorned each ear giving her the appearance of a very hip, carefree player. Lauren had worn gray suede pants with a matching bolero jacket and had twisted her hair up into a loosely woven French knot high at the back of her head. Loose tendrils of hair fell around her face which only enhanced the small diamond studs in her ears. She, too, looked quite cavalier, not at all concerned, and appeared as if she were out to have one heck of a good time. Inwardly though, she cringed every time the thought of seeing a certain someone crossed her mind.

She could not believe that she had agreed to come. Gloria had had to beg, plead, cajole and convince her to accompany her this evening. Finally, after she'd reminded her of that fact that this would be the first time since the death of her father that she'd be entering the "social" scene and if left to do it alone it wouldn't happen, Lauren had acquiesced and agreed to join her.

She had gotten Gloria to promise one thing though. If at anytime she gave the signal, she would hustle her out of there pronto—no questions asked. The signal was to grab her purse, rummage through it frantically and say, "I left my cell phone at home." Barring that, they each promised the other that they'd try and tough it out although they realized that, for very different reasons, this evening would be a trial of magnanimous proportions on how well they were able to handle situations which were not particularly comfortable. Gloria was worried that she'd feel pressured when people came up to her, as she knew they invariably would, to express their sorrow on the loss of her father. She didn't want anyone to feel sorry for her, pity her or wonder what was to take place next under the guise of the Sorrentino empire. And she knew that beneath their comforting words, their unasked questions always signified that they wanted to know more. There had always been the "un-answered" questions surrounding the Sorrentino name. She, unfortunately, had never gotten used to it.

Morgan brought their drinks over then, joining the little group that had somehow formed and was deep in discussion on the new magazine *O*.

"It's not only well written, covering the full gamut of issues that pertain to us, our lives, our careers, even our social quandaries, but it offers somewhat of a different slant on political issues as well," Susan offered.

"Yes, I was really impressed with the first issue and have been picking it up since," Gloria said, glad to be discussing anything other than her family and its prob-lems.

"I took a look at your copy and found it visually ex-citing. The photography is certainly well done—even the ads are appealing to the feminine eye," Lauren said as she sipped her drink. She was taking no further chances with her stomach and its stability. Although she'd been able to keep her food down in the past sev-eral days, she'd still felt a little queasy at times. Each time she planned to call and make an appointment with her doctor, something of more urgency would come up and interrupt her thoughts. She made a mental note to call Dr. Forman's office the following day come hell or high water.

Duke, having just finished talking to the an on-air personality at WQCD named Deborah Rath made his way toward the bar and spotted Gloria and Lauren's group in conversation.

He approached them, realizing he still found his new partner's younger sister very attractive. She looked like a female version of a pirate with the dangling hoop earrings she was wearing and the white shirt and he couldn't resist his impulses any longer.

"Well, no one told me you were going to be here," he said as he walked up with a big smile on his face.

"Really, well Morgan usually thinks it's somehow necessary for me to attend any business function that he throws of a social nature, so here I am," Gloria responded smiling and offering her hand. Duke took it, but smoothly pulled her into a soft embrace too. Gloria then introduced him to Lauren, Danton and Susan, effectively covering her surprise at his familiarity. Duke then graciously offered to freshen everyone's drinks at the bar and they moved in that direction. A few moments passed as drink orders were placed, and the conversations resumed.

"So, you're Michael's partner. It's good to finally meet you," Danton offered as the three women continued talking.

"Danton, you obviously don't remember me from school. I attended Northwestern too. I was a business major," Duke offered as they started on their new drinks.

"Oh my God, you're Duke Hayes! How could I forget you? You and Michael were inseparable even then. Man, we all go back a long way. And isn't it great that we all ended up in New York?" Danton said, rushing through each sentence as if it were his last.

"Yeah, this town is the only one big enough for so much talent," Duke said laughing.

"How the heck is Michael anyway?" Danton asked then.

"Actually, I am going to get him because we were having a conversation about you just the other day and I don't want him to miss seeing you. Wait right here," Duke said and headed into the lounge area of Zanzibar where he'd last seen Michael.

He found him quickly surrounded by three agency

executives, all female, all beautiful and all vying for his attention.

"Need any help?" Duke mumbled under his breath so that only Michael's ears would pick up his obvious snide remark.

"No, I'm doing just fine—unless you want to get me another drink," he said.

"Listen, I hate to break up this little party and please don't hold it against me, but I just found a long-lost comrade that my partner and I need to talk to. I promise he'll be back in about five minutes though," Duke offered, smiling at each of the attractive women. They all smiled graciously, nodded in approval and waved them off realizing they'd been competing against themselves while talking to him at the same time anyway.

"Who or what is it that you have over here that's causing the fire?" Michael asked, a little annoyed at having been pulled away from the circle of beauty which had surrounded him.

"You'll see," Duke promised as they made their way back to the other side stopping occasionally to shake hands and accept the congratulations of various individuals present.

"Danton. You old dog. Duke and I must have talked you up," Michael said shaking his hand quickly before both men reached out to give a mutual bear hug.

"Well, I suspect Northwestern is duly represented at this time," Duke said laughing at the three of them.

"I congratulate you both on your latest accomplishment. I hear CBN is going to be doing great things in the near future," Danton offered sincerely.

"Yeah, we're both excited at the prospect of this kind of expansion for the station. It actually means a whole new level of exposure for us both," Michael said while Duke nodded his head in agreement.

Lauren and Gloria were in conversation with Susan.

They turned as Michael acknowledged that portion of the group which had taken center stage in one small section of the restaurant.

"Hello, Michael—it's good to see you," Gloria offered as he quickly kissed her cheek.

"Yes, it's good to see you too. It was nice to share dinner with you a couple of weeks ago," he added, realizing that he hadn't seen her since that time, but that he hadn't seen Lauren since even before that.

He turned to Lauren then, bracing himself, but it was not nearly enough because in the four weeks since he'd seen her, talked to her, been in her presence, she'd become even more beautiful—if that was at all possible. Her hair had grown and she had it piled upon her head, carelessly, but somehow gracefully, and it only magnified her sensuality. Her coloring had paled somewhat from the sun-filled days they'd shared, yet the warm bronze tones were still there and only served to highlight the almond color of her eyes. He couldn't seem to tear his eyes away from her and suddenly his heart was pounding rapidly in his chest. His outward appearance did not give any clue to the inner turmoil he was experiencing.

"Hello, Michael," she said carefully, holding out her hand in an informal businesslike stance.

"Hello yourself," he said as he reached for it, totally unprepared for the warmth, the electricity that it brought forth.

Their eyes met and held for what seemed an eternity. Neither moved, their bodies polarized by uncertainty, their smiles frozen in place by emotions so deep that tears or laughter would have been more appropriate.

"So how have you been?" Michael asked breaking the ice as others around them continued their conversations, unaware and unconcerned with the emotional drama that was playing itself out in their midst.

"I'm fine. I've been working like a madwoman lately though," she said quickly, hoping to ease the tension.

"Well, haven't we all," he countered, a little annoyed that she seemed ready to issue excuses if he seemed ready to press the issue. There'd be no excuses offered nor accepted. He'd decided that long before this moment.

"Yes, and I'd like to congratulate you on your success with the deal. It seems that everything worked out in your favor after all," Lauren offered, sincerity plainly etched in her voice.

"Yes, it did after all. My partner and I are very pleased."

"Well you should be—you worked hard for this."

Not wanting the contact to end, but also not absolutely sure he knew where it would lead if it continued, Michael took a deep breath.

"Would you like another drink? I think I'm due for a refill," he said casually.

"Yes, thank you. I think I'll have a glass of champagne," she said then surprising herself. But suddenly, she wanted a drink and champagne was her drink of choice.

"Fine, be right back," Michael promised as he headed toward the bar.

Lauren turned back to the group at large and joined the on-going conversation which centered around internet music sites and the ability to download music for free.

"I think we're getting into dangerous ground when John Q Public no longer has to pay for music that's new to the marketplace," Duke offered.

"Napster is something to be reckoned with. The courts have the case now and it'll be decided in the coming months, but it doesn't look good for the industry," Danton responded.

"Hey, whatever happened to America, home of free enterprise?" Gloria said partly in jest and partly to throw some combustion on the fire.

"There's free enterprise and there's pirating. That's downright illegal," Lauren offered.

Michael returned then only hearing her proclamation of illegal and asked, "What's illegal?" handing her the glass of champagne.

"Lots of things, but some of them we do anyway now don't we?" Gloria responded with a particularly mischievous glint in her eye. She'd spotted the champagne Lauren was getting ready to consume and wondered why her roommate had chosen to switch poisons. Gloria was also aware that this was the first time that Lauren had seen or spoken to Michael in weeks and was hoping not to see any sparks fly. She knew Lauren could take care of herself; she was just hoping Michael could handle himself as well.

"We were discussing downloading music for free and its effects on the industry overall," Lauren explained.

"Well, in the long run it'll have a negative impact on the entire industry, causing the price of CDs to skyrocket to make up for the lackluster sales which will result from half the population being able to download them for free. That's exactly how you create an unfair marketplace," Michael said.

"I wonder how many people outside the industry feel that way?" Susan, Danton's companion offered.

"She's right. That's going to be the deciding factor when it comes right down to it," Duke said. "The recording industry versus John Q. Public is the issue," he added.

There was a call to dinner then and everyone moved into the dining area. Morgan approached them, pointing out a table which served as the anchor table and directed Duke, Michael, Gloria and Lauren to it. He joined them along with several principal members of CBN's executive board whom Michael and Duke had met only the week before.

Dinner consisted of four courses beginning with Caesar salad. Mussels marinara were served as an appetizer with peasant bread for dipping into the sauce, and two choices of entrees consisting of veal marsala, saffron rice with mushrooms or shrimp scampi accompanied by the pasta of your choice were available, followed by Italian cheesecake for dessert and coffee.

Throughout dinner, conversation flowed around the table evenly with Michael and Lauren sitting directly across from each other. .

Lauren found it difficult to keep her eyes from meeting with his. Every time she did, she found that he was looking at her. It not only made her uncomfortable, it made her heart beat faster. The champagne she'd drunk earlier had somehow seemed to calm her nerves so she'd had another glass during dinner. The food had been delicious and she'd eaten heartily, not realizing how hungry she'd been. She'd forgotten how handsome Michael was, forgotten how tall he was, most of all forgotten the affect he seemed to always have on her. She wanted to hear everything he had to say, know everything he was thinking. At the same time, warning bells were going off in her head which she couldn't ignore.

As the table disbanded and moved to the now cleared area where the music and dancing had already gotten started, Michael walked over to Lauren, took her elbow gently and steered her away from the group.

"I just wanted you to know that no matter what happens tonight, I forgive you for the past weeks," he said softly, looking into her eyes.

His touch on her arm was heated and brought to mind how it had felt to be touched by him at other times. Lauren's face colored as her body betrayed her mind.

"Well, that certainly takes a load off my mind," she said lightly, trying to cover up the thought patterns that were forming in her head. Thoughts of his kisses, his caresses, his body were foremost in her mind and there seemed to be nothing she could do about it.

"Great, I'm glad we have that cleared up. Now we can go on to enjoy the remainder of the evening," he added smiling.

Lauren felt her heart do a double beat. His smile had done that to her before, but she'd somehow forgotten that. This wasn't going to be easy, but she'd handle it. She knew she had to for the sake of going forward.

The music, which had been started while dinner was being served, was good. A dee-jay, the same one Morgan had hired for the dinner party held at Gloria and Lauren's apartment was pulling out all the stops in getting the party started right.

The dance floor, which was small, was already almost filled to capacity with normally stiff-backed, conscientious business types, all gyrating and dancing to the beat.

"Can I get you anything from the bar?" Michael offered as he and Lauren found seats at a booth.

"Sure, champagne please," Lauren said.

"Okay, be back in a minute," Michael said wondering what the hell he was doing. He'd vowed to be aloof, standoffish and downright hostile, but when he looked at her, it just wasn't possible. And on a night when he should be the happiest of his life, he didn't want to interject misery into it by trying to do something that felt totally unnatural. He didn't care if he never saw her again after tonight. He just wanted to be in her presence for the here—the now.

When he returned with the drinks, Duke and Gloria

had found their way to the dance floor and waved at them as he sat down. They seemed to be having a good time and the conversations he and Duke had shared earlier came to mind.

I hope he knows what he's doing, Michael thought to himself. *But do any of us really know what we're doing or why we're doing it.* He immediately dismissed both thoughts realizing that now was not the time to analyze—nor was it the time to think.

"Here you go, miss. Drink this one slowly. I think it's your third or fourth, but never let it be said that I am counting," he added.

"Don't worry, I can handle myself—champagne or no champagne." Lauren laughed.

"Oh, no doubt. Look, I wasn't trying to suggest anything otherwise. I do know that champagne has an unpredictable effect on you though so I just thought a word of caution might be in order," he said, not wanting to remind her that he'd seen her after four glasses of champagne in the past.

"Okay, point taken. I'll switch to ginger ale after this one," she said.

"You know, I'd love to dance. " Lauren took Michael's hand, led him to the floor and they joined the crowd already dancing to the old-school classic "I Found Love." Four records later, they were still on the floor and Michael was easily reminded of the fact that Lauren was one hell of a good dancer. Her hair, which had been artfully pinned up early in the evening, had come down and now tumbled around her shoulders. She'd removed the suede bolero jacket and was now only wearing a sleeveless black halter top with the gray suede pants.

Michael, whose gray suit jacket lay across the seat of their booth, also had removed his tie and opened the top button of the shirt he was wearing. His hair, shiny and black in the darkness of the dance floor lights, made Lauren want to run her hands through it. She watched him as he danced, concentrating on his moves, smooth and tight and felt a familiar throbbing in her body. She wanted him. It was that simple and yet it was complicated too.

They silently communicated that the time for dancing was over. Duke and Gloria had taken up residence at the other side of the bar and were deep in conversation.

Lauren finished the remaining champagne in her glass in one gulp, feeling hot, thirsty and in need of more.

"I think I'm going to need that ginger ale now," she whispered into Michael's ear to be heard over the loudly blaring music.

"Okay, I can use a refill myself," Michael said as he started toward the bar.

Duke walked over then with an especially triumphant smile on his face.

"I'm going to drive Gloria home so I wanted to check with you on Lauren. Is everything okay? I mean can you get her home okay because they came together?" Duke asked.

"Really, well let me just check. I don't want it to be said that I misread any signals, " he laughed.

"Lauren, Duke is going to drop Gloria home. It seems they're ready to leave now. I can drop you whenever you're ready to go. Is that okay with you?" he asked, wondering how and why he'd gotten into this position. He'd promised himself that he wouldn't press anything, wouldn't stick his neck out and here he was offering to drive her home. If she turned him down, he'd feel like a fool. If she accepted, he'd still be confused . . . What the hell was he doing? he asked himself in the thirty seconds it took for Lauren to respond.

"Sure, if it's no trouble to you, Michael," she said, looking at him with those catlike eyes. His heart melted.

"No, no trouble at all," he said automatically as Duke reached out to her, taking her hand and saying good night. Duke clasped Michael's shoulder, told him he'd speak with him over the weekend and quickly returned to Gloria who was waiting at the bar. She waved at Michael, gave a little thumbs-up sign and he realized that she was actually rooting for him with Lauren. That brought a smile to his face.

So, he had his work cut out for him.

He ordered the ginger ale and a Coke for himself. He wanted to be of sound mind and body for anything else that was to take place this evening.

Lauren was waiting patiently when he returned with their drinks and they continued to enjoy the music, just listening to it and watching some of the others on the dance floor.

Looking at his watch sometime later, Michael noted it was almost midnight and asked Lauren if she was ready to leave.

"Sure, if you are."

He realized that they'd both enjoyed the evening and neither wanted it to end. He also knew he didn't want it to end at Zanzibar.

"Come on, it's getting late," he said as he gathered their jackets.

His car was in a garage on 44th Street and as they walked the one-half block, Lauren timidly took his arm. It felt good. The weight of her hand felt natural as if it belonged there and he once again asked himself what the hell he was doing.

Michael was quiet as he drove, sensing that Lauren's thoughts were of a mixed nature as were his own. They'd shared an entire evening in each other's company, enjoyed themselves immensely, yet neither knew where this evening would end and it was on the minds of both. As Michael approached the Brooklyn Bridge, Lauren said quietly, "I don't want to go home."

"Are you sure?"

"I'm sure." She looked at him silently, pleading for his understanding.

Michael turned the car around without another word and headed toward the FDR Drive North.

"Hey, listen to this. It's the new CD from Boney James and Rick Braun, 'Shake It Up,' " he said while turning up the volume. The music served as a buffer for both their thoughts. Michael wondered if he would regret the entire evening. And Lauren wondered if she knew what she was doing. She did know that she'd enjoyed his company and did not want the evening to end. They arrived at his house in less than fifteen minutes, not having said another word the entire time.

"Would you like something to drink?" he asked as they entered the living room which was bathed in moonlight stretching diagonally along the polished wood floors. He hit the wall switch and the track lighting which he'd recently installed added strategic spotlights of illumination which enhanced the beauty of the room.

"Yes, how about a cup of coffee. By the way, the track lighting is wonderful. I remember you said that was the one thing you really wanted to add," Lauren said as she admired the effect it had on the entire interior space.

"That's right, I did tell you about it. I was still getting estimates from electricians at that point, but I finally found the right people and they completed the project in two days. Coffee coming right up," he added walking toward the kitchen.

"Need any help?" Lauren offered graciously as she followed him. She leaned against one wall as she watched him begin to prepare the coffee.

"No, but you can have a seat and keep me company though."

Something about the way he looked, head bent in concentration over the amount of coffee he added to the mixture, caught Lauren off guard and she came toward him with one thought in her mind. She wanted to be in his arms at that moment and nothing else mattered.

She walked up to him just as he turned from the sink after having filled the coffeepot with water, and took it from his hands, setting the pot on the counter. Surprise was written on his face as she simply looked into his eyes and he knew. He felt it too. They came together wordlessly. Their mouths seeking, their hands reaching, their bodies molding themselves one into the other.

Lauren felt as if she were on fire the moment their lips touched. She couldn't get close enough to him as she fit herself to him, daringly encouraging his response without heed or caution.

Michael, caught a little off guard by her total lack of inhibition, responded in spite of himself. A cautionary bell went off in his head, but he ignored it. His body was in control and his mind had been overridden. Lauren continued to kiss him passionately as she began unbuttoning his shirt, his tie dangling around his neck from earlier in the evening. She placed kisses all along his neck, trailed them down his chest and reached for his belt buckle.

Michael, realizing that she had somehow taken control, continued to kiss her while removing her jacket. The halter top she'd worn underneath had no back and her shoulders were exposed expansively. Michael looked at her through eyes filled with desire, carefully appreciating her beauty as he slowly kissed he shoulders, her neck and the swell of her breasts above the fabric of the scanty top. He desperately wanted to take his time in making love to her, but knew that the fires which burned in each of them at the moment would not allow for lovemaking which was either slow or casual.

"I think we should go upstairs now," he said pulling her hips against his arousal which was quite evident. She responded by rhythmically moving her hips against his in a slow and seductive manner which only heightened both their passions.

"I don't think I can get that far," Lauren said, reaching this time for the zipper on his pants. For the second time that evening, she caught Michael totally off guard as she reached for him and freed him from the confines of his slacks, caressing him slowly.

"God, Lauren—if you don't stop it, we're not going to make it out of this kitchen," he said hoarsely now, unable to control any of what was to happen.

"Beds are highly overrated," she said into his mouth, pulling him down to the floor.

Michael reached for her then, pulling her on top of him so that she lay cushioned against his body. They both removed her slacks, hands impatiently pushing aside any impediment to their passion. When he positioned her astride him, he marveled at the beauty she represented to him. Her hair hung down onto her shoulders, freed from its earlier restraints by the dancing and frolicking they'd done. He removed the halter top easily in one stroke of the two strings which laced in the back holding it together. Her breasts rose above him like two cone shaped orbs, the nipples a toasty brown color calling to him for sampling. He rose up encircling one with is tongue while his hands covered the other in a tantalizing circular motion. Lauren moaned as she ground her hips against his slowly, the heat building between them like a bonfire with more than adequate kindling. Michael paused, uttered a few words of unintelligible frustration and hastily reached into his pocket while still holding Lauren closely to him.

"Here, let me," she uttered breathlessly in his ear, while taking the small packet from him. Carefully, and with the lack of finesse exhibited by a first-timer, she applied the tightly rolled sheath.

Michael watched her with something akin to pride, passion and wonder. She was amazingly resilient and he knew that it had taken a tremendous amount of growth for her to reach the point at which they now stood.

Lauren kissed him triumphantly, passion escalating instantly as she slowly lowered herself onto him, feeling him enter her, all heat and solid smoothness. He allowed her to control the depth, the tempo, the beat and she quickly mastered the required technique. She realized that by leaning slightly forward, it created a sensation so pleasurable that she almost cried out. She leaned down, fitting her mouth to Michael's in a kiss that was both steamy and teasing. Their tongues played havoc with their senses as the tempo of their lovemaking increased. Lauren felt a now-familiar tension gathering in her belly as Michael continued to caress her breasts with both hands. She leaned forward, pressing herself tightly against the length of him and shower bursts went off in her head and her body. The sensations sent Michael over the edge as he erupted in one deep final thrust.

Lauren's body went limp as she leaned down toward Michael, kissing him softly on the lips once, then twice. His eyes were closed, his breathing still labored somewhat and she wondered what he was thinking.

"You're trying to kill me, right?" he asked, reaching up to hold her to him tightly.

Lauren laughed then and said slowly. "Now, whatever gave you that idea?"

"First you disappear for more than a month—no

phone calls, no letters, no e-mail—no sex. Then you ravish me on my kitchen floor," he said reaching up to smooth her hair back while looking into her eyes for answers to so many of the questions that remained unasked.

"First of all, I did not ravish you. We just weren't able to make it to the bedroom this time," she said matter-of-factly as she reached for the halter top.

"Oh, I see; so this is just an everyday, ordinary occurrence for you is it?" he said, his eyes darkening as he sat up and adjusted his clothing.

"No, Michael, you know that's not the case. I just meant I'm not ready to talk about it just yet, okay? What we just shared was wonderful, fantastic, unbelievably great, but I can't talk about the past month right now. Just give me a little time, sweetheart. I promise I'll try and explain everything to you soon," she said. Looking into his eyes as they sat only an arms length from each other trying to figure out what had just happened, each felt anxiety, yet they were filled with hope by their passion.

"Look. I'm beat. Why don't you come upstairs where we can at least be comfortable," he offered, taking her hand and helping her to her feet.

"I'd love to," she said surprising both herself and him.

They made love again during the night. And in the early morning hours, just as dawn's light was beginning to change the shape of the ensuing day, Michael felt the warmth of her body next to his and reached for her. Their lovemaking was dreamlike and slow, the intensity soulful and satisfying. It was as if neither could get enough of the other and it was late Saturday morning when they finally awakened.

Lauren turned over, smiled at the look of complete and utter peace on Michael's sleeping face and felt a wave of nausea overtake her. Hoping to overcome it by just remaining quiet and still, she took several deep breaths to quell her stomach. It did not help and she jumped out of the bed, making it just in time to the master bathroom, which adjoined Michael's bedroom.

Michael thought he heard her coughing and it awakened him. He lay there silently thinking of the night before and all it had encompassed. He smiled then, realizing that she was in love with him and fighting it like hell. He also realized that she was retching, not coughing in the bathroom.

"Lauren, are you okay" he called out, thinking she'd probably drunk a little too much champagne the night before, but also realizing that she'd only had about three drinks—nothing that should cause her to become ill the following day.

When there was no answer, Michael got out of bed, pulling on a navy blue terry-cloth robe and knocked at the closed bathroom door.

"Lauren, is everything okay? Do you need anything?" he asked not wanting to disturb her privacy, but wanting to be of help if she needed it.

"No, I'm okay. Go on back to bed," she called out in a strained voice.

"Can I get you anything?" he persisted, now becoming increasingly alarmed at the thought of her really being ill.

"Ginger ale if you have it and some crackers," she managed to croak out.

"Okay, I'll be right back," he said to the closed door as he turned to go downstairs to the kitchen.

He searched the kitchen cabinets and came up with an unopened box of Pilot crackers, then found a large bottle of Schweppes ginger ale. He put on the pot of coffee they'd never gotten around to the night before, smiling at the thought of what had occurred in his kitchen. He then prepared a tray with the crackers, the ginger ale and two cups of coffee, taking it up to the bedroom.

Lauren had come out of the bathroom, was propped up on several pillows in the bed looking pale and uncertain.

"Are you feeling okay?" Michael asked as he put the tray on an old steamer trunk he had at the foot of the bed.

"I'm fine. I guess something served at the dinner last night didn't agree with me," she said quickly. "Do you have a shirt or something I can put on for now?" she asked, realizing she was totally naked under the down-filled comforter and sheets of his bed.

"Yeah, of course," Michael said quickly, removing a GAP T-shirt from one of the dresser drawers. He also found a pair of royal blue silk boxer shorts which he never wore anymore and handed those to Lauren too.

"Listen, I can make you an Alka Seltzer if you'd like," he said as he watched her attempt to down the ginger ale and crackers. Something about it didn't seem right to him. She'd been drinking ginger ale the night before too. Almost as if she knew her stomach wasn't one hundred percent.

She turned to him then, her coloring beginning to return to normal as she put on the T-shirt and pulled on the shorts.

"Michael, please don't worry about me. I'm fine. Just too much champagne and celebration," she offered.

"Well, I hope the celebrating part isn't what made you sick," he said thinking of all that had transpired during the night and into the early morning hours. And then, like a flash he knew. She could very well be pregnant. She'd been a virgin the first night they'd slept together but he hadn't known that and had assumed she was on the pill. They had used condoms in subsequent times of lovemaking, but that was never one hundred percent effective and it had been so infrequent and unexpected that he'd never gotten around to asking her about her method of choice. And on his part, he'd slept with women of the world who were used to these things, knew how to take care of themselves and did a very good job doing just that.

"Lauren, when was the last time you had your period?" he asked softly as he joined her at the end of the bed for a cup of coffee.

"Michael, just what are you getting at?" she asked impatiently then, realizing that it had been a bad idea to wake up in his bed, allowing him to see how most mornings were with her and not expect him to ask questions. The very same questions she was beginning to ask herself the longer this occasional nausea plagued her.

"Look, Lauren, I'm just a little concerned that's all. Is this the first time you've thrown up in the morning like this?" he asked then, putting the cup down. He then looked her directly in the eye awaiting her answer.

"It's nothing to worry about. I told you it was probably something I ate at the party that didn't agree with me," she said earnestly. "I think I'll take you up on that Alka Seltzer though," she added hoping to effectively change the subject.

"Fine, listen, I know this was a little unexpected, but would you like to do something today?" he asked as he searched his medicine cabinet for the antacid. He found the packages, ran some cold water and added the tablets.

"I'd love to but, I promised Gloria I'd spend the day with her out on Long Island. She told her stepmother, Cora that she'd come out and do lunch. She asked me along to keep her company," she said while drinking the fizzing liquid.

"Okay, perhaps another time soon," Michael said with the emphasis on the last word as he looked at Lauren with a searching look in his dark eyes. For the life of him, he couldn't figure her out. She'd practically raped him the night before although force had not been at all necessary. Now, here she was erecting barriers between them as if she couldn't get away fast enough.

"Look, I had a terrific time last night and I want to see you again soon," she said then as if reading his thoughts.

"Fine, Lauren, however you want to play it. Just remember one thing, you came to me last night," he said meaningfully, his eyes dark with passion and a glint of anger.

"That's right; I did, didn't I?" she said boldly. Lauren then kissed him softly on the lips as she headed toward the bathroom to shower and dress.

Twenty-three

Lauren shook her head slowly as if to ward off the effects of what she'd just read. Unfortunately, it didn't change anything. Didn't change the fact that she was onboard the D328 jet and ready to work the 32 passenger flight out of New York's Kennedy Airport en route to Fort Lauderdale, Florida. Didn't change the fact that it was a full two-day layover in that Florida city with the return trip taking place on Monday morning. And certainly didn't change the fact that the organization they'd be flying today would be the Radio Engineers Annual Golf Tournament and Convention. Odds were, her passenger list would most probably include Michael Townsend and there was nothing she could do about it.

She'd managed to avoid seeing him in the weeks past since the "coming-out party" although she had spoken to him twice. In those conversations, she'd been warm and friendly, but unavailable. She knew she was being unreasonable, even selfish, but each time she was in his presence, she no longer held any control over her actions or reactions.

And in the scheme of things, that scenario was unacceptable. Especially now that she knew what she knew. Lauren was six weeks pregnant. She'd finally gone in to see Dr. Forman and he'd examined her, performed several routine tests and then asked what brought her into his office since she wasn't due for an annual physical exam for another five months. After describing the symptoms that were causing her concern, he'd asked for a urine sample.

Two days later, Lauren had received a phone call from Dr. Forman's nurse informing her that her pregnancy test had come back positive with the additional question of whether she would be able to come back into the office for consultation anytime that week. Not knowing what she wanted to do, she'd postponed making that appointment.

Lauren was terrified. And confused. What the hell had happened? She knew that she should have started to use some standard form of birth control; that condoms only offered a limited measure of security and had definitely thought of it during the many times that she and Michael had made love, but she'd never considered its permanent state. And then she remembered, vividly, that the very first time they'd made love onboard *Megahertz*, no birth control, no condoms, no protection of any kind had even entered the picture.

Lauren was not at all sure of what she was going to do, what she even wanted to do, or was in a position to do. She did know that she hadn't ever really believed in abortion. Not for herself anyway. But that was mainly because she'd never considered becoming pregnant and being caught off guard this way.

How could I have been so careless, she thought, realizing that she'd bought herself a slice of reality for which she'd surely have to pay a premium price.

Above all, she knew she couldn't let a breath of this get out because if Michael found out, she didn't know what he was capable of doing, saying or expecting her to do.

The passengers were beginning to board, mostly

male, successful radio entrepreneurs, on-air personalities, programmers, general managers and other communications executives. She was engaged in welcoming the boarding passengers and handing out the Charter Division's signature ballpoint pens when she heard a familiar voice call out, "Lauren, is that you?"

Morgan seemed genuinely glad to see her, accompanied by one of his upper level managers, Colin Gates, who was busy stowing his carry-on bag in the overhead bin.

"Yes, Morgan, it's good to see you. When I realized this flight was being chartered by the Radio Engineering Convention, I thought you might be on board," she said smiling, not adding that her thoughts had also included a certain other communications/radio entrepreneur who also might be in attendance.

"Yeah, how have you been? I haven't seen you since the party at Zanzibar," he said as he deposited his carry-on bags into the overhead bins before him.

"Actually, I'm fine and looking forward to Florida for the next couple of days," she answered.

"Yeah, me too. Fort Lauderdale's weather will be a definite improvement on what we've had in the past couple of days. Forty-degree temperatures in November is not my idea of any kind of comfort zone," he added, taking his seat.

"Tell me about it. Can I get either of you anything?" Lauren asked as she prepared to continue getting the remaining passengers seated and organized.

"No, I'm fine. How about you, Colin?" Morgan asked his colleague and seat companion.

"Actually, I would like a Coke," he said, pushing his glasses back onto the bridge of his nose. He was all of five-feet five-inches with blond hair, blue eyes and a slightly receding hairline which seemed to regress farther and farther each year as the hassles and stresses of managing the station took their toll.

"Not a problem," Lauren said, smiling quickly and giving them both the thumbs-up sign.

"She's my sister's roommate," Morgan said in explanation as she walked away.

"Wow, you should be trying to date her," Colin offered as he removed his glasses, wiping them for a better view of Lauren's profile as she walked up the narrow aisle of the aircraft.

"Naw, she's more like a sister at this point. Anyway, I think she's involved with one of our new partners who I think I see boarding at this very moment," Morgan said as he noticed both Michael and Duke entering the front of the plane. They'd shared a cab straight from the station after having worked the entire day making sure programming was in place for the weekend to come.

Their seats were located mid-plane on the opposite aisle and they found them without incident, loading their overhead items and fastening their seat belts in short order.

Lauren returned with the soft drink for Colin Gates as well as for several other passengers and continued making the arriving passengers welcome and comfortable. Michael, his head bent over paperwork he needed to complete and fax back to the station immediately upon his arrival in Ft. Lauderdale, did not take notice of her as she passed his seat in the opposite aisle of the aircraft. Neither did Duke, the proverbial "bean counter," as he continued to work on the annual projections, his laptop computer and calculator in full operation. He knew he had only a few minutes more of the use of the computer before the flight was airborne and was trying to at least put an end to the quarter's numbers.

The flight got underway without further incident and was less than halfway to its sunny destination when Lauren began distributing drinks and snacks. Michael, head still bent in concentration on the paperwork he was attempting to finish up, looked up quickly as he heard her familiar voice ask, "Can I get either of you gentlemen a soft drink?"

A moment of pure unadulterated discomfort passed between all three persons, Duke, Michael and Lauren. Duke didn't know if Michael had spoken to her recently or not, but he did know he hadn't expected to see her on this flight. And he was also pretty sure that she hadn't expected to see him either by the expression on her still-beautiful face. Quick on the uptake, Duke broke the silence by laughing. "Well, this is almost too good to be true. Sure, I'll have a white wine," he said waiting for his partner to collect his thoughts.

"Hello, Duke. I thought you guys might be on this flight once I saw Morgan board and realized that this is your annual convention and golf outing," she offered easily. Inwardly, her heart was pounding and she hoped Michael wouldn't notice the way her skirt fit her just a little more snugly than it had the last time he'd seen her in uniform.

"Well, Miss Traynor, it is nice to see you again," Michael offered in measured clips. Clearly he was not amused and was not going to be mollified by her businesslike personna.

"Can I get you anything to drink?" she offered. Lauren honestly hoped for the ability to at least be cordial in this unexpected encounter, which she would have avoided at all costs if she'd only known ahead of time so that she could have canceled today's assignment.

"Sure, why don't you pick something for me?" he

said suggestively. Now seemingly ready to do battle, his eyes flashed danger into hers and she knew he was more than angry with her.

"Okay, I will. How about red wine?" she offered thinking of the blood he'd probably like to spill. She knew he was furious with her, but also knew he'd never show it no matter how provoking the situation.

"That sounds fine—red wine," he repeated, looking at her meaningfully which also reinforced the fact that he was not only furious with her, but that at some point in the coming hours, she'd know the extent of that fury.

She served their drinks then and moved on to the next row of passengers all the while painfully aware of the scrutiny she was receiving.

Michael watched her as she moved up the aisle methodically doing her job, and he knew true torment. On the one hand, he wanted to say to her, "It's over—I don't want to continue this anymore." But on the other hand, he wanted to understand what her motivations were for continuously breaking the ties that bound them each and every time they were in each other's presence. Somehow, he knew this time he'd find out just what was to be in this on again-off again relationship with Miss Lauren Traynor.

They landed at Ft. Lauderdale's airport at 7:30 that evening and five limousines which had been chartered to take them to the Wyndham Resport and Spa, boasting two PGA managed golf courses, were awaiting the arrival of their thirty-five passengers. Another flight due in from the west coast later that evening would also add another thirty-five executives, programmers and engineers to the convention mayhem.

As the passengers deplaned and Lauren took her post to bid them farewell, Michael walked up, took her arm and said in a slightly lowered voice, "Where are you staying?" He knew he was taking a chance that she would not answer him or, worse, would give him an incorrect answer, but he had to take that chance.

"I'll be at the Marriott," she said, looking at him as if she knew exactly what he was thinking.

"Good. Perhaps we'll see each other before the return trip," he said meaningfully.

"Fine. I don't return to New York before Monday morning so I'll certainly be in the vicinity," she said without any commitment. But her eyes said something far different. Something he couldn't read.

Michael had watched as she'd canvassed the aisles, helping other passengers with simple requests during the flight. Her uniform, still tailored to fit and accentuate her professional air, seemed to have become more defined. Her bust and her hips which had always seemed slim, now seemed more voluptuous. He'd found himself responding to the mere presence of her form. He had to mentally ground himself, remind himself to stay in check, rein himself in so to speak, but his thoughts were filled with the memory of the last time they'd been together in his kitchen.

He had no doubt that he wanted to make love to her again—over and over again just as they had the last time they'd been together. He didn't know whether that was what she was afraid of and he didn't care. He only knew that every time he was in her presence, every time he saw her, the need to have her, possess her and ultimately make love to her became paramount in his mind.

"Fine. Great flight by the way," he said casually as he stepped into the jetway leading into the airport.

* * *

Sunny skies, eighty-two degrees with winds blowing out of the southeast at five miles per hour was the forecast for Saturday's weather and the golfers loved it. Hitting the course at 7:30 A.M. after a breakfast buffet which began at 7:00, they were in top form. Each group commandeered golf carts with their respective station logo on banner on the side with CBN/WJZZ housing Morgan, Michael, Duke, and Colin efficiently. They played until twelve noon, then broke for a buffet luncheon which consisted of seafood salads, fruits, a carving station including hot roast beef, roasted turkey and pastrami, and lots and lots of announcements, industry awards and all the latest reports on who was doing what in the radio/broadcast realm. Returning to the course for the final rounds to be played to the eighteenth hole, each participant welcomed this respite from their everyday world of broadcasting, programming, music selection and advertising requirements.

Duke loved golf and had played it often with his father back in Chicago before leaving for Northwestern. Michael, on the other hand, played just well enough to keep his business associates in check when it came time for a little rivalry. And although the course itself was absolutely breathtaking, he had something else on his mind.

There was an award's dinner planned for that evening which he knew he did not want to attend, but it was business and that meant it was mandatory. After leaving Duke and Morgan at the front desk of the hotel and heading toward his room, he showered and then lay across the bed. A quick nap would do him good he thought looking at the clock on the bed stand which read 6:30. A cocktail hour was scheduled for 7:30 with dinner beginning at 8:00. *The awards ceremony will be underway by nine o'clock and things should be settling down by ten,* he calculated mentally while reaching for the phone.

"Connect me with the Ft. Lauderdale Marriott, please," he said quickly.

"Your connection is on the line sir," the hotel operator said after some twenty seconds.

"Marriott."

"Please connect me with the room of Lauren Traynor," he said into the phone, one arm covering his eyes. He was tired, but wanted to set things straight so that if this evening made sense, they'd at least get to spend it together.

"Hello," she answered sleepily.

"Hello yourself," he replied, not able to stop the blood from coursing through his veins heatedly in response to the sound of her sleep-filled voice.

"Michael, what time is it?" she asked sleepily, obviously having been asleep for some time.

"Six-thirty. I was just about to take a nap myself then I figured I'd give you a call and find out what your plans are for this evening," he said.

"Wow. I laid down about four o'clock after having a huge lobster salad for lunch. It must have knocked me out like turkey does to some people," she laughed.

"Oh, I never heard that one before. That's a good one." He liked the fact that she could make jokes within minutes of being awakened from a sound sleep. A good sense of humor was a great asset in the scheme of things, he reasoned.

"Anyway, I don't really have any plans for the evening. I just thought I might take a swim down at the pool when I woke up. It's still sunny outside so I probably will, but just for a quick minute, you know," she said breathlessly into the phone.

He loved her voice. "Yeah, listen I'm going to be tied up here for the next couple of hours until about ten or so. What do you say we have a late dinner or drinks about ten-thirty? That's probably the earliest I can get over there because we have an award's dinner tonight for the golf tournament that was held today," he explained.

"Okay. That doesn't sound too late, after all I don't have to be up early tomorrow morning for anything anyway," she offered.

"Good. Meet me in the lounge area of the bar, okay? Ten-thirty, don't be late," he said then and hung up.

Michael's eyes slowly adjusted to the darkened lounge area as he looked for Lauren within its confines. She sat in a corner booth, the overstuffed red leather upholstery seeming to swallow her for some reason. She was wearing a white eyelet dress with tiny shoulder straps which exposed the natural beauty of her shoulders and neck. It hung to just above her ankles which were wrapped with strappy black and white sandals and had a matching shoulder bag. Her hair, which she'd just washed and blown dry after having indeed gone swimming, hung to her shoulders, the ends curling slightly. She looked simple, elegant and stunning.

"You made it," she said as Michael slid into the booth beside her.

"Yes, and so did you," he said meaningfully.

"Well, I don't think you can say that I've ever stood you up now," she offered in defense of her behavior thus far.

"No, but you play a pretty mean game of cat and mouse, Miss Traynor. Let's not get into this right now. What are you drinking?" he asked then, stopping himself from going any further.

"I'll have ginger ale for now," she said quickly.

"So, you're still nursing a bad stomach," he countered before she realized her mistake in reminding him of the last time they'd spent together.

"No, not really, I just figured I'd start out with ginger ale and work my way up to wine or champagne later," she said defensively.

"Oh, I see," he said, noting that she seemed to be a bit nervous as if there were something unspoken going on this evening.

"Look, Lauren let's call a truce. Every time we get together, we have a fantastic time after which you find it necessary to bolt for the sky. I'm tired of not knowing whether I should call you, date you, sleep with you, you know what I'm talking about," he offered, unable to allow the uncertainties of their relationship to lie still for even the beginning of this evening.

"I know and I apologize. I really do. I don't mean to be such a pain in the ass, but I'm trying to work some things out. Bear with me, Michael," she said in earnest, placing her hand on his arm in a reassuring gesture.

The waiter arrived and took their drink orders. They continued to talk mainly about work, their new positions each representing a challenge which neither had been able to foresee prior to the changes taking place.

"So you really like working with the Charter Division. Doesn't the fact that you have to stay over with the whole flight detail bother you some times if it's a boring destination?" he asked as Lauren described her new assignments in detail.

"Not really. Each city has so much to offer and I get a kick out of travel—I always have ever since my childhood with my dad's Army obligations. As a result, I love being in new places, exploring, investigating and sightseeing for a couple of days. It really inspires you to appreciate this great country we live in," she offered.

"Only a nut like you would like that. Don't you ever get lonely or scared in a totally foreign city by yourself?" Michael asked in amazement at her sense of adventure.

"Not really. You always have another crew member with you first of all and even if you and that person don't hit it off, you can shop, sightsee, visit various points of interest, etc. You know I really get into it," she said laughing at his response which was to shake his head in wonder.

"You're one for the books, Lauren. Let's get out of here and go down to Las Olas Blvd for some dinner. I ate much earlier," he said then finishing his white wine.

"Fine," she said as she sipped her drink. He took her hand, helping her to her feet and whistled softly. "Wow, I hadn't realized how pretty you look this evening," he said taking in the softness of her dress, the sexiness of her sandals and the overall affect it had. It never ceased to amaze him that she was indeed, beautiful.

"Well, thank you," Lauren responded, inwardly pleased that he'd noticed the extra care she'd taken to dress this evening.

The car which Michael had hired for the evening waited at the hotel's entrance. Smaller than the limousines which had been hired to transport the conventioneers from the airport, the Lincoln Town Car was relaxing and smooth as they made their way toward one of Ft. Lauderdale's most popular tourist areas. Twenty minutes later, they reached "old" Las Olas Blvd, a strip which was riddled on either side with upscale shops, restaurants, nightclubs, art galleries and which stayed open and alive until the early morning hours.

Preferring to walk, they marveled at the interesting blend of modern, yet thoroughly enchanting shops and restaurants they passed on either side. Hand in hand, they continued to stroll, until they approached a restaurant which had a particularly interesting décor. Done in the design of far eastern cultural pieces with Indian artifacts and huge palm trees placed strategically throughout, Michael asked if she'd like to try their cuisine.

"Indigo—it looks interesting and you know I'm all for the exotic," Lauren answered rising to the challenge immediately.

"I thought that would be your response," he said smiling as they took seats at one of the outdoor rattan tables. It was a beautiful night. Warm, with only a slight glimmer of a breeze and a full moon which lit up the sky brilliantly.

As they scanned the menus, each deep in thought, Lauren came to a conclusion. She'd definitely keep her newfound medical condition a secret until she really decided exactly what it was that she should do. She realized at that moment that Michael would feel some kind of compulsion to do the right thing and she didn't want that from him. She didn't want that any more than she wanted him to feel that she'd somehow trapped him by getting pregnant. She knew that he'd never let her know that that was how he felt, but it would hover over their lives and she couldn't live with that thought or that possibility.

They ordered their food and drinks and continued to talk aimlessly about the past, the present and the future, each feeling that this evening was somehow a watershed point for them both. Perhaps it was that they were both out of their elements. A different city, an exotic restaurant, a time away from the routine of their everyday existence which allowed them to open up in a new and different way.

"Why don't we take the car and go down to the waterfront area after dinner? I hear they have an interesting blend of shops, cultural effects and Ft. Lauderdale history down there," Michael suggested as they sipped coffee at the end of their dinner.

"Great," Lauren responded. "What's your day like tomorrow?" she asked curious as to the time commitment these conventions kept their participants on.

"We play golf again in the morning, but it's not mandatory. Today's tournament was finalized already. Then we have another luncheon at about one P.M. and we're actually on our own after three P.M. Why, are you trying to account for my time tomorrow too?" he asked, laughing in spite of himself.

Lauren just looked at him at that point, knowing he was doing his best at getting her back for all the times she'd avoided spending quality time with him; needling her just to see what her reaction would be.

"Actually, I was only curious as to how much work and business actually gets done when major corporations take their top-level employees away on trips that span several days. I guess it depends on the industry," she said.

"Yeah, I'm sure that if this was an accountant's annual convention, they'd spend a lot more time going over actuals, projections and the bottom line so that next year's results would be better. Radio is a little more laid back, although we are getting exposed to some important feedback and information on the markets across the U.S. just being in each other's company," Michael offered.

They reached the "new Las Olas" area shortly after and began exploring its various nuances which included more shops, restaurants and art outlets. Built to resemble a Spanish waterfront landing, there were two levels to choose from, each offering a wide variety of items on display. Boats for charter were also available, including one which left the marina every hour on the hour headed into the nearby inlet for an hour-long tour of local "celebrity homes."

"Come on, let's take the tour. I feel like being on a boat and *Megahertz* is nowhere within reach," he said as they watched the eleven P.M. boat leave the dock.

"Are you suggesting a midnight boat ride, Mr. Townsend?" Lauren countered playfully.

"Exactly. It'll be fun, romantic and midnight; what more could you ask for?" he said as they approached the harbormaster's booth and purchased their tickets for the next scheduled boat to leave.

The ride, the scenery, the atmosphere was beautiful. They sat below deck, watching the shoreline and the sights their guide so eloquently pointed out, hands intertwined throughout. It was a magical night, with stars dotting the Florida skyline like rhinestones on dark blue velvet. Each felt the magic that was in their presence and knew that this night would signal a new stage in their until now, turbulent relationship.

"Would you ever want to live on the water?" Michael asked as he held her in front of him, surrounding her with his arms as the evening breeze softly threaded its way through the air.

"Sure, it's lovely, but who could afford it? These homes are all owned by millionaires as our tour guide pointed out and if not, they've been in their families for generations," she stated practically.

"You're right, but a girl could get lucky too," he said and laughed as he played with her hand, threading his fingers through hers, liking the feel and weight of her response.

"You know, I never think about things like that. Re-

ally, I mean I'd just as soon work my way up the airline
ladder, buy a co-op or a condo in the city perhaps and
let each day unfold as it will," Lauren said.

"Well, that's practical and clearheaded and no one
ever said you were anything but," he said, kissing the
palm of her hand as the boat returned to the dock. The
hour had gone too quickly, but they each had enjoyed
it immensely.

"Hey, this was great. Maybe we should come back
tomorrow and do it again in the daytime," Michael said
as they prepared to return to the shore.

"Now you're going a bit overboard." Lauren laughed
as she took his hand. "Where to now?"

"Well, it looks as if we've closed down half the places
around here, but let's walk along the promenade for a
while."

It was well past two A.M. when, as they sat astride a
bench beneath a large tree filled with twinkling lights,
Michael lifted Lauren's face, kissed her softly and whispered, "Can I count on you to understand that I have
some very real and deep feelings for you, Lauren? We
both need to act like adults in this relationship and accept the fact that there is more going on here than
casual sex, good times or physical attraction," he said,
earnestly looking into her eyes.

"Michael, I never said anything between us was casual. It's just that I get so scared of coming to depend
on your being there and then the possibility of that not
being the case makes me want to break all ties—no matter how close we've been." Sharing her feelings with
him honestly for the first time, Lauren felt as if a weight
had been lifted from her heart.

She couldn't imagine what he would think if she told
him of her most recent development. That would com-
plicate everything and complications were not welcome
at this point. They had made a major breakthrough,

she thought, and needed to be able to build on that before anything further developed.

"Let's go back to the hotel. It's getting late," she said as she pulled him up from his seated stance.

"I'm sure our driver has probably taken one heck of a nap by now waiting for us to return," he said as they found their way back to the parking area of the water-front attraction.

As they entered Lauren's hotel suite sometime later, Michael closed the door behind them, took Lauren's hand and pulled her tightly to him.

"I want you, Lauren," he whispered as he kissed her hungrily, trailing kisses from her lips to her throat and across the expanse of the exposed flesh above her dress. He lowered the strap on one side, then the other and reached around to the back to lower the zipper. The dress fell to the floor as Lauren felt her knees weaken. His kisses were heated and penetrated her consciousness deliciously.

"I wanted to do this all night," he said as he gently raked his fingers through her hair, holding her mouth in place as he gave undivided attention to her lips.

They had not moved from the tiny alcove entrance-way and the only light in the room came from the huge expanse of windows on the other side of the bedroom.

Lauren wound her arms upward around his neck, gently pressing her body against his and felt his desire. She reached under his jacket, her hands finding their way to his sports shirt and pulled it in short order, from its tucked in position. She wanted to feel the muscles of his back, his chest in her hands. Now clad in only a strapless white Victoria's Secret eyelet bra and matching panties, she looked lovely in the lighting provided.

"I think you have on too many clothes," she murmured as they moved as one toward the bed.

"I think you're right." Michael removed his jacket and shirt in two short maneuvers. He reached for his belt buckle, but Lauren stopped him.

"No, let me do that," she said smiling and his response was more than evident.

"Lauren Traynor, you're off the hook," he said as she unbuckled, unzipped and helped him step out of his pants.

"You inspire me," she said laughing as they both got into bed.

"I am so glad to hear you say that," he answered, kissing her softly while still laughing at the insanity which always seemed to surround their lovemaking. Inwardly he thought of how lovely she looked in the moonlight which streamed in from the windows which covered one wall. The stark white of the scantily cut bra and panties against her skin provided sharp contrast, enhancing the almond brown of her skin. The sun she'd received that day after frolicking in the pool now made its presence known in the golden hues radiating all over her body.

Looking down at her, Michael knew that he wanted this night to be different and wondered if Lauren too felt the uniqueness of what they shared. He gathered her into his arms and nuzzled her neck, willing himself to slow everything down, take his time, and savor each moment to come.

"I love you," he said then, meaning it, knowing it and feeling it for the first time.

"And I love you too, Michael." Lauren covered his face with tiny kisses, laughing, then suddenly crying softly, the tears falling unexpectedly as Michael wiped them away first with his hands, then his lips.

They continued to hold each other, looking deeply

into one another's eyes marveling at the depth of feelings shared, until they each fell asleep. And they made love slowly, passionately as the sun rose, spreading golden sunlight across the expanse of the room christening their bond.

Twenty-four

"Lauren, please don't pack everything you own—just enough for two days," Michael called from the living room interrupting Lauren's train of thought. The room, normally neat and organized, was in total disarray with clothes strewn across the bed and the chair in addition to several dresser drawers remaining in an open position.

"I am packing only the essentials," she replied while she mentally ticked off the two outfits she'd slipped inside her garment bag, realizing that she could pack one pair of sandals to go with both. She also threw in a short sundress which doubled as a beach cover, then threw in two bathing suits, two pairs of shorts with matching tops, a straw hat, and a long black halter dress for evening.

"Michael, for the last time where are we going?" she called to him over her shoulder attempting to sound threatening, but actually thrilled to be getting away on something other than a working flight. Not to mention that it was with Michael.

"Now that would be telling wouldn't it," he said entering the bedlam of her bedroom.

"I'm only prepared to tell you that it will be hot so pack a bathing suit or two. It will also be will be casual, infinitely relaxing and very romantic," he added, obviously quite amused at her total confusion and lack of information.

Since their return from Fort Lauderdale only two weeks before, he and Lauren had reached a new understanding, talking by telephone each night, seeing each other for a brief lunch at his office once and having dinner at the trendy new downtown eatery "America."

Michael crossed the room to where she stood, impatiently sorting through the closet full of assorted dresses, slacks and blouses.

"Lauren," he called softly as he lifted her hair from her shoulders and neck. He kissed her shoulder softly and tasted the now-familiar flavor of her skin.

"All right, all right," she responded, turning into his arms.

"If you're in that much of a hurry, I may have to pick up most of my clothing when we get to our destination which you haven't seen fit to inform me of," she said, issuing a challenge. Her eyes were a glistening pool of warm amber and Michael quickly stepped back from her still holding her loosely in an attempt to quiet the urge to make love to her right there among the mounds of clothing she'd so carelessly strewn all over the bed. He knew she wanted him to, could tell by the way she looked at him, lips parted and moist, her eyes issuing an unspoken challenge.

"Come on, young lady, we do not have time," he heard himself say. What he really wanted to do was strip that ridiculously sexy black lace undergarment off her body and feel the response he knew she was capable of giving. Instead he muttered, "You're dangerous."

"Come on, you are going to have to get a move on because our flight leaves in exactly one hour and forty-five minutes. I shouldn't have to tell you that we should be on our way to the airport," he said, helping her close the bags she'd carefully filled with clothing for a weekend that could very well span one week in the amount of interchangeable outfits she'd managed to fit in.

"Okay, okay. I'm ready. You know it's not my fault that you decided to put together this little rendezvous without any previous notice." Lauren pulled on a pair of Gap jeans and a white silk shirt which she tied at the waist. She then pulled her hair into a ponytail which Michael had come to love.

"Honey, where we're going, you are not going to need half this stuff," he teased as they left the apartment some moments later.

Their taxi reached Kennedy Airport in only thirty-five minutes. Michael and Lauren were able to check in, search for magazines, buy bottled water and sunscreen and still reach their boarding gate on time.

"Barbados. You know I've never been there," Lauren said as she finally was able to realize their destination as they obtained their seat assignments and boarding passes.

"Well, it was my mother's birthplace and we still have a house there so I thought it might be nice to get away for a short spell."

"You never told me that your mother was from the islands," she said then, thinking that there were lots of things they probably didn't know about each other even at this point.

"Well, now you are informed and you should also know that my dad is from Trinidad," he added.

"So, that's where you got all that curly black hair from," she said reaching up and running her fingers through the back of it as she often did.

"Yeah, my dad's is turning white now so I guess I have that to look forward to in about thirty or so years," he laughed.

* * *

The small house they entered sometime later was painted a beautiful tropical blue with white, yellow and tiny purple flowers bordering the slate walkway. White-washed shutters framed each window with ivy climbing the uppermost portion, ending in trails on both sides. Lauren walked into the sun-filled living room and gasped in delight.

"Oh, Michael, its beautiful," she exclaimed. Several large plants filled each corner with terra cotta pots containing flowering shrubs dotting the length of one wall. The floors, hardwood polished to a gleaming shine, were covered by large colorful throw rugs in bright pastel colors. Two small potted bushes stood alongside an eighteenth-century oak secretary replete with brass knobs and hardware. A large brass-framed mirror hung above it giving the room a feel of expansiveness, though it was in fact quite cozy and intimate. The stone fireplace in one corner dominated one wall with two white Haitian cotton love seats facing each other. Filled with pillows covered in shantung silk done in varying colors from lemon yellow to deep purple, they contrasted beautifully with the stark-white stucco of the walls. Separated by a circular glass coffee table, it created a sitting area which encouraged interaction while pampering its inhabitants with a full view of the room's offerings.

The dining room, entered by stepping down two wide steps off to the right, was just large enough to accommodate a table which seated six comfortably. A matching sideboard filled the expanse of one wall. Carved from the remnants of a ship's discarded cargo door, the table was heavy oak with its brass door polls still intact and visible which gave it definitive character. Six heavy oak chairs were placed around it, but the room was softened by the splashes of color offered by the throw rugs on the floors, the yellow, blue, orange, and lavender dinner plates coordinating the two place settings now visible on the table, and by the lovely arrangement of birds of paradise which adorned the sideboard along with two bowls of native fruits.

Michael held Lauren's hand, leading her from room to room, area to area as she touched everything much as a small child would in wonderment.

A narrow, wooden winding staircase curved upwards from the farthest corner of the room leading to the bedroom upstairs. The large brass bed with a snowy white coverlet dominated the room which opened off into a yellow and white tiled bathroom. A small veranda with old fashioned French doors ran the length of one wall overlooking the ocean. In one corner stood a huge crystal vase filled with native flowers currently in bloom.

Lauren walked into Michael's arms and laid her head on his chest. She felt tears come to her eyes and knew that her emotions were out of control, but no longer cared.

"This is so beautiful. Thank you for bringing me here, Michael," she managed to croak out.

"Hey, why are you crying? Kitten, I thought this would make you happy. It certainly makes me happy to have you here," he said as he brushed a tear from her cheek.

"I know it's silly, but I seem to cry at the most ridiculous things lately."

"Come on, let's take a walk along the beach before the sun sets," he said taking her hand and leading her down the stairs to the first floor.

"Sonia," he called toward the back of the house toward the kitchen. A young girl of about nineteen emerged hesitantly, dressed in a cotton skirt and camisole, wiping her hands hurriedly on a cloth tied around her waist and hips.

"Oh, Mr. Michael, I didn't know you'd arrived," she said excitedly as she moved forward to greet her employer.

Michael hugged her and then turned, eager to introduce Lauren to the daughter of the family who cared for the house in his absence.

"Sonia, this is a very good friend of mine, Miss Lauren Traynor. She's from New York also," he said as Lauren extended her hand to the young girl. She took it warmly in hers, placed her other one on top and said graciously, "I am very pleased to meet you."

"We're going out to take a walk on the beach. Did Reynaud give you instructions as to what I'd need for the next couple of days?"

"Mr. Michael, don't you worry about anything. We've got the cupboards stocked, the refrigerator's full and I was even able to get some of those wines you asked us for," she said smiling.

"Wow, I'm impressed and especially on such short notice," Michael said, taking Lauren's hand.

"Should I prepare something for dinner for the two of you?" she asked.

"Actually, I think we will be eating in this evening. Just something simple is fine," Michael said as he led Lauren to the door. This place always made him happy. It reminded him of his mother. She'd loved it here and so had his father during the times when they'd vacationed or come over to visit other family members. He hadn't done that in a long time and realized that he'd missed Barbados.

The sun cast a reddish-orange glow over the island and the deep blue green of the water contrasted sharply with the overhead sky. It was like a scene depicted in some colorful, talent-ridden oil painting. Only it was real. The sand, still warm and dry from the day-long sun was a rich pearl-colored beige. The stretch of beach on which they walked was deserted by humankind and, hand in hand, Lauren and Michael gloried in the absolute peace and tranquility which engulfed them. Except for the occasional squawk of a seagull and the chantlike sounds of the pounding surf, there was quiet. No car horns honking, no buses with air brakes, no trucks with heavy transmission gears cranking, no airplanes overhead, no helicopters, no ambulances or police cars with sirens wailing, just quiet. And as they walked, soaking in the incredibly rejuvenating calm of the environment, each was deep in the private world of their own thoughts.

"Lauren, there's another reason I brought you down here—more than just to show you my mom's birthplace and have a relaxing couple of days," Michael said softly.

"What is it? You sound very serious all of a sudden," Lauren said hearing something in his voice which had not been there earlier.

"Okay, listen, I don't want to seem like I'm rushing anything, but we have had an incredible few weeks which was started off by a couple months of incredible punctuated by unpredictable. I know now that what I feel for you is the real thing. It's going to last for a very long time—forever. Do you feel the same way about me?" He searched her face for the answer knowing in his heart that she loved him too. He just wasn't sure if she was ready to acknowledge it—either to him or to herself.

"Michael, you know I do. I can only ask you to forgive me about the past because I really behaved badly, but I think you understand where I was coming from," she said, hoping that he did.

"I think I do. I used to do some of the same things when I dated people I could only take in small stretches. Then I met you and my whole modus operandi changed," he admitted candidly. "That's the pure, unadulterated truth."

"Well, I was probably sensing your former prototype because I definitely had you pegged as a player. And I was not about to get played or any of that. It's too much trouble to pull yourself back together, dust yourself off, and have to carry on after having been through the emotional upheaval that a failed relationship calls for," she said as they sat on the sand, watching the rising tide come in.

"Your defense mechanisms were most definitely at work," he laughed and then kissed her on the forehead. "I didn't plan to fall in love with you, Lauren, but it happened and I'm fully prepared to deal with it. Come on, I'll race you back to the house. Let's go into the pool," he said helping to raise her to her feet. "All this talk about love and relationships is making me want to swim to safety," he added, his laughter lightening the mood significantly.

"I didn't see a pool. Was it around the back or something?" she said as they headed toward the house.

"Actually, my dad and I had it put in only a couple of years ago. Yeah, it's toward the back of the property."

They changed into swimsuits quickly, noting the aroma of some delicious fare wafting through the house and realizing that they would indeed be ready for dinner by the time they finished swimming.

The pool was a study in grandeur. Michael and his father had not spared any expense when they'd decided that it was the one element that their Barbados retreat had lacked. Olympic-size with depths of twelve feet, it was rimmed with blue and green ceramic tile with a large dolphin-topped waterfall in one corner. It was also fully enclosed by a sun-shielding screen which they'd had shipped in from a Florida-based company.

"Oh my God, this is gorgeous," Lauren exclaimed as she took in the beauty of its design, the ripples of blue water and the magnificent atmosphere it created.

"And so are you," Michael added as she dove in wearing a one-piece white maillot with tiny indented cutouts at the waist, hip and high up on one of her ribs. The suit accentuated her body as if by design and although it was certainly not as revealing as a two-piece, the cutouts accentuated just enough skin to have a similar effect.

They swam, played water tag, ducked under the waterfall to be drenched by its cascade and cavorted for well over an hour until hunger drove them to the chaise lounges to dry off.

"I don't think I can move from this spot," Lauren said as the water, the sun, the day's endeavors took their toll on her body.

"Yes, you can because Sonia probably has one hell of a fine meal cooked up for us by now and I, for one, am famished," Michael said taking his towel off and twisting it into a snap dragon to torture Lauren with.

"If you don't stop that I'm going to throw you back into the pool," she threatened, her eyes hidden by dark sunglasses. "I'm getting hungry too though," she said then and began to gather her towel around her.

"Okay, let's just shower and change into something comfortable for dinner. We'll be informal since we're our own guests," he said as they entered the cool shade of the interior of the house.

Sonia approached as they made their way upstairs asking if they were ready to be served dinner.

"Sure, just give us fifteen minutes to shower off the chlorine from the pool," Michael said.

Lauren stepped into the bathroom, stripped off the damp bathing suit and reached inside the shower stall to turn on the water.

"Hey, who said you could go first?" Michael teased as he entered the bathroom.

"Girls are first. Everybody knows that." She laughed.

"Not this time. But I have a solution," he said, stepping out of his bathing trunks and joining her in the shower. Lauren laughed.

"I should know that you'd have something like this up your sleeve." She began rinsing her hair, knowing that she would have to work with it really quickly to be able to eat dinner any time soon.

"I am so sorry that I told Sonia we'd be ready in fifteen minutes," Michael said as he reached out and circled one of Lauren's breasts. "This could take a lot longer," he said meaningfully, his hands now becoming very busy, very focused and not at all engaged in any washing techniques.

"Michael, you're incorrigible," Lauren laughed as the evidence of his desire became totally apparent. She then rinsed the soap from her hair and wrung some of the water out.

"I can't help it. It's your fault," he said caressing her buttocks, sliding his hands around her waist to encompass her stomach and then reaching lower.

"Maybe we should postpone dinner altogether," Lauren said as his hands found her and she leaned back against the expanse of his chest. Michael continued to fondle her and Lauren gasped at the response her body gave in short order.

He turned her around, sealing their mouths with a kiss that was scalding as she still trembled with response. Bracing one hand on the shower stall wall, Lauren and Michael made love with the heat and steam of the water enhancing each and every sensation. The cascading water, the feel of his hands kneading her breasts as well as the thrusts of his body took her over the edge again in minutes. She leaned limply against him as he shuddered his release into her body.

"We're gonna drown in here if we don't get out soon," he murmured into her ear.

"It was your idea," she said laughing then, as she carefully stepped from the stall and reached for a towel. They were stacked atop a wicker shelf, all yellow in varying stripes, and hues. They complimented the bathroom perfectly.

"I am starving," Michael said as he too stepped out and reached for a heavy Egyptian cotton towel.

"You cannot be hungrier than I am," Lauren said, briskly drying her hair and body simultaneously. She'd blow-dry it quickly, leaving it to hang straight for the time being. For now, all she wanted was to get to the delicious aromas they'd detected since they'd entered the house earlier.

Entering the dining room sometime later, they were both pleased to see a bottle of Robert Mondavi white Zinfandel, two loaves of bread with butter and blue cheese on the breadboard, and several large clusters of both red and green grapes.

Sonia, hearing them come into the room, began bringing in large steaming bowls of jerked chicken, rice and peas with coconut, a mixture of native vegetables, and a platter of flying fish, a native dish of Barbados, placing them on the sideboard from which they served themselves.

They were both ravenous and ate several helpings of the spicy food, marveling at how good everything tasted, laughing deliriously at how hungry they were.

They then took their wineglasses into the living room and sat on the love seats facing one another, listening to several CDs which Michael had brought and talked.

"Can I ask you something, Michael?" Lauren said as they continued opening the newfound understanding they had of each other.

"Sure, anything," he answered.

"Have you ever brought anyone else here?" she said then and he knew that his answer would mean everything to her.

"No I haven't. You're the first person I've brought here," he said honestly.

"And why did you bring me?" she asked without missing a beat.

"Because I love you and I wanted to ask you to marry me, but I felt you should get to know me a little better first. This house represents my mother to me and so I thought if you were exposed to it you'd see that side of me and understand that I can love you so thoroughly, so completely, that you can stop running away from what you must know by now is the love you've been looking for all your life," he said looking into her eyes.

"Am I to understand that you are asking me to marry you, Michael?" Lauren asked then, her eyes tearing slightly with the joy that she felt.

"Yes. I love you and I know that I can make you happy. Will you be my wife, Lauren?" he asked.

She crossed the room then, throwing herself into his arms and kissing him fully on his lips, her joy etched into every fiber of her being.

"Yes, yes, yes, I will be your wife, if that's what you want. I love you so much it hurts to look at you sometimes," she said then, finally admitting what she'd known in her heart from the moment he kissed her on that first night in the foyer of her apartment.

Michael gathered Lauren into his arms and smoothed her hair away from her face. "You've been fighting this thing since it started, Lauren. I can't say that I blame you because it's a jungle out there and you have to protect yourself," he said tenderly, holding her chin in his hands.

"Michael, I think there's something that you ought to know. I was trying to figure out the best way to tell you. Trying to figure out if I should tell you, but the right time just never seemed to come up. I think this might be as good a time as any though, now. I'm going to have a baby—your baby," she said quietly, holding her breath for his reaction.

Several moments passed in which a multitude of thoughts passed through their minds.

"I know," he said evenly, looking directly into her eyes where the love she sought was mirrored and multiplied many times over.

"What—why—how could you know—no one but me knows," she said then, rising to her feet in an awkward gesture.

"I've known since the night of the CBN party when you spent the night at my house, threw up, and then ran home in a panic. I put two and two together. Look baby, we've been making love like crazy for the past three months. And although we used condoms every time we made love after the first time, you and I both know they're not one hundred percent effective. Not to mention that the first time was monumental. I had no idea that you weren't the woman of the world you pretended to be so I figured you had taken care of everything," he added, laughing now at the look of denial on her face.

"Seriously, Lauren, by the time we realized we might be doing something that could prove to be disastrous, I was already in love with you. So I just figured I'd let the chips fall where they would. But then I started to get nervous when you'd pull your disappearing acts on me. I realized that you might be pregnant and go off and have an abortion without even letting me know. That's honestly when I realized that I loved you and wanted to marry you. I couldn't bear the thought of your discarding anything that you and I had created together, Lauren," he said, walking over to gather her into his arms once again.

"Even with all the confusion going on about the merger and our acquisition of the other stations we acquired, KSSU in L.A. and WTTS in Atlanta, I was really unable to block out thoughts of you and believe me, I tried," he admitted.

"I've been so confused, Michael," she said as he continued to hold her, comfort her and allow her to unburden the last couple of weeks of hidden uncertainty.

"I couldn't tell you about the baby. I've been miserable not knowing how long I could keep it from you, but I also realized that I couldn't abort our child," she said, tears softly falling now.

"You don't have to worry about that. I love you and we're going to be married," he said as he kissed her lips softly. And now that I know for sure, it's ginger ale only for you, young lady," he said going back into the dining room to pour a glass for her.

Lauren watched Michael walk away, the long legs trim and appealing in his jeans and a simple T-shirt, and knew that she was truly blessed. She could finally stop running away from love and turn toward it, embracing the life that they'd created together. She'd come a long way on a wing and a prayer but it had paid off.

Dear Readers:

I hope you enjoyed this romantic novel, set in the heart of New York City with brief stops in Atlanta, Fort Lauderdale, Los Angeles, and Barbados.

Intrigue, romance, passion, and oftentimes turmoil can be at the core of any intense relationship. In my own friendship with several flight attendants, I came to realize that the glamour, excitement and aura the airline industry generally presents would probably make for good reading. I hope you'll agree.

Enjoy!
Linda Walters

ABOUT THE AUTHOR

A New York photojournalist who contributes regularly to local newspapers and national magazines, Linda Walters's coverage of Caribbean jazz festivals, culinary events, and restaurant reviews are eagerly awaited by readers.

Linda attended Fordham University at Lincoln Center, is a certified access producer with Time Warner Cable, and is a wholesale account manager with one of the nation's top mortgage lenders. She resides in Queens, New York. This is her first romantic novel.

Do You Have the Entire
SHIRLEY HAILSTOCK
Collection?

__Legacy

                0-7860-0415-0 $4.99US/$6.50CAN

__Mirror Image

                1-58314-178-2 $5.99US/$7.99CAN

__More Than Gold

                1-58314-120-0 $5.99US/$7.99CAN

__Whispers of Love

                0-7860-0055-4 $4.99US/$5.99CAN

More Sizzling Romance From
Brenda Jackson